Praise for STUPID ALABAMA

IF YOU DON'T think a New York kid spending the summer with his biologist uncle in the wilds of Alabama is snort-out-loud funny, you need to read *Stupid Alabama*. From gorilla spankings to gator heists, man-eating hound dogs to midnight salamander raids, the uber-snarking Melvin is my new hero.

--**Suzanne Johnson, author of the *Sentinel of New Orleans Series* of urban fantasy published by Tor Books**

Enjoy the story!
Mike

Stupid Alabama

A "Laugh-So-Hard-You-Will-Snot" Tale About Growing Up
to Discover Not All Things are "Stupid"
but a lot of them are.

Michael P. Wines

Wildlife Illustrations by Claire Floyd

The Ardent Writer Press, LLC
Brownsboro, Alabama

Visit Michael Wines' Author Page at

www.ArdentWriterPress.com

For general information about publishing with The Ardent Writer Press contact *steve@ardentwriterpress.com* or forward mail to: The Ardent Writer Press, Box 25, Brownsboro, Alabama 35741.

ISBN 978-1-938667-13-8

Library of Congress Control Number: 2013944406
Library of Congress subject headings:
- Humorous Fiction
- Humorous stories Juvenile fiction
- Humorous stories
- Humorous stories, American--Alabama
- Reptiles--Fiction

First Edition

ACKNOWLEDGEMENTS

This book is entirely Larry Williamson's fault. He edited, suggested, corrected, emphasized, modified, reworded, cut, rearranged, and generally organized a bunch of words about farts and alligators into something pseudo-understandable. Larry introduced me to the Auburn Writer's Circle, a group including Suzanne Johnson, Peter Wolf, Julia Thompson, Robin Governo, Shawn Jacobsen, and Matt Kearley, who put up with reading about vomit and animal poop every week for several years to help me write this story. Larry didn't stop there; he also introduced me to Steve Gierhart, who patiently published me. Steve's lovely daughter, Stephanie Gierhart, came up with the cover art through countless emails about shirt color. Claire Floyd is the best illustrator ever to pick up a pencil and will forever be my favorite adopted sister. There are also a few hundred friends that gave me advice after I shoved a page in front of their face. Some of those people are Mike Moore, Heather Hughes, Sherri Nicole Marshal, and KT Pierfelice.

There are a plethora of people who either inspired me to embellish things I did with them or to them. My former fellow zookeepers, including, Deanna Lance, Steve Reichling, and Michelle Keck, should be thanked for their various musings. The keepers from the Memphis Zoo and Aquarium, the Bronx Zoo, Zoo Atlanta, and the Montgomery Zoo (which are all way more professional in real life than I gave them credit for) inspired tidbits of the book. Auburn University and Craig Guyer's lab, grad students (past and present), and undergrad students all had huge roles in the invention of this book whether they knew it or not. Some of those people include Jimmy and Sierra Stiles, Jim Godwin, Roger Birkhead, Lindsay Adams, and Eric Wheeler. I shouldn't leave out Jennifer Lolly and the Louise Kreher Forest Ecology Preserve.

A special thanks to my family. Many of the stories in this book were based on family events. I considered apologizing but, looking back, I would certainly throw up in Jim's cowboy boot again if ever given the chance. I love you all, and realize you must love me after putting up with me for all these years. Thanks to my nephew, Web, for inspiring me to create Melvin. Though you are very different in real life, you both share the fine quality of pointing and laughing when I do something stupid. Thanks, Mom, for asking me how the book is coming every time I talk to you, then relaying it to Bill, Uncle Jim, and Aunt Diane. My siblings (Jim, Anne, Kelly, Megan, Alison, Brad, and Chelsea) were a big part of my often under-exaggerated characters.

Lastly, I'd like to thank real kids who made a difference. All of these charities were started by real kids. Look them up and help, or start your own. You can do it.

1. Kids Saving the Rainforest
   http://kidssavingtherainforest.org/
2. The Ladybug Foundation
   http://www.ladybugfoundation.ca/
3. Free the Children
   http://www.freethechildren.com/
4. Alex's Lemonade Stand
   http://www.alexslemonade.org/
5. Care Bags Foundation
   http://www.carebags4kids.org/
6. The Orianne Society
   http://www.oriannesociety.org/
7. Project Leonardo
   http://www.panthera.org/programs/lion/project-leonardo
8. Hoops of Hope
   http://www.hoopsofhope.org/

Contents

This book is dedicated to the great state of Alabama.
Your wildlife (human and otherwise), culture, and landscape
are among the most beautiful and diverse on the planet.
I hope it always stays that way.

CHAPTER ONE

I think I'm in Love

A half-grown, eighth-grade mustache is not intimidating to most people. Melvin Fitzpatrick, a scrawny, nerdy, wallflower of a sixth-grader, however, was not most people.

At that moment, the front of Melvin's favorite blue t-shirt was wadded up in the hairy knuckles of Rusty Castleman. The thirty-seven quarter-inch hairs of Rusty's half-stache scratched at Melvin's forehead. Rusty's dirt brown eyes were as intense as a subway train's high beam. Melvin felt like a rat with his tail caught in the track.

The toes of Melvin's worn sneakers dangled hopelessly inches above the floor. The corner of the books in his overstuffed backpack dug into his kidney. He was pinioned between a set of sturdy lockers and the ruffian, Rusty Castleman.

Melvin never gave his heart much thought before. He knew he had one but wasn't truly aware of it. It thumped in his bony, eleven-year-old chest. It motored faster with every "Hit him!" or "Punch him!" or "Go on and get him, Rusty!" the bully's posse chanted. Those shouts were the only thing he could hear above his own panicked panting. Melvin hung for what seemed like hours. He wanted the torture to stop but knew it would get worse before it got better. Unfortunately, Melvin was right.

Rusty slammed him against the lockers, harder than before. "Think you're a hero, Fartzpatrick?" Jerk-face snarled. His breath smelled like garlic-crusted armpit. The back of Melvin's head clanged against the locker door. Rusty pulled a club of a fist back, still pinning Melvin against the locker.

Melvin turned his head and closed his eyes, expecting a punch to his face. Instead, the punk folded him in half with an uppercut to his ribs. The hit replaced the air in his lungs with panic. Rusty pushed him to the floor, scattering the contents of Melvin's backpack among dozens of unfriendly feet. He curled up in a ball trying to catch his wind. The only fight he had left was to hold the tears back batting at his eyelids.

Rusty wasn't finished. "Get a pen," the pest said with a horrible yellow sneer. He pinned Melvin to the ground with a dirty knee. Then he drew roughly on Melvin's face with a smelly, black, permanent marker. He finished, picked Melvin up by the back of the collar, and guided him into a headlock. Melvin welcomed the ink's smell, anything to cover up the sourness of Rusty's body odor. It was bad enough getting beaten up, but getting whipped by a jerk that smelled like warm buffalo vomit was intolerable.

Stinky Castleman dragged his prey in a small circle, showing him off to the bloodthirsty crowd. Melvin couldn't hear anything. He was trapped under Rusty's arm with his mouth, nose, and ears covered. He took short, shallow gasps, unable to get the deep breaths he needed.

Panicked, Melvin did the only thing he could to escape, besides peeing his pants. He bit. "Get off me!" he hissed through a mouth full of hairy forearm. The headlock was instantly broken. Melvin was shoved to his knees as he gasped and gulped air into his burning lungs.

"The little twerp bit me!" Everyone around looked at Rusty's wrist. A perfect set of teeth were imprinted deep into the skin. A single drop of blood slowly ballooned out of a tooth mark. Rusty turned green, let out a girly "meep" sound, and fainted.

"Yo! You killed him, Homie," Melvin's best friend Chucky Goldstein said while picking himself off the ground, also a victim of Rusty Castleman.

"Shut up! I did not." Melvin was angry at Chucky for getting him into the situation.

"I told you to call me DJ Chuck-N-Stuff," said Chucky. The two boys nudged Rusty's unconscious body with their feet. By the time they noticed the crowd had vanished, it was too late. An iron clamp landed on each boy's shoulder. It was the unmistakable death-grip of Coach Hornsby.

"What the heck happened to Castleman?" snorted Coach. He lived for these moments. He had smelling salts, an unlimited supply of white medical tape and no less than six air-pump needles on his person at all times. No one could figure out where he kept them, considering he wore skin-tight red shorts with no pockets. He had a tight white t-shirt tucked in, knee-high white socks with red stripes, sneakers, and a whistle. He wore this self-imposed uniform every day. The winters in Brooklyn got darn cold but Coach Hornsby was ever-vigilant in his attire. Melvin often wondered if he would wear the same thing if the school's colors weren't red and white. Coach Hornsby knelt, waving smelling salts under Rusty's nose.

"Eeewww!" Rusty spat. "What happened?" he whimpered as Coach Hornsby pulled him to his feet.

"Yo, my boy, Melvin straight-up knocked you out," Chucky said with a laugh as he pointed at Rusty.

Melvin felt the hole he had been digging with Rusty had become a grave. "Shut up, Chucky. I did not. Castleman fainted when he saw blood."

Rusty glared, slowly getting his legs back. "I didn't faint! I just … I just slipped."

Mr. Hornsby had had enough. Melvin could tell because Coach yelled, "I've had enough! We'll let Principal Decker figure out what happened. Gather your stuff, Fitzpatrick." He managed to give the shoulder death grip to all three boys at once, while dragging them down the hall. "Sit," Coach ordered as they arrived at the dreaded office. Melvin and Chucky squatted on one side of the hallway of shame. Rusty Castleman sat on the other, still glaring at the two boys.

"This ain't over, Fartzpatrick, you little puke," Rusty said, pinning Melvin to the wall with his eyes the second Coach Hornsby disappeared behind a door.

Stupid Alabama by Michael P. Wines

Chucky stood up and looked at his reflection in the office window, nervously grooming his curly, red bulb of hair. "Ha! What are you going to do, squish him when you pass out again? I'm glad you didn't wet your pants, Nancy," Chucky said to a growling Rusty. Chucky straightened his over-sized New York Knicks jersey and wiped the scuffs off his high tops.

Melvin felt Rusty's glare. He furiously rubbed at the ink on his face with the front of his t-shirt to hide the giggles escaping as a result of Chucky's jeer.

"Get in here," Coach Hornsby said, holding the office door open. The tension wasn't broken, but seemed to have changed focus. The boys shuffled in and were directed to several plastic chairs chained together behind the main counter. Coach Hornsby grabbed Rusty's arm and cleaned it with an alcohol wipe. He handed one to Melvin to remove the recently acquired Fu Manchu and the large 'L' smeared on his forehead.

Janita Johnson, a tall uncompromising girl, sat at the counter playing Sudoku. Smart, well mannered, eighth-grade students got to spend one period as an office worker instead of sitting in class. Her duties included answering the phone and filing mail into teachers' boxes. "Oooo, you gonna be in trouble," she said to the boys, pouting her lips while shaking her head.

Rusty gave Janita his patented glare. His face might have stuck that way. Chucky smiled, strutting a little. Melvin shrank even more than before, trying not to look at anyone or anything in particular.

"You boys couldn't wait to beat each other up for one more day," came from Principal Decker's cracked office door at the back of the room. "I was hoping to get through this last day of school without any foolishness."

Coach Hornsby stood outside the door, arms crossed. He looked like a troll guarding a bridge.

"Castleman and Goldstein I could have guessed, but Fitzpatrick, too? I'm disappointed in you, Melvin. You know better than to get into fights." Principal Decker looked down her nose as she came out of her office. "Your mother is going to be very upset when I talk to her. What happened?" She licked her thumb and rubbed hard on Melvin's forehead.

Ew. Melvin squirmed. His stomach twisted while his face turned red with frustration. He wasn't sure if it was because of the inevitable principal and parent phone conference or from the beating Rusty gave him.

Melvin was never a bad kid, and had been particularly good over the past month. He heard about a six-week computer camp at New York University this summer and had been begging his parents since. "We'll see," was their standard reply.

"They started it!" Rusty blurted, pleading his case before the two younger boys had a chance. "I was just going to class."

"That's some bull!" Chucky said, leaning back and crossing his arms.

"Watch that language, young man," Principal Decker interrupted, "You are in enough trouble already." She scribbled something down on an incident report attached to a clipboard.

"Sorry, but it's true," Chucky pouted.

Melvin pleaded, seeing computer camp slip away. "Ms. Decker, you don't need to call my mom. I didn't do anything."

"If you didn't do anything, why does Castleman have bite marks on his arm?"

"Yeah," Rusty said. "I told you I didn't do anything. He bit me."

"Don't look at it, Rusty. Yo, you might slip again," Chucky said, making air quotes with his fingers on the word *slip*.

"Shut up, Chucky," Rusty, Melvin, Coach Hornsby, and Principal Decker said in unison.

Janita stood up from the counter. "Ms. Decker, I can tell you what happened." All eyes looked to her. "Rusty was picking on that confused, little Jewish boy when Melvin told him to stop. Rusty drew on Melvin, punched him in the stomach, and put him in a headlock. Melvin bit Rusty. Rusty saw blood and fainted like those inbred goats do after hearing a loud noise. So I got Coach Hornsby. It was all kind of funny really," she added, grinning.

Principal Decker strained to hold back a smile. "Violence is never funny, Ms. Johnson. Thank you for straightening it out."

Janita added, "I think Rusty was mad because he failed the eighth grade and has to repeat it. Again."

Rusty gave her a nasty stare.

"Oh, don't think you can scare me! I'm not afraid of you," Janita said with a snap.

Melvin and Chucky shared an I-can't-wait-to-talk-about-this-later look.

"That's enough of that for now," Principal Decker said.

"See, you don't have to call my mom," Melvin reminded. He was not afraid of redundancy. "It was self-defense."

Principal Decker lectured Melvin. "Even if you were defending yourself, you still bit Rusty. I'm going to call all of your mothers. You should never have needed to defend yourself in the first place. At the first sign of trouble, what should you have done?"

"Tell a teacher," Melvin moaned in defeat.

"Right," she nodded, scribbling hard on her ever-present clipboard. The final bell rang. The halls vibrated with kids running out the doors enjoying that 'school's out for the summer' feeling. "Sit here while I finish some paperwork. Castleman, we are going to have a long talk." She turned back to her office.

Chucky straightened his shirt and checked his breath. "What's happenin' this summer, Sweet Thang?" he said to Janita, leaning back into his chair. "Give me your digits. Maybe we can kick it."

Melvin cringed, learning his daily lesson on how not to talk to girls. Chucky had an honorary PhD in the subject.

Janita gathered some things into her backpack. She finished, turned, and walked over to Chucky. She towered over him but bent down to look into his eyes. "As if," was all she said and walked out the door.

Chucky was so startled his chair fell over backward. "I think I'm in love," he said with stars in his eyes, after he crashed to the floor.

CHAPTER TWO
Coprolite Happened

"People rejoice! I'm finally released from captivity!" Chucky exclaimed as he and Melvin walked out the front door of the quiet school.

Melvin rubbed more ink onto his once favorite t-shirt. His face seemed to have a never-ending supply. "Stupid Rusty Castleman is going to be here again next year! That sucks. I had hoped to be rid of him."

"Bro, that was hilarious when you bit Rusty. He went out like three strikes! You didn't have to get into it, though. I had him right where I wanted him. That sucka' was falling into my trap," Chucky boasted.

"What trap was that? You didn't look like you could do much, hanging from a locker by your underwear."

"Whateves. He's just lucky you showed up to distract him. I was about to bust a flying knee on his cranium when you jumped in. Did you really think he was smart enough to pass the eighth grade? That knuckle-dragger can't even pass gas without cheating," Chucky snickered. "Are you going to that computer camp you've been yappin' about all month?"

"I don't know. I better get home to do some damage control before Old Lady Decker calls my mom."

19

"I'm getting out of here, too, before she lets Stinky Castleman out. Hopefully, he'll forget about me making fun of him. He's about as sharp as a bowling ball, but hits just as hard."

Melvin's cell phone vibrated. The text message from his mother read *Get home now*. His heart and stomach switched places. "She already called. I've got to go. Call you tomorrow if I'm still alive," Melvin said as he turned.

Chucky held up two fingers. "Peace, yo." His phone announced a text message with a repeating line from "No sleep till Brooklyn" by the Beastie Boys. Chucky idolized them. "Aw crap. She called my moms, too."

Melvin ran the four blocks home, stopping only once to rearrange the contents of his backpack. He wanted to avoid as many giggles from onlookers as possible. He hadn't seen his own face but knew it couldn't be good.

He got to his building and climbed the three floors to his small apartment hoping one of the Franks wouldn't come out for a chat. The two apartments below him and most of the apartments around him were occupied by old men named Frank. Apparently, a singer named Frank Sinatra was popular at the time these guys were born. A chat with one of the Franks usually meant he would have to move boxes or fix an ancient VCR as a favor.

His stomach and heart had almost returned to normal, just to switch places again once he got to the top of the narrow wooden stairway. It was the last day of school for his mother, too. She taught art history at a private school in Manhattan. Today was a half day for her. He pulled the key dangling from a chain around his neck. "Mom, I'm home," he said quietly, prodding for a hint of his mother's mood.

He was suddenly grabbed from the side and pulled into a full-on bear hug that rivaled Rusty Castleman's headlock. "Are you okay? Did you get hurt?" Shea asked, like only a mother can. Then the inevitable licked thumb came out to spread more ink around on Melvin's face. Principal Decker must have assured her of Melvin's safety during their phone call, but Shea had to see for herself.

Melvin squirmed, blocking the slimy thumb as much as he could. "Yes, I'm fine. It's no big deal."

"What about the other boy? Is he okay? Ms. Decker said you bit him! Why would anyone want to hurt another human being?" Shea abhorred violence. She couldn't watch scary movies or contact sports. She wouldn't even let Melvin and his father wrestle in her presence.

"The jerk is fine, too, Mom," Melvin pouted. "He's more of a gorilla with pants than a human being."

"Good. Go to your room then, after you wash your face." Shea stepped back since her immediate worries were over, slapping him with the you-are-in-so-much-trouble look. Shea normally had a kind smile and a pretty face, but her current expression made him think of a T-Rex with a pocket full of hand grenades. Melvin hadn't gotten that look in a while. "We'll have a discussion when your dad gets home."

Melvin knew not to argue with the mom look, especially with a dreaded discussion in the near future. He sulked along the short, narrow hallway to the bathroom, trying not to stomp his feet or slam doors. He scrubbed the smeared mustache and blotch of an "L" for what seemed like hours. Most of it eventually came off with help from his mom's makeup remover.

Melvin pushed on his door. It wouldn't open all the way, blocked by the random mounds of things on the floor. He had to squeeze to get his backpack through. That dislodged a stack of CompuGeek magazines topped with one crusty old shoe and a rubber rat his father had given him to annoy his mother. The pile avalanched through the open door. He chunked his backpack on the bed covered in clean clothes he was supposed to put away days ago. He bent over in the doorway, hiking the magazines to an invisible quarterback who fumbled them all over the room. He closed the door, trying not to slam it.

The movement in the room woke his computer from sleep mode. The monitor hummed to life, flashing a reminder of one day, one hour, and forty-seven minutes until the registration deadline for computer camp. He'd also installed the screensaver on his parents' computer. It was another way to market his wants since, thankfully, they didn't come into his room often.

Strategically placed computer camp flyers and brochures littered the small apartment. They went to the refrigerator, the table near the front door, the bathroom taped to the inside of the medicine cabinet, the inside of the pantry door, and in his dad's backpack and mom's purse. He also set up a reminder to be sent to both parents' emails and cell phones around lunchtime every day. Melvin liked to be thorough.

Two hours until his dad got home from work. Most kids, being banished to their rooms, would have a hard time of it, but Melvin had more electronic gadgets than he could ever use.

Both his grandfathers were tech geeks. When the latest gadget came out, they bought it and sent the old model to Melvin. He often had two of the same cell phone or GPS or whatever, everything USB wireless compatible, which gave him one model to use and one to take apart. Lately, they had sent him computer drives, DVD burners, graphics cards, web cams, and anything else that could be technologically tinkered with. From the hodgepodge of random bits came his two favorite things, Frankenstein and Igor.

Frankenstein, his desktop computer, was actually more of a desk top, bottom, both sides, and some under-the-bed computer. Parts attached everywhere, leading to ports for all the gadgets to upload and download information.

Igor was his laptop. It wasn't quite the physical specimen of Frankenstein, but could get most jobs done with great efficiency, and had a steady link to the big boy in case of emergencies.

Melvin busied himself with the gizmos, constantly learning how to use, improve, and combine properties. He could do amazing things with technology; that is, if he would ever go somewhere and do anything besides learning how to do amazing things with technology.

When Melvin's father, Briar, eventually got home, he wasn't alone. Briar was usually lenient when it came to Melvin's punishment. He had a sixth sense, always seeming to know what Melvin was thinking when he did things that got him into trouble. Melvin had never been in a fight before, nor had the principal ever called his parents. Still, Briar came down hard in a few circumstances, like the time Melvin and Chucky took the subway into Times Square without supervision. A toy robot convention at FAO Schwarz led the boys astray.

A month of snow shoveling, sweeping, moving furniture, reorganizing ancient record collections, and dozens of other tasks for the Franks was almost worth it. Briar referred to it as community service. Before the punishment, the Franks paid Melvin a couple of bucks for the odd jobs he did. After a month of servitude, the Franks expected the work for free. He made considerably less money lately, for the same or more work than before. His father lectured: *If you can't do the time, then don't do the crime.*

Melvin felt nervous about the imminent talk, anything but the dreaded discussion. *Why couldn't they just spank him and be done with it?* He mulled this while listening through his bedroom door. Unable to hear, Melvin decided to bite the bullet and leave the relative safety of his man cave.

Briar turned down the hall to greet Melvin. "Come say hello to your Uncle Petro, then back to your room. Your mom told me what happened while she paced the house worrying about you. You're not off the hook just because we have company," Briar's authoritative tone made Melvin feel like a dog that got caught laying logs on the new carpet.

"Hey, Gas Man, what are you doing here?" Melvin tried to sound upbeat and not in any way scared for the fate of his foreseeable future, including computer camp. He hugged his uncle, who didn't smell anything like campfires and pine trees.

Melvin called his Uncle Petro Gas Man in jest. Petro was such a strange name that people associated it with oil, hence the name Gas Man. Showing up unannounced wasn't like Petro, especially in the summer. He was a biologist in Alabama or Arkansas or someplace where there was nothing to do but be a biologist. He sent things like snake fangs or huge beetles mounted in frames to Melvin for his birthday and Christmas. Once he sent an 'owl pellet' for Melvin to dissect. It was full of tiny rodent skulls and bones. Petro later told him an owl pellet was a nice term for owl puke.

Melvin realized he, Petro, and Briar had a lot in common. They each had a strange first name taken from long-dead relatives. All three had thin, wiry builds with scruffy, light brown hair. Each had a cowlick atop of his head that wouldn't tame down no matter how much gel was applied. They had a similar sense of humor and had an affinity for strange t-shirts. Petro wore a t-shirt with a triceratops skeleton pooping. The words 'Coprolite Happened' were printed underneath.

Briar, the older of the two brothers, had a slightly larger nose than Petro. Petro loved to remind him by calling him "The Nose." Melvin also had a horrible nickname his father bestowed upon him as a toddler. Briar gave it to him so he could use it in front of Melvin's first girlfriend when and if that ever happened.

"Well, hello, Koo Koo Butt!" Petro returned the usual greeting. "I'm here to bust you out. I heard you got yourself in trouble."

Melvin was about to start pleading his case when Briar interrupted. "We haven't heard the story from him yet, so that's still a touchy subject. Okay, Kiddo, you said 'Hi' to your uncle; now, back to your room until our family discussion." Briar was still using his adult voice.

"All right," Melvin pouted. He touched the keyboard on the computer in the multi-room to wake it up. The screensaver appeared, flashing that there were only twenty-two hours, thirteen minutes left to register for computer camp, just in case they had missed it before.

CHAPTER THREE

Guilt Trip

Melvin closed the door to his room and turned on Frankenstein. He had networked all the computers in the apartment together so he could watch and, more importantly, listen to his parents' conversations via the webcam on top of the computer in the multi-room. He hoped listening to his parents' conversation about the day's events would help him prepare a logical self-defense.

Melvin inherited the art of arguing from his mother's side of the family. Other than the times she worried about her son, Shea's logic skills were legendary.

Melvin watched and listened to the adults in the other room, taking better notes than he ever had in class.

"So, what brings you to the big city?" Shea asked, giving Petro one of her patented welcome hugs.

"I'm doing courier work for the city of Montgomery. I have to drive some packages back to Alabama tomorrow. I hope you don't mind shacking me up for the night."

"You're always welcome. You know that. It's great to see you."

Briar interrupted. "Melvin doesn't look like he was beaten up. Who did he bite, and why?" Melvin's dad liked to kill a few hundred zombies on the Xbox, but was disgusted by real violence. To him there was always a way around it. He seemed disappointed Melvin had been in a fight.

"He bit that Castleman bully, an eighth grader. Principal Decker said he was defending Chucky. She also said it was more self-defense than a fight, and thought Melvin should have found a teacher before getting in the middle of it. She said the Castleman boy fainted at the sight of his own blood after Melvin bit him."

Melvin heard several giggles, even one from his mother. He didn't expect his parents to find any of this funny.

Petro snorted. "Can I call him Jaws?"

"No, we don't want him to think it's funny, even though it is," Briar said after a belly laugh.

Petro smiled at Briar, which Melvin could see, thanks to his high-def web-cam.

"It sounds like you as a kid," his uncle said.

"I never bit anybody," Briar said with a hearty chuckle.

"No, but you defended me plenty of times. You always beat me up later, but sure wouldn't let anyone else do it."

"I have no idea what you're talking about," Briar said through a toothy grin.

Shea scolded him with her eyes.

"Do you remember the time you got into a spat with Shelly Zimmerman?" Petro continued. "She was your age."

"What? I have no recollection of such a circumstance," Briar said in an attempt to avoid the story. Too late. His smile grew as his hands rose, open-palmed, like a politician passing the blame.

Shea looked past Briar to Petro. "What happened next?"

"Well, Briar made Shelly Zimmerman so mad she wanted to fight. I thought she was going to kill him. Briar, on the other hand, was scared to death of the girl."

"I was not scared of her! I just wouldn't punch a girl. It's called chivalry."

Shea's eyebrows rose. "So, now you remember?"

Briar shrugged, grinning as if attempting to look innocent.

"Busted!" Melvin said. Then he slapped a hand over his own mouth, remembering he wasn't supposed to be listening. Luckily, they didn't seem to notice or react.

Petro continued. "Anyway, the two of them decided they couldn't fight. Shelly had a younger brother the same age as me. She made him fight in her place. Briar took it easy on him. He was four years older and way outmatched little Scotty Zimmerman. After a few minutes of the smaller boy running at Briar and getting knocked down, they decided it would be more of a fair fight between Scotty and me. I was never asked my opinion."

"You did what?" Shea asked, astounded, turning back to Briar.

Briar squirmed, holding his hands up with a smile. "He's making the whole thing up. I will never admit to anything, uh, especially the next part."

"I absolutely believe you made a girl so mad she wanted to hurt you. It sounds like you're lucky Shelly Zimmerman didn't have an older sibling. I can't believe you brought your little brother into it," Shea said.

"Hey, isn't Melvin the one in trouble here?" Briar said, throwing his own son under the bus.

"What happened next?" Shea asked, not letting Briar off the hook.

"Well, Scotty and I started fighting. We grabbed each other and rolled around on the ground. We both got covered in dirt and I got grass stains on my brand new jeans. A teacher took us to the office. I got in trouble for the whole thing, while Captain Chivalry here got nothing."

Shea gave Briar the mom look. Briar seemed to shrink while maintaining his toothy grin.

"The worst part was when Mom asked what happened to my jeans. Briar told her I got into a fight!" Petro reported, seeming happy to get revenge on his brother.

Shea intensified the mom look. "Really?"

"He didn't mention he and Scotty became best friends after that," Briar protested. "Okay, okay, let's get back to Melvin's fight. I'll give him a good talking to along with more community service."

"I think he's worried we aren't going to let him go to computer camp," Shea said. There was a pause in the conversation, as if they taunted Melvin on purpose.

Melvin's heart pumped faster. His fate was being decided. He compiled a list of reasons why he should be allowed to attend, even though he had gotten in a fight.

His Dad said, "I'd let him go to computer camp. Melvin's a great kid. Growing up is hard. I'm surprised he hasn't gotten in more trouble. He knows the difference between right and wrong, and usually makes the right choices. He only got into a fight today because of his good intentions to help Chucky."

Melvin highlighted the parts of his mental list already mentioned. Camp seemed within reach. His emotions bounced up and down, as if on a pogo stick, reaching higher every minute.

Briar shrunk a little, saying, almost to himself, "The problem is, I don't know how we can afford it."

"How much is it?" Petro asked.

Shea hesitated. "It's eight-hundred and fifty."

"Ouch."

Briar continued, sounding defeated. "I had to cut hours for everybody at the shop, including myself. No one's getting any overtime or even full time in the foreseeable future, but hopefully nobody's going to lose their job."

"I had no idea business was so bad," Petro said.

"It's bad everywhere, which is why I have to keep my employees employed."

Shea shrugged. "I'm off for the summer. So, I'm not bringing any money in at the moment."

Petro apologized. "I would help if I could, but I don't make much either. I'm doing odd jobs, like the one that brought me here, to help pay for my research."

"We wouldn't ask anyway," Briar said.

"Why don't you borrow the money from Mom?" Petro asked.

"She'd lend us the money, but we would still have to pay it back. We don't have the money now, and I don't know if we'll have it six months from now. Heck, I still owe her from grad school."

Petro admitted. "I'm in that club, too."

"It's the same with my parents," Shea said.

Melvin felt as if someone kicked the pogo stick out from under him while in mid-bounce. He was so busy trying to get permission to go to computer camp he didn't think about whether or not they could afford it. Guilt pounced on him like a jungle cat. He had pestered his parents constantly for a month.

"The really sad part is Melvin wouldn't learn anything," Briar said. "He already knows more about computers than anyone I've met. He would end up teaching them."

Melvin had not thought of that. He'd imagined computer camp as a technological heaven, where everyone got to use the most advanced systems and hardware.

"I looked at the schedule on their home page," Briar continued. "The high point of the camp for each kid was building his or her own website using HTML. Melvin mastered that three years ago. Heck, he made a website about robots. Melvinsworld.com still gets several thousand hits a day, even though he hasn't updated it in months. He was just messing around, figuring out how Flash works. The camp would be a huge letdown for him. He hasn't stopped talking about the camp since he heard about it. I haven't had the heart to tell him he wouldn't learn anything new."

Melvin was already looking up the schedule on the computer camp website. Surely his dad was mistaken. Week one's classes included: 'Computer Set Up,' 'Getting started with Windows,' 'Exploring the Internet for Beginners,' and a few more titles not even worth mentioning. Where was the 'Basic Lasers,' 'Hologram Video Game Design,' or 'Flying Droids 101' that Melvin imagined several hundred times a day?

Melvin's emotions stopped bouncing, and began hitting him with the pogo stick. He looked around his bedroom. The way things were going, a meteor, piano, safe, or all three could fall from the sky at any second. He would need to find cover.

"Crap." Melvin pouted a little louder than he meant to as he explored further into the itinerary.

His dad's head turned toward Melvin's room. He paused, then looked directly at the webcam on top of the monitor in the big room.

Melvin froze, seeing his father's eyes look directly at him on the screen.

Briar finally looked away from the camera and continued the conversation. "I thought computer camp would be great for him until I did some research on it. I'm surprised he even wants to go, considering how basic it is."

Melvin released the breath he didn't realize he'd been holding.

"He doesn't have anything else to do this summer," Shea said. "He's going to have to stay home, which means I am, too."

Briar wrung his hands together. "Shea planned on giving painting lessons at the studio this summer for extra cash. We could have managed the cost of computer camp until today, when I had to make the cutbacks at work."

"Melvin should come to Alabama with me. It'll be great," Petro spat out excitedly.

"No, we couldn't ask that. Besides, you haven't ever taken care of a kid before," Shea said with more than a little concern.

Petro assured her. "He's not an infant anymore. He takes care of himself now. He just needs a little supervision."

"He'd get in the way of your work. He's a full-time job," Briar said, shaking his head.

"Heck no. He could help me with my research. I'm starting a huge project, hoping to help save the Red Hills Salamander. It's more responsibility than the biology department has ever given me. I've got to write grants, organize government agencies, and research tons of old journal articles. It's also a chance to make a difference. Melvin can help out with some of my other projects while I focus on this new one. I bet he'd even learn something. He can earn his food and I can house him easily."

Shea looked worried. "He's not a puppy. Melvin probably wouldn't want to go out to the country, anyway. He's a city boy."

"Why don't we ask him?" Petro suggested.

Briar shrugged. "Melvin has computer camp on the brain. I doubt he'll even consider it. But it can't hurt to ask."

The guilt panther tugged Melvin's small intestines out like spaghetti. He wished he hadn't listened in on their conversation.

A knock came to Melvin's door. He quickly powered off the monitor and turned the speakers down. "Can we come in?" Shea asked.

"I guess."

Shea squeezed through the door and stumbled over piles of gadgets and clothes on the floor. "You really need to clean your room."

"Sorry," was all Melvin could muster.

Petro remained in the kitchen, which somehow lessened Melvin's shame.

Briar used his authoritative voice again. "We need to talk about a few things. First off, I thought you knew better than to get into fights."

Melvin responded more sharply than he meant to. "I didn't do anything except tell stupid Rusty Castleman to leave Chucky alone."

Shea poured the salt of shame on Melvin's tasty parts for the gnawing panther. "Watch that tone with us. We know you didn't start it. You should have told a teacher instead of getting in the middle of it, though. I don't know what we would have done if you were hurt."

Melvin began to think the punch to the stomach was the least painful thing that happened to him that day. Realizing computer camp was a bust and getting eaten up with guilt was much worse.

Briar's voice lost its edge. "You need to work on your judgment. You get a couple weeks of community service for the fight."

"Fine," Melvin whined.

"Now, about computer camp…"

Melvin interrupted, not wanting to say the words. "I looked into it a little more. It seems kind of dumb."

Shea wrapped a consoling arm around Melvin. "What are you going to do for the summer? You could stay here, or your Uncle Petro said you could stay with him in Alabama."

There wasn't enough time to think about the option of going with Uncle Petro. Melvin twitched, his neck caught in the jaws of guilt. He just wanted to be finished with the entire, awful, stupid day before the locusts showed up. "I guess I can go with Uncle Petro," he said, still feeling betrayed by computer camp and wishing Rusty Castleman would come down with a sudden and incurable case of face warts.

Stupid Alabama by Michael P. Wines

Melvin's head hung low, not making eye contact with his parents. Briar's and Shea's eyebrows lifted simultaneously, having taken in the unexpected news. "All right then, I'm going to go get dinner ready. You've had a hard day, darling. Want some lasagna?" Shea rubbed Melvin's messy hair.

All Melvin could come up with was "Sure," though he wasn't hungry. She kissed him on the head, then wiggled through his partially opened bedroom door.

Melvin's dad showed no sign of leaving with her. "I'm jealous I can't go with you."

Melvin couldn't put more than one word together. "Why?"

"I wasn't born a city kid like you. I grew up having all sorts of adventures with your Uncle Petro. Now, you get to have your own. I wish I could go with you guys."

Melvin's head lifted at the word adventure.

"You're going to be in a different world this summer. You have to listen to your uncle and use good judgment. I know your mom has taught you to be careful."

Briar always had life advice. Melvin learned from a toddler to look people in the eye when shaking hands and always try to remember people's names. 'Little respectful gestures can make all the difference,' was one of Briar's mantras.

His father shuffled past the random piles on the floor toward the door. "You'd better start packing. You two are leaving for Alabama in the morning."

The word, Alabama, seemed to poke Melvin in the chest. He imagined people with no shoes chewing on wheat straw and spitting a lot.

Briar almost made it through the door only to turn back. "Oh. And son, if you listen in on our conversation again through that webcam, I'm going to make you eat it."

Melvin gulped. "Okay."

"Good. Now we're clear." His dad closed the door.

Melvin shook off the sudden fright, then googled *Alabama*. Frankenstein always had answers. Words like: *Bible-Belt, Heart of Dixie,* and *Yellowhammer* immediately popped up.

He pondered Frankenstein's strange response. "Why would the Bible need a belt? Who is Dixie? Why would anyone need a yellow hammer instead of any other color?"

Melvin had set up one of his extra webcams on Chucky's computer so they could Skype over the Internet. His best friend liked to answer each video call by mooning the camera. After the second time, Melvin threatened to email a picture of Chucky's butt to the entire school. Chucky answered with his face this time, thankfully. "What's up, yo?"

"I have to go to Alabama tomorrow with my uncle. No computer camp."

Chucky put his hands on his head. "Whoa! Yo' moms must'a been pissed about toothin' up Rusty."

Melvin was still pouty. "A little bit. Mostly, they just can't afford to keep me here."

Chucky had a knack for not helping during any and every situation. "Did you ever see that movie *Deliverance*? I think it was about Alabama."

"No. What's that?"

"It's an old gross movie about people who played the banjo and married their sisters."

"Great." Melvin stretched the word to fill it with as much sarcasm as possible. "Did you get in trouble?"

"Pops told me not to get into fights unless I plan on winning. Ma heard and got mad at him instead of me. Ha! Now, every time she brings it up, I just tell her Dad said it was okay because I plan on winning every fight. Then her face gets all twisted up and she storms off to yell at him."

"Lucky! I've got to go pack for stupid Alabama. I'll text you tomorrow."

Chucky held two fingers to his chest. "Peace."

Melvin spent the rest of the night munching on lasagna and packing a pile of gadgets Radio Shack would be jealous of. He uploaded and updated as much software as he could onto Igor. Frankenstein would have to stay here, but he could still uplink to it with Igor as long as there was an Internet connection. Melvin packed his backpack and two small duffle bags with the hardware. He saved one extra duffle bag for some clothes, extra shoes, bathroom stuff, and his oversized R2D2 beach towel.

Melvin's favorite author, Douglas Adams, wrote: *A towel is about the most massively useful thing an interstellar hitchhiker can have.* Melvin might not be an interstellar hitchhiker, but he knew a towel couldn't hurt.

The night passed slowly, filled with dreams of banjos and tractors. Briar woke him just after dawn for a goodbye hug. Melvin sleepily hugged back, but snapped awake when his father put a fifty-dollar bill in his hand. "This is for emergencies and to buy something nice for your mother. Have fun, Koo Koo Butt. I have to go to work. Love you."

Melvin didn't protest the nickname this early in the morning, when nobody else was around. "Okay. Thanks, Dad. Love you, too." He stretched the grogginess from his bones. The apartment was quiet, though everyone else was already awake.

Petro and Shea sat in the kitchen sipping coffee. "Morning," they grumbled in unison as Melvin entered the room. Shea still wore her fuzzy pink bathrobe and slippers, while Petro sported the Fitzpatrick male standard uniform of jeans and t-shirt.

"Good morning," Melvin rasped back, preparing his uber-healthy breakfast of Cocoa Puffs and a Red Bull.

"That's healthy." Shea tried to tame Melvin's hair with her freshly licked thumb. "Are you almost ready to go, darling?"

"Yup."

"You'll need a hat, a belt, some boots, and lots of socks," Uncle Petro said ominously.

Melvin's rasp turned to a whine. "A belt? I don't have to dress up in Alabama, do I?"

"No, it's so I can more easily tie you to the top of the van on the trip down," Petro added with no hint of fun in his voice.

Shea got that worried Mom look. "Listen to your uncle when he tells you to do something."

For the next hour she followed Melvin around, cautioning him of things to do and not to do and finally gave him a fifty dollar bill. "This is only for emergencies, and to buy your father something nice."

Melvin tried to hide his smile while taking the money. He didn't mention the fifty his dad gave him already. After a few more minutes of hugs, I-love-yous, and promising to do and not do way too many things to remember, he packed his bags into a large, empty rental van. Shea waved frantically from the sidewalk, still in her bathrobe, as they drove away.

"We just have to make one quick stop."

"Where's that?"

Petro grinned. "We have to pick up a couple of Chinese alligators from the Bronx Zoo."

CHAPTER FOUR
I Pity th' Fool

Petro had a dangerous twinkle in his eye. Melvin recognized it as the same look his father got around April First each year. It usually meant Melvin would unexpectedly be covered in green slime, have his shoes nailed to the ceiling, or come home to find his room filled with packing peanuts.

Melvin sank into the van's warm vinyl seat, not looking forward to the long drive. "Where are we really going?" He knew better than to believe everything his uncle told him. They were related, after all.

"I told you we're going to the Bronx Zoo. You get to be my navigator. I can't read the map and drive at the same time. Hopefully, I can get a little use out of you this summer."

Melvin turned to the back of the van. It was completely empty except for Melvin's bags and a few rays of sunshine lighting the floor. There wasn't the new car smell that came with most rentals. The floor and walls were covered with a dirty, scratched black liner.

Melvin rifled through the gadgets in one of his bags, mumbling excitedly. "Wait a second, I have just the thing!" He popped back into the front seat, plugging a cord into the cigarette lighter. He frantically pecked at the screen of a gadget attached to the cord. "I'm putting in the Bronx Zoo as our destination." He licked a suction cup on the back of the device and stuck it on the dashboard for Petro to see. It was a GPS.

A green path lit on the screen for Petro to follow. "I pity th' fool who don't turn right in two-hundred yards," the machine said.

Melvin folded his arms, contentedly. "I rigged it to sound like Mr. T. It can do a whole bunch of voices like Lord Voldomort's, Gandalf's, and Darth Vader's."

Petro looked genuinely impressed. "You're not completely useless after all."

"Quit yo' Jibba Jabba and turn left at the next light; Recalibratin', Sucka," and the occasional, "Take it from me, Mr. T. Merge to ya' left," got the travelers through the congested streets of New York and to the Bronx Zoo in less than an hour.

Petro pulled up to the guardhouse near the front entrance. "I'm here to pick up a couple of gators for the Montgomery Zoo," he said to the guard.

Melvin's eyes widened. He thought Petro was joking about the alligators. "Cool."

The large, curly-haired woman looked up from a *Glamour* magazine. She said something incoherent into her walkie-talkie and waited for a response, not breaking eye contact with Petro. It burped back a reply. "Oh, honey, you need to go around to the service entrance." She pointed with a four-inch long fingernail painted purple, dotted with rhinestones.

"Thank you." Petro weaved through twenty minutes of traffic to get two blocks.

An older gentleman stood at the gate in a spotless uniform at full attention. He looked as though he needed a tall hat. "State your business," came out in a blunt, but not unfriendly tone.

"I'm here to pick up a couple of Chinese alligators for the Montgomery Zoo."

There was more chatter over the walkie-talkies. Petro presented paperwork to the guard. He read every single word on both pages, checked Petro's ID, and commenced to walk slowly around the van looking in all the windows. He snapped back beside Petro's window, surprising both occupants. "This seems to be in order. Who's that?" He nodded at Melvin with a distrustful look.

Petro tried to loosen up the guard. "This is my assistant, Melvin. He'll be used as bait to lure the gators back into the van if they manage to escape."

The guard showed no sign of acknowledging the jest. "Young man, you had better hope the *Alligator sinensis* do not get loose." He chattered more into his radio while giving Petro directions on where to drive, how fast to drive and, more importantly, where not to drive. The walkie-talkie squawked again as the gate opened.

Melvin was confused by the guard's reply. "I thought we were getting whole alligators, not just their sinuses."

Petro laughed. "No, *Alligator sinensis* is just the fancy Latin term for Chinese alligator. All species of living things have their own scientific name. Most of the names mean something that helps describe them, tells where they live, or says who discovered them. The person who discovers the species gets to name it."

"Yawn," Melvin said, glad to be out of school for the summer.

Petro followed the strict path. "You keep being a smart aleck, and I will feed you to the gators."

A stocky man dressed in stained khaki shorts, knee-high black rubber boots, and a dirty, wet, Bronx Zoo polo waved them down. Melvin noticed most of the people behind the fence were dressed this way, dirt and all. The nametag identified him simply as Joe. "You here for the gators? Back in over there." The man pointed to a pair of double steel doors sunk into a large, partially underground building marked *Herpetarium*.

CHAPTER FIVE
Gator Gas

The doors swung open, revealing a wet concrete floor with a drain along one wall. The center of the room held two long stainless steel tables. One was covered with piles of fruits and vegetables. The other had hundreds of dead rats, a few rabbits, and one pig the size of a really fat Labrador. They were frozen, piled on newspapers, thawing. Melvin felt like he walked into Hell's cafeteria on fruit and ratsicle day.

The overwhelming heat in the building didn't help the musky rodent smell. Other than the pile of dead animals, the place was spotless. The shelves and cabinets lining the walls shined as if someone hosed them down daily. Two refrigerators, one marked *People* the other marked *Not People* sat next to each other against one wall. Melvin thought it best not to ask why, and hoped no one ever confused the two.

Crickets chirped from three large wooden boxes in the far corner. A big blue lizard with red dots clung to the wall above the crickets. Melvin looked twice, deciding it was a plastic one someone had placed on the wall as a joke.

Someone had cut the heads off a set of golf clubs, and replaced them with different shaped hooks. The hooks were hung on the wall in order, according to size, along with several large sets of snake tongs. A double door centered each wall. Each door had a large glass window that seemed out of place. Melvin wondered why anyone would put a window in a heavy steel door on the inside of a building. As Melvin pondered, the suddenly not-fake lizard darted to the floor faster than Melvin could blink. It chomped a cricket that had managed its way out of one of the boxes. Melvin stared, open mouthed, at the creature crunching down a second escapee.

"That's Chompers. He's our free-range Tokay Gecko. He eats all the crickets that escape the boxes. Don't try to pet him, though. He's got a nasty bite." Joe reached his hand out to Melvin.

Melvin made a conscious effort to close his mouth. He shook Joe's hand, which, like everything else, was wet. "Hi, Joe. I'm Melvin Fitzpatrick."

Petro and Joe seemed to recognize each other. "Hey there, Petro! Long time no see. I'm sorry, but today is feeding day. I don't have much time to show you guys around. If I had known you were bringing Melvin, I would have made time."

"That's fine. We have a long haul ahead of us anyways. Are the kids almost ready?"

"All the health checks and paperwork are done. We just have to catch and crate them up. I'll help you unload the crates from the van."

A raised eyebrow brought the mischievous look back to Petro's face. "They are going to ride free-range. I flew in and rented the van here, so no crates."

"Looks like you two are going to have a fun drive back. If you crank up the A/C, the gators ought to get nice and sleepy."

"That's the plan. I brought a roll of electrical tape for their snouts." Petro handed Melvin the roll of tape from his pocket.

Melvin's voice got higher than usual. "What am I supposed to do with this?"

"I figured you'd want to wrap their mouths. We can leave it off if you want, but I don't want to have to clean your blood out of the van before I return it."

Melvin broke into chipmunk talk. "No, wrap their mouths. I didn't think I would be the one close enough to wrap them."

Petro put on his serious face. "Here's the plan. I'm going to jump on the big gator. I'll hold its mouth shut while you tape it. Joe will guard us from the other gator while we work. Once that gator is taped, we jump the other one, doing the same thing. Now, I just need a towel."

"I've got one!" Melvin made Douglas Adams proud. He ran back to the van, grabbed it and rearranged his bags so the gators couldn't climb, eat, or sit on them.

Melvin returned with the image of *Star Wars* droid emblazoned on the sail-sized beach cloth. "Nice towel," both Petro and Joe said.

Melvin grinned. "I know, right?" He couldn't help feeling proud of his planning, even if it was just a towel.

Joe shrugged. "Follow me."

Melvin trailed after Petro and Joe. Cages and aquariums lined the right wall of the hallway. The left side was lined with the back doors of larger exhibits. Each door had a card labeled with the creature contained within. Some had the word 'VENOMOUS' printed in big orange letters under what looked like a sliding window built into the door. Electrical outlets every few feet overflowed with cords from heat lamps.

Joe cracked open a door, peeked through, then closed it. He held it as if something was going to burst out any second to rip his arms off. He secured the outside lock with great gusto and maybe a little drama. Next he pulled up a grate in the floor beside the door. He reached in up to his armpit, and turned a spigot of some sort. "This'll drain the water in the room."

"Are you trying to catch flies?" Petro asked Melvin with a grin.

'Catching flies' was a term his father used when Melvin left his mouth hanging open. Apparently, it was a family saying. Melvin shut his mouth but couldn't keep his hands from sweating. *What if he couldn't get a grip on the electrical tape? What if the gators really could smell fear like they do in movies?* Melvin's hands weren't wet because he was hot; they were slimy with a nervous sweat. *If he couldn't concentrate long enough to keep his mouth closed, how was he supposed to keep an alligator's mouth shut?*

"Okay, are you two ready?" Joe asked, interrupting Melvin's mental hysterics.

"Wait, wait, wait, not yet," Melvin stammered, sounding like he was at the doctor about to get a vaccination in the butt. "I want to go over the plan again, uh … for safety."

The two men smiled at each other.

Petro waved Joe and Melvin into a huddle. "Joe will open the door. Melvin, you be ready with the towel. You are going to toss it on the head of the closest gator. I will jump on it, covering its eyes and holding its mouth closed. Then you tape it up." He nodded to Melvin. "Joe, are the gators ready?"

"I guess we could ask them. I wish this door had a window like the others." Joe used the side of his fist to bang loudly three times on the heavy metal door.

Melvin felt as if his uncle had a new partner in messing with him. He was just about to tell the pair he couldn't be fooled so easily, when the gators answered back. The sound was so loud and unexpected that Melvin made his own girly yelp as he jumped.

"Boom! Boom! Boom!" came from behind the door. It sounded like an elephant after drinking a few hundred gallons of soda pop and swallowing half a ton of Pop Rocks, as it relieved itself with a thunderous burp.

Melvin felt the reverberations in his chest. Just when he thought it was over, the same sound came from several far-off locations. Melvin jumped and ducked at the same time, with each mighty gator belch. "Was that them?" He knew it was, but couldn't help asking.

"That was them, and several other pairs that live in the building. They're talking to each other. We aren't certain, but we think they're being territorial. The alligators make that noise to let others know to stay away," explained Joe.

"So, now they know we're coming and have told us several times, very loudly, to stay away." It took Melvin a second to realize he said that out loud. He was a jittery wreck, still surfing the wave of adrenaline from the scare he got.

"Right," Joe said. He took a four-foot-long snake hook off the wall. Faster than Melvin had hoped, Joe pulled the door open.

Melvin closed his mouth and readied the towel. Whatever made that sound had to be absolutely massive. He half expected the beasts to storm the door in a bloodthirsty rage the very instant the lock was disengaged. No sounds of movement came from the room. Maybe Melvin would have a few more precious seconds with his arms and legs attached. He wished he hadn't had that Red Bull with breakfast this morning. His hands were slimy with sweat. He didn't need them to be twitchy from caffeine, too.

CHAPTER SIX
Days Without an Accident ...

Joe entered the room casually, which bolstered Melvin's confidence he would survive the next few minutes. Petro followed, also not apparently worried about sudden evisceration. Melvin peeked into the narrow concrete room, holding R2D2 as if he was a matador and the gators were bulls.

A ledge inside the door jutted out three feet before a steep down-slope in the floor. It was a small wet room with a drain set in polished concrete at the bottom of the slope. Sunlight shone through a skylight, causing green, slimy algae to grow on the part of the floor that was generally underwater.

Melvin pulled out his cell phone, turning it to video record mode. Chucky would never believe him unless he actually saw it.

Two of the shortest, fattest alligators Melvin had ever seen lay side-by-side at the bottom of the recently drained floor. The closest was about five feet long. It had its mouth barely open. The other was maybe four feet long, slightly plumper and closed-mouthed.

Joe gestured proudly toward the pair of crocodilians. "Here they are. The big boy is named Avalanche. The little fat girl is Loki."

The pair was less impressive than Melvin imagined. Still, nothing but a ten-foot slope separated Melvin from the alligators, which kept the intimidation factor pretty high.

"I'll separate them so you can …," Joe said as he started down the slope. His big rubber boots slipped out from under him as he stepped on the slimy green algae. Joe slid a million miles an hour towards the waiting jaws of the angry reptile. The slick concrete walls and floor gave him nothing to grab on to. He tried to swing the hook around to get it between himself and Avalanche. When he fell, both hands went up, along with the hook.

Avalanche turned quickly in anticipation of his coming target. His mouth opened, ready for a boot-wrapped human-ka-bob.

Petro started down the slope to help Joe, but he couldn't get there in time.

Melvin threw the towel as if throwing a shuffle pass at a pterodactyl. Another girly yip came from Melvin as he did. This sissy squeaking was getting to be too frequent for his liking, though he doubted anyone noticed this one.

The towel hit Avalanche in his gaping mouth a millisecond before Joe's foot slid in. Avalanche snapped his toothy pink jaws shut on the wrinkled droid like a bear trap. As Joe began to get his footing, Petro lost his. Avalanche didn't notice what he had wasn't a tasty foot burger. He spun his body on the towel as if ripping the leg from a delicious gazelle. Death rolls are more effective in water than out. Mostly, Avalanche wrapped his own head in the towel while awkwardly rotating on the slippery floor.

Loki seemed to be annoyed by everything going on. She didn't charge Petro as he slid down knees first into an upside-down Avalanche. The reptile lifted off her generous belly, pointing her snout to the ceiling. She reared back, as if preparing to pounce. Her throat swelled with air. She let out another boisterous gator belch, much louder in the little concrete room than outside of it.

Petro and Joe scrambled to their feet on the opposite side of the reservoir. They were about four feet away from the grumpy varmints.

Loki seemed pleased the two men backed off, and Avalanche stopped his goofy spinning. She laid down, content and quiet while her upside-down mate slowly scratched at his encumbered head with one claw-tipped foot. He didn't seem to be in a hurry to escape the cotton clutches of R2D2.

Joe stabilized himself with a few deep breaths. "Right. Shall we proceed with the original plan, then?" He said with flushed cheeks. Both he and Petro had wet shirts and soggy butts from sliding down the slope. Joe separated Avalanche from Loki by pulling him gently with the hook.

Petro grabbed Avalanche's towel-wrapped snout. He maneuvered the finally docile gator over to right-side up, then sat on his back, all the while holding the snout shut. "Toss me the tape. Don't come down here. You need to stay up there to help us back up." As if Melvin wanted to climb into the alligator pit.

Petro pulled a roll of purple gauze from one of his overflowing, cargo pants pockets. He wrapped the male's toothy grin in purple, then applied an outer layer of duct tape. Loki got wrapped the same way, with Joe's help.

Joe and Petro made a few entertaining attempts to scale the short, algae-covered slope. In the effort, they managed to soak the parts of their clothes that were still dry.

"Melvin, will you go get the big python hook?" Joe asked with a frustrated grimace. "We can use it to pull ourselves out. It's six feet long, and hanging on the wall of the main room."

"Sure. Be right back." Melvin felt hesitant walking down the hallway alone. He turned off his camera to pay closer attention to his surroundings. "Snakes, lizards and gators, oh my," he mumbled nervously. After seeing the free-range gecko earlier he wondered what else was wandering around the cluttered hallways of the Herpetarium. He finally arrived at the big, wet, smelly room through the door with the window. Two zookeepers Melvin hadn't seen before were sorting through the pile of dead rats as he walked in.

"Hey there, kid. Can we help you with something?" asked one of them with a friendly but confused smile. She was barely over five feet tall, thin and as dirty as the other keepers Melvin had seen. He wondered how someone the same size as himself could do the job here. She couldn't be much of a gator-wrestler.

"Joe and my Uncle Petro are stuck in the pool with the Chinese alligators. Joe sent me after the python hook to help them out." Melvin felt like Lassie.

"Are they okay?"

"Yup, they keep falling down the slope, though, so they're kind of wet and annoyed," Melvin reported.

The woman's face lit into a wide grin. The other keeper's face did, too. He was an older man, skinny and muscular with a large graying red mustache. They seemed to conspire with each other saying, "Really?"

Melvin wondered if he had said too much.

"I guess we ought to help them out," the man said. "I'll grab the hook." He looked like Avalanche did as Joe's foot was sliding to his mouth, excited and mischievous. "Deanna, you might want to get the others in case we need to make a human chain. Oh, and bring the camera."

Melvin followed 'Jim', according to his nametag, down the hallway. The radio on Jim's belt crackled to life with a static beep as Deanna's voice crackled out. "All reptile keepers please report to the west Chinese alligator room. Joe requires our assistance." Though her voice was barely clear enough to be understood, Melvin could tell there was a giggle behind her announcement.

Melvin thought he definitely said too much.

Jim's eyes devilishly squinted. "Joe's plagued us all with practical jokes over the years. His favorite thing is to set one of us up, while waiting close by with a camera to take our picture. He filled my locker with meal worms once. He loves to take pictures of us in difficult situations before helping us out. He has a wall of these pictures in his office. He calls it the wall of shame."

As they arrived at the gator room, "I heard you needed some help getting up the big bad hill," Jim said in a mocking voice as he maneuvered the six-foot-long hook through the door.

"Aw, crap," Joe mumbled through a reddening face.

A small crowd gathered at the door, each taking a turn to get a picture of Joe and Petro with digital cameras and cell phones. They all giggled and snickered at the two slumping men. No one seemed interested in helping them out.

"This is going on the wall of shame," Deanna said with a huge smile.

"All right, you finally got me," Joe said. "Now will you help us out?"

Joe and Petro pushed Avalanche up the slimy slope as far as they could. Jim and Deanna pulled him up farther with hooks. Another man grabbed his front leg and tugged him up the rest of the way. They were running out of space on the ledge by the door. The keeper slid Avalanche to the corner Melvin had wiggled into.

"Here, kid, sit on him a minute," the keeper said as he slid the suddenly ginourmous reptile at Melvin. He turned around to reach for Loki.

Melvin climbed on top of Avalanche like he had seen his uncle do. He straddled the gator and wrapped his hands over the taped muzzle before he thought about what he was doing. Melvin felt very alone at that moment, even with people standing all around. He had been scared before, like during the fight with Rusty. This was a different kind of fear. He worried about the tape breaking or sliding off. He worried about the other people in the room if the gator managed to escape. His eyes focused on his hands, willing them to hold tight. He could not, would not let the beast free. Avalanche's head felt like there was no meat between the strangely soft scales and his boney skull. Melvin held on, expecting the krakon to buck him off at any second.

After what seemed like weeks, but was probably half a minute, Petro and Joe were out of the pool. The other keepers left, laughing.

"Melvin, loosen up a bit, buddy. You're going to suffocate the poor little guy," his uncle said. Petro had noticed how intensely focused Melvin was on top of the gator. His eyes were wide and his knuckles white. Petro flipped his phone open, pointing it at the gargoyle Melvin had become. "Smile."

The flash and click snapped Melvin out of his trance. "Can you take him?" Melvin asked, not moving his eyes from the boney green head.

Petro grabbed Avalanche's snout with one hand as he pried Melvin's away with the other. "I've got him. You can get off."

Melvin didn't stand up so much as jump off and over Petro. Joe had Loki in his arms like a long pile of squirmy green firewood. Petro struggled with Avalanche, but managed him into the same position.

Once Melvin was free from his impromptu job of beast-master, a shudder went up his spine. It seemed to shake the willies away, starting with his feet and ending in the tips of his outstretched fingers. He caught himself panting. He peeled R2D2 off the floor. R2 looked worse than after landing in the swamps of Dagobah.

Joe started down the hall with Loki. He had to walk sideways not to smack her head on every cage they passed. Loki swung her tail out at every lamp, cord, or spray bottle. She easily had a .700 batting average by the time they got through the hallway. Petro had to step through the debris. Luckily, Avalanche was a scaly sack of potatoes that put up no fight or argument.

Melvin picked up and straightened what he could as he followed the strange parade. Once back in the large room, Melvin ran ahead, opening the van's back doors. The gators slid in easily. Loki gave Joe one departing tail slap, leaving a pink mark across the left side of his neck.

Joe grabbed a couple of towels, handing one to Petro. The two men dried themselves off as much as possible. Petro pulled something out of his shirt pocket. "I found this in the bottom of the pool while we were waiting for you to get us out. I thought you might like it."

Melvin held out his hand. A white Chinese alligator tooth rolled onto his palm. "Cool!"

"I can do one better than that," Joe said. "I owe you for saving me from Avalanche. I'll be right back. I need to clear a spot on my wall." He disappeared around the corner.

A minute later he returned with a 'Bronx Zoo' baseball hat and a picture frame. He put the hat on Melvin's head and handed him the small frame. It had a pair of real snake fangs mounted inside. The caption read 'Gaboon Viper, *Bitis gabonica,* The largest fangs in the world.'

"If you hadn't thrown that towel on his head, I would've had to reset that." Joe pointed at a dry-erase board on the wall. It read 'Days without an accident … 3.'

A young man walking-by grumbled as Joe pointed at the sign. His entire left hand was bandaged.

"Freaking cool! Thanks, Joe!" Melvin exclaimed.

Petro's Field Notes
CHINESE ALLIGATOR

Chinese Alligator *(Alligator sinensis)* is one of only two kinds of alligators in the world, the American and the Chinese. The Chinese gets around five feet long and about eighty pounds. It is critically endangered, which means it is close to extinction. In fact, there may be more Chinese alligators in zoos than in the wild. They used to be more common, but people liked to eat them. So, I guess they taste good, too. I'm sure if they could talk, they'd say, "Do I look like a waffle or a pile of nachos? No! So quit eating us, you jerks!" Unfortunately, the only noises they can make sound like a walrus burping through a megaphone.

CHAPTER SEVEN
Recalibratin' Sucka

"**Great. We're all** set. We need to start moving. We've got to get these guys to Montgomery," Petro said, shaking Joe's hand.

Joe smiled. "Take care of 'em. It was good to see you guys, even if I'm going to be made fun of for the next two weeks. Nice to meet you, Melvin. Thanks again for the assist back there."

"No problem. Thanks for the fangs, oh, and the hat." Petro and Melvin hopped in the van. The gators huddled together near the back, wide-eyed.

"Are they going to be all right back there?" Melvin asked.

"Sure. They'll be fine. I'll turn the A/C up to high. That should make them nice and sleepy."

Melvin wrapped his framed fangs in a t-shirt and stuffed it deep into his duffle bag full of clothes. Petro shifted the van into drive and pulled away from the Herpetarium.

"See there. This should be an easy trip," Petro jinxed. The van lumbered over the first speed bump. Avalanche and Loki didn't care for it. Avalanche instantly went into a death roll, which seemed to be his go-to move during any time of confusion. Loki ran for the front of the van. She hit the pile of luggage at full speed, which is pretty darn fast considering she only had a five-foot start. Instead of going over the bags, she went right through the middle. Her short, powerful legs spun boots, ditty bags, and backpacks in every direction. Luckily, her back legs tangled in the strap of Petro's big, army-green duffle. She landed between Melvin and Petro's seats, stuck and thrashing wildly.

Melvin squeaked, "I don't think free range is such a good idea."

Petro reached down, pinning the angry gator's head to the floor with his right hand, his left still steering. Melvin slung the sopping wet R2D2 towel over her head, resoaking Petro's arm in the process. Petro released Loki's head long enough to get his arm on the other side of the towel. Once her eyes were covered, she calmed a bit. She thrashed a few more times, half-heartedly.

Petro coasted over the last few speed bumps. Avalanche tangled himself in one of the seatbelts attached to the floor where the van seats should be. "Be cool. I don't want the guard to think we don't know what we're doing."

"Do we know what we're doing?"

"Mostly. Just stay calm. I can fix'em once we get away from the zoo." Petro waved at the guard with his left hand as he pulled up to the gate.

The guard gave Petro a suspicious, stink-eyed look as he approached. Melvin thought the man's face must have stuck that way as a child.

"Papers?"

"I was just getting those. Melvin, where did I put those papers?" Petro's arm shook with a small tremor from Loki.

Melvin pulled the papers from the glove box. Petro had to reach across with his left hand, which probably seemed awkward to the guard. His look intensified.

The guard's radio beeped to life. "You can let them go, Tom. They have clearance."

His eyes narrowed to a ridiculous slit. He pulled the radio from his belt and spoke into it. "On whose authority?"

"This is Joe in the Herpetarium," the radio crackled.

Melvin desperately wanted to say, "These are not the droids you're looking for. Move along." But he didn't dare.

The guard scanned the papers and handed them back. His eyes squinted with the assurance that all was well on his watch. "Thanks for visiting the Bronx Zoo." The gate opened. The travelers put on their sunglasses and were off.

Petro pulled into New York City traffic while wrestling an alligator with one arm. At the first traffic light, he put the van in park. He unbuckled his belt, and managed to turn Loki around. Melvin tried to untangle her back leg from the duffle. Once she was pointed in another direction, she took off again, taking the bag with her. Petro shifted the van back into drive. The light turned green. Horns began half a second after. The insistent beeps seemed to fluster Petro more than two alligators running free in the vehicle. The van lurched forward as he struggled to put his seatbelt back on.

The sound of the horns inspired Avalanche to release one of his deafening throat burps, though he was upside down and tangled in a seatbelt. Petro jumped, but kept the van under control. Melvin flinched, but smiled, starting to feel as though his summer trip wouldn't be as bad as he thought.

He dialed the destination of Montgomery, Alabama, into Mr. T's console, suction cupped to the dash. Although the temperature was well into the nineties outside, the A/C on full blast made the van quite chilly. Melvin searched one of his strewn bags for a hoodie. He ventured into the back to find one for his uncle, too. They had matching black sweatshirts, with the hoods pulled tight over their heads to stay warm.

"I've got to pull over to secure the gators," Petro said after a mile of city blocks. Four blocks later he pulled into the first spot he found. He parallel parked on the pedestrian-filled street. He switched off the van and maneuvered his way into the back. Petro quickly untangled Loki from the duffle. Avalanche was more of a challenge.

Melvin built a blockade out of luggage so Loki couldn't burst through again. He hooked backpack straps though the arms of the seats, weaving the bags into an impenetrable net.

The gators became docile once the air cooled all the way to the back of the van. Petro and Melvin had everything and everyone secure, finally. They were, however, stuck in the back of the van.

"I guess we have to go out the back door to get back in the front. Make sure the doors are unlocked. I'll block the gators while we get out," Petro said. It sounded like a good plan.

Melvin hit the unlock button, while Petro pushed the two tired reptiles to one side of the van. Melvin swung the back door open and backed into the street. Petro followed, having to open the other side of the back door to hold the gators in place while he backed out. A beam of sunlight shone through the open doors, landing on Loki's head. Excited, she lifted up, bellowing a deep, throaty boom.

New Yorkers are used to lots of noise on the streets. Car horns, loud music, yelling, and jackhammers are common everywhere in the city. A huge growling boom, coming from the back of a van was not something people were used to. Two guys dressed in black hoods in the middle of summer and wearing sunglasses were worrisome. Give those same guys a pair of alligators and it's downright scary.

"Dude's got a crocodile!" a man yelled as he backed away, running over people. In his hurry to flee, he ran squarely into a telephone pole. His head glanced off the immovable object, and he landed on his butt. He reached up to his scalp and found blood on his fingers from the layers of staples attaching years of flyers. "I'm bleeding! I've been attacked! It was those dudes with the crocs!" He yelped, while flapping his arms as if he could levitate.

"Don't let it eat my baby!" a woman screamed. Her baby was a two-hundred pound sweaty kid sucking on an ice cream cone. The boy's eyes widened as his mother grabbed his plump hand and dragged him away from the van. He dropped his ice cream and began to wail.

Most people walking by didn't notice much until they saw the blood on the man's face and heard the chubbster squawking. Mass panic ensued. People fell over one another to get away from whatever everyone else was trying to get away from. It was a New York City stampede.

"It's okay, folks. These are just Chinese alligators in transport. Nothing to worry about." Petro attempted to calm the fleeing crowd. "We should probably go."

"Yah," Melvin agreed. They closed the back doors and hopped in the front seat. Dozens of people pointed and yelled at the van as if it were about to explode. Others fumbled clumsily about, seemingly scared out of their mind, but not sure why. Luckily, people blindly running away stopped traffic so Petro had a clear shot for a block.

Stupid Alabama by Michael P. Wines

He turned right at the first chance, then left, and right again. All the while, Mr. T repeated, "Recalibrating, Sucka."

"That was weird."

"Yah," Melvin agreed again.

CHAPTER EIGHT

Communist Crocodiles

A few quiet minutes passed. The gators seemed content with the mischief they caused and settled in for a nap.

Petro's stomach grumbled. "If you see a good place to get a calzone, tell me. I've got to have one before I leave the city. It's tradition."

Melvin reached over and snatched the cell phone out of Petro's shirt pocket. "Okay. Let me see your phone."

"Don't change my ring to a fart, like you did last Thanksgiving. I got lots of weird looks. I didn't know how to change it back. It was days before I could get to my cell store to get it fixed. It didn't help that you and your dad called me every ten minutes, either."

Melvin paused from fiddling with the cellular to smile proudly at Petro. "I want the picture you took of me while I was sitting on Avalanche." Melvin found the picture quickly, even though the phone was ancient. Proudly pulling out his newer cell, he texted it to himself. "I'm surprised this phone has a camera on it. It's so old."

"I got that phone six months ago. It was brand new then."

"It might as well be a cup with a string. It won't hold mp3s or video, and only has a three megapixel camera. Lame." He handed it back to Petro.

"Sorry, I don't get spoiled by my grandparents like you do. And don't let your mom see that picture. If she finds out we're transporting gators, this'll be a short, painful trip. So that means don't paste it on Facebook."

Melvin cringed as he looked at the picture. He knew it would end badly if his mom saw it. Avalanche's mouth looked like the only thing holding it shut was Melvin's hands. The tape was covered by his grip. He really wanted to show it off. "I'm going to send it to Chucky. I'll tell him not to send it to anybody."

Melvin's phone surprised him with a beep before he could send the picture. It was an oddly timed text from Chucky. "Did you hear!? Two guys are terrorizing New York with giant crocodiles."

"I think we are going to have to skip the calzone this time." Melvin turned on the van radio.

"What? Why?"

"Just listen." Melvin tuned from station to crackly station. He scanned pop, rap, alternative, Spanish, and a few other stations until he got to the broadcast of a cable news channel.

"This breaking news just in. Two men assaulted a crowd of people in the South Bronx with huge crocodiles. They jumped out of a van wearing black hoods and sunglasses. Our lead crime reporter, Mitch Mitchum, is on his way to the scene as we speak."

Petro's stomach grumbled again, but not with hunger. "Crap, your mother is going to kill me."

Melvin's phone rang as if on cue. "Hi, Mom, what's up?" He tried to sound cheerful and ignorant of the fact that he could be facing the electric chair soon, which was decidedly better than his mother's worry-wrath twice in two days.

"Are you two out of town yet? If not, hurry it up. We may be under attack again. There are men with crocodiles chasing children."

Melvin thought the last thing his mother needed was more ideas on how he could die at any second of any day. "I heard about that. It's on the radio. I doubt it's anything to worry about, probably just a misunderstanding." He knew it wouldn't stop his mom from twitching with mental images of him being gulped down by giant reptiles. "We're almost into New Jersey. No worries, Mom."

"Oh, thank goodness. You stay away from men in vans," Shea said as if it were a mantra she hadn't told Melvin since before he could crawl.

"But I'm in a van right now with a man." He couldn't help but annoy his parents sometimes.

"Your Uncle Petro doesn't count."

Melvin jumped at the opportunity to annoy both his uncle and his mother. "Mom just said you aren't a man."

"What?" Petro asked, truly confused, having only heard Melvin's side of the conversation.

"Oh, stop that. I'm serious about staying away from strangers in vans."

"Sorry, I know, Mom. I'm careful. Besides, who better to be with than Uncle Petro if we are attacked by giant crocodiles?"

"Good point. Just be careful. You know I worry."

Melvin and half the eastern seaboard knew his mother worried. A few minutes of "Wear your seatbelt," "Look before crossing," and "Mind your uncle," finished off the conversation.

"She doesn't suspect yet," Melvin said, feeling ashamed for not telling his mother the whole truth. He pulled Igor from his backpack, flipped him open and typed 'Rusty is a buttwart' into the password log-on space. Igor hummed to life.

Petro said, "Joe called me while you were talking to your mother. He wanted to know why a dozen reporters were banging down his door for information on the crocodiles being used as weapons by two men. He suggested if we were asked about it to say we don't know a thing. We have permits and aren't doing anything illegal, end of story." Petro's stomach growled again. Though he wasn't doing anything wrong, he still felt too guilty to stop for that calzone.

"We should probably take off these hoodies for a while."

Melvin googled 'Crocodiles in New York'. Several links came up. He clicked on the first one, which was a thirty second video of a witness' account.

Mitch Mitchum stood with dashingly mussed hair, a butt-chin, and a microphone next to the same guy who yelled, "Dude's got a crocodile," before running over several people to get away. Both men look proud of themselves for being on TV.

"This is Mitch Mitchum on the scene with a firsthand witness to the brutal attack," Mitch reported with a twinkle to his huge freakishly white teeth. "Tell us what you saw, sir."

"Dude had a crocodile!"

"What happened next?" Concern flooded Mitchum's face.

"Two dudes with crocodiles came out of a van. He said he was Chinese, but you couldn't tell, because they was wearing black hoods and dark glasses. They was goin' after a lady's baby. I jumped in between them, so the baby wouldn't get gobbled up. He's really lucky I was there. That's how I got this gash in my skull, protectin' the babies!" The man's eyes looked as if he almost believed it himself.

"You heard it here first, New York. Keep a look out for two Chinese men, in a van wearing black hoods and sunglasses. If you should see the culprits, stay back for your own safety, and call 911. Wait, this just in, we have a picture of the van and the men that another witness took with his camera phone."

Melvin and Petro gulped. The signal stopped. Petro was driving through the Holland Tunnel, into New Jersey, so there was no way Igor's satellite feed could continue until they were through. A few agonizing minutes passed. The only sound was the hum of the tunnel walls whizzing by. The tube opened to a blue sky in Jersey City and the slow, steady traffic of I-78 westbound.

Igor found the signal. A picture came on the screen of confused people running away from the area of the van. The unhelpful witness was about to bounce into the fat eight year-old because he wasn't looking where he was going. The kid's mother pointed at the back of the van where Petro and Melvin in black sweatshirts faced the other direction. The doors to the van were closed and the license plate was blocked by Melvin as he turned to get into the front seat. There was no way to identify Melvin, Petro, or the van from the camera-phone photo.

Melvin exhaled the breath he didn't realize he was holding. "That's a horrible picture. You can't tell anything by it. Whoever took it must have a phone like yours."

Mitch Mitchum continued. "There you have it, folks, evil men hatching an evil plot to bring down our wonderful city. Even crocodiles can't break the spirit of this town. No terrorist organization has claimed responsibility for the attacks yet. There are whispers on the street it could be the communists trying to restart the cold war, and what better way to do it than with cold-blooded dragons as weapons. I, Mitch Mitchum, lead investigative reporter with channel 5 news, will be here and anywhere to report that we aren't scared. We will not be intimidated by these communist crocodiles. I swear to get to the bottom of this story, and bring those responsible to justice. Back to you, Tina."

"Mitch Mitchum is an idiot," Melvin said.

CHAPTER NINE
Onion Rings are for Rookies

New Jersey flew by in a haze of smokestacks, warehouses, and parking lots as Petro drove west on I-78. "Do they call this the Garden State because there's only one garden?"

"I think they're being hopeful that someone will start one someday," Melvin replied, settling in for a long ride. The van was an icebox on wheels. It worked great for the gators, putting them into slow motion -- well actually, no motion.

The last fifteen minutes of the state surprised the travelers with lush green hills and fields. "I think somebody is playing a joke on New Jersey. They moved the Welcome to Pennsylvania signs twenty miles to the east."

Petro's nervousness eased a bit as they drove farther from the city. He'd been sitting rigidly, clutching the wheel with white knuckles since the Holland Tunnel. He, unlike Melvin, was out of his element in the city.

'Welcome to Pennsylvania, the Keystone State,' the sign read. Petro was almost back to his normal comfort level, or at least acting like the Petro Melvin knew.

"What does keystone mean?" Melvin wondered, having nothing else to do.

"No idea. I do know a keystone species is one that's really important to its environment, compared to others in the same place.

So, maybe Pennsylvania being the Keystone State means it is more important than the others. Heck, I don't know."

"What did you say, Sucka? I was looking up Pennsylvania on *Wikipedia*." Melvin soaked up Mr. T's gift of gab like a Mohawk-shaped sponge. "The short version is the state was in the middle of the original thirteen colonies and lots of government stuff was done here. Big woop. It's also known as the chocolate state. If I were the sign-making guy, that's what I would put on the sign, instead of that keystone jibba-jabba."

"What's Wiki … what's huh?"

"You don't know *Wikipedia*? It's an online encyclopedia that anyone can edit. I use it all the time."

"If anyone can edit it, how do you know the information is right?"

"If it's wrong, somebody changes it back quickly. Usually, people edit it to correct small mistakes, like dates or places, in an effort to get the information as correct as possible."

"Sounds cool," Petro said. Conversation lulled as Petro thought. A smile crinkled onto his mug as he scratched at the place a mustache should be, but wasn't.

Melvin wondered why he wasn't pulling at the hair under his lip instead. He recognized the evil grin spreading across his uncle's face. He knew it well. His father had the same grin when he was plotting. Melvin caught himself doing the same squinty-eyed half smile a couple of times while planting a plastic cockroach or putting a rubber band on the sprayer nozzle on the kitchen sink. He better break his uncle's train of thought before the train ran him over. Food was one of the better distractions for a Fitzpatrick male. "You still hungry for that calzone?"

Petro snapped out of his devilish haze. Melvin knew he looked forward to a huge New York-style calzone every time he visited his brother. Usually, when Briar went south for a visit, he would take a fresh calzone on the plane. That would usually insure Petro would be there to pick him up from the airport. Petro called it a wheel tax. "I think I missed my chance for the wheel tax."

"What?"

"Never mind, I'm hungry. Be on the lookout for some tasty victuals."

"What's a victuals?" Melvin almost busted out *Wikipedia* again.

"Victuals is a term for food, cooked up Southern style."

"You mean like opossum or deep fried frog legs? I don't think they make that in Pennsylvania. Eww, and I'm glad."

"Just look for a place to eat, you little twerp. Too bad we aren't anywhere near Philly. We could get cheese steaks. Let's get through Allentown. We can get something on the road after." Petro's stomach howled and growled, but he wanted to avoid anything that could pass for a large town or city after the alligator incident earlier.

Melvin was hungry, too, but it subsided at the thought of opossum parts. "I'll google the map ahead. How about we stop in Hamburg? There has to be good food there and it's not too far."

"I can dig it. You're the navigator. Tell me when to pull off."

A few miles later the travelers looked over menus at a greasy spoon. "Let's get this to go. We don't want the car to get too warm." Petro avoided any discussion of the alligators in front of the locals, just to be safe.

The diner had the typical menu. Melvin's eyes narrowed as the corners of his mouth twisted with the taste of a plot forming. His mother forbade him from eating onion rings due to the offensive effects Melvin produced as a result. He realized his mother wasn't around for the vile aftermath, but his unsuspecting uncle was. "I'll have a cheeseburger and an extra large order of onion rings, please, ma'am." He felt like an old west gunslinger loading the chambers of his six-shooter pooter. "Extra pickles and a Mello Yello."

The waitress looked at him funny for ordering so dramatically. "Sure, sweetie, and for you?" She turned to Petro.

"Cheeseburger, fries, and a Coke for me, please." After a pause, Petro added, "Can I have a cup of chili with that, too?" Petro settled the bill while Melvin managed his drink, a large cardboard cup of chili, and two paper bags soaked through with grease.

They hopped back in the van. The gators were still in the back, although Loki had turned around. They were behaving themselves. Petro got back onto the interstate before eating.

Meanwhile, Melvin inhaled his onion rings, barely stopping to chew. He preferred fries, but was willing to make the sacrifice on such an occasion. He finished the rings off with a handful of sliced pickles, which would provide a nice sour tinge to his developing gas grenade.

He let out a giggle, thinking of the fine line between farting and pooping in front of someone. One was the funniest thing on the planet. A fart could make a nun laugh. The other was Melvin's worst nightmare. He had a phobia about pooping in public bathrooms. Luckily, the bomb he was about to detonate was all gas. He chewed the cheeseburger slowly, enjoying the flavor of oncoming victory.

"You must really like onion rings," Petro said with what could have been a nervous laugh. Melvin hoped his uncle didn't sense anything amiss while watching Melvin suck his food down like a zombie with a fresh plate of brain soufflé.

"I eat them every chance I get," Melvin said, truthfully. He pulled this prank on Chucky once during a sleepover. It was the only time Melvin saw him cry.

They finished their meals and picked up I-81 south in Harrisburg. A few miles past town, orange signs appeared warning of construction ahead. Two lanes of traffic flowed steadily while the third veered off at an exit. Cars slowed as a sign read, 'Right lane ends one-half mile, merge now'. The van crawled, already in the left lane. A few minutes later they were stopped in the single narrow lane, concrete barriers on either side of them.

Melvin felt his bowels expanding with buildup of onion and pickle gas. It was almost high noon and the faceoff was about to begin. He couldn't help grinning at the perfect trap he laid. Petro couldn't get out of the van even if he wanted to. He couldn't roll the windows down for long because the heat would wake up the gators. A few seconds of strong wind while driving on the interstate may knock most of the smell out, but they were sitting still, no breeze.

Melvin watched his uncle. He seemed to be having a daydream. He was rubbing his upper lip, as if he had a mustache.

Mr. T broke the silence after a couple minutes of sitting still. "You betta' check yo'self. There is construction ahead."

"Thanks for the warning, genius," Petro said.

Melvin's stomach contracted with a tiny giggle. That's all he needed. The pressure had nowhere to go but out. He grabbed the seat handles, leaning forward into a truly maniacal laugh.

Petro looked over, confused. His joke hadn't been that funny.

Melvin attacked with a sound rivaling one of Avalanche's throat burps. The note continued for a second, going up in pitch then finishing with a machine-gun crescendo. It smelled like an inside-out warthog got tossed into a meeting of skunks who have a fear of inside out-warthogs. Melvin cried with laughter, releasing little stragglers with every cackle.

Petro wept as a defense mechanism to keep his eyes from imploding. "It was the onion rings, wasn't it?" he gasped, realizing his mistake. "Well played, young man. That was truly disgusting. You are your father's son. I think you floated off the seat."

Melvin's pride was apparent, even through the sweatshirt he held over his nose and mouth. "Mom won't let me have onion rings."

"I have to tell you something, boy," Petro said seriously as the smell finally began to dissipate.

Melvin became somewhat nervous. His uncle had never been mad at him. Petro's tone and staunch face pulled him out of his laughing fit. "What?"

"I. Hate. Chili." Petro released a counterstrike that could have been Genghis Khan's battle cry. The stench was thick, warm, and wrong. It put Melvin's putrescence to shame. The windows steamed. The gators buried their snouts in luggage, tired of the awful human games.

Melvin broke first. He hung his head out the window, gasping for shameful relief.

"This is going to be a long trip, Rookie," Petro said. Crying but smiling, he rolled down his own window. The line of cars mercifully began to move.

CHAPTER TEN
Curse of the Cowboy Boot

Petro was right, much to Melvin's dismay. It was a long, long trip. I-81 took them through a thin slice of Maryland and into Virginia. The Great Smoky Mountains crept around them like a half-frozen turtle crawling through a molasses swamp.

Having grown up in one of the busiest and most bustling cities in the world gave Melvin an attention span of zero. There was always something to distract him from boredom. The slow hum of the engine, mixed with miles and miles of stretched-out interstate grated his patience down to a thickness of a flea's whisker.

"Quit squirming and read a book or something," Petro suggested. He fiddled with the stereo buttons. "National Public Radio never comes in unless you're close to a city," he pouted in defeat, turning off the static.

N.P.R. was the only station Petro listened to and Melvin was glad the van couldn't pick it up. He could have tuned it in on any number of electronics devices besides the radio, but thought better of mentioning it. Melvin could only take so many hours of two guys gabbing about cars, or a group of dorks singing about some lake in Minnesota. The news shows were the worst. All they talked about were money, and people growing gardens in new ways or places that Melvin couldn't pronounce, much less find on a map. He was familiar with all the shows because it was the only station his parents listened to, as well. Maybe only old people can appreciate talk radio that doesn't include bodily function sounds and prank calls.

Melvin warmed up Igor, his laptop, for a distracting game of Ranger's Assassin. He plugged in his ear-buds to get the full effect of decapitating cave-trolls and dismembering bumble-orcs.

Petro piloted the van up hills and down valleys. They went around cliffs and over bridges. Melvin played on, happily slaughtering everything his seventeenth-level shaman-warrior came across. His mind was contentedly occupied. His stomach, however, was still in the van. Melvin noticed the butterflies gingerly flitting around in his stomach. He ignored them like he did every time he read a book on the subway. They always went away.

There were two problems with using the same strategy he used in the subway. The first was he never opened his computer to play a video game while on public transportation. He always kept it hidden in his backpack. His father warned him of thieves. Lots of people wanted a sleek-looking computer, but no one would steal a paperback. While reading is a good distraction for a long ride, it didn't absorb Melvin's attention like Ranger's Assassin.

The other problem was the movement of the van through the mountains was much different from the movement of a subway car through the city. The stops and starts forced a person to focus on his surroundings; otherwise, he would be sent sprawling onto the floor or into the next person. People don't like to touch each other, or even acknowledge one another's existence in the city. So flying into a stranger on a subway was frowned upon.

The van ride was vastly different. It was smooth, without sudden jerks and frequent breaks to let people on and off. A subtle, sneaky nausea was building. Eventually, the butterflies flitting became pterodactyls flapping. Melvin paused the game, folding the computer shut.

"I think we need to pull over," he spat. His mouth began to water. His stomach rang alarm bells, wailed sirens, and set off screeching foghorns in his mind. Emergency!

Petro returned from his own far-off place, not realizing the regurgitative apocalypse was upon him. "What's up, buddy? Gotta pee? There's an exit coming up."

An exit wasn't the only thing coming up. Melvin didn't have time to roll down the window, nor did he think of it in his sudden panic. He had half of a precious second to shove Igor off his lap and out of the way. Then it came. Melvin's mouth and nose boiled bubbling crude. His stomach felt like a dumpster full of cats and firecrackers after someone dropped in a torch.

"Aaaagggghhh," Petro yelled in response to the sound of the sickening splat.

"Aaaagggghhh," Melvin gurgled. He didn't have anywhere to project but couldn't stop himself. He looked about frantically for a receptacle, finding nothing. He tried covering the geyser with his hands, only to have the awful chunky juice spray from between his fingers. When he realized vomit was on his hands, he let go, flinging slimy bits as he did.

His eyes widened in horror. The sour plume wouldn't stop. He looked to Petro for answers.

"Don't point it at me!" Petro began maneuvering the van to the side of the road while frantically pushing buttons in a futile attempt to lower the passenger window. Each second seemed like hours as his nephew lobbed cream of onion ring soup bombs all over the interior.

Melvin turned his sprinkler head of goo back to the front, spritzing the windshield and dash as he turned. After several years and at least half of Melvin's weight in puke, Petro found the right button. Melvin noticed, with relief, the window going down. It lowered almost fast enough to keep up with Melvin's turning head. Almost. The amazingly steady stream hit the window as it lowered, sending up a misty rainbow of onion ring, soda pop, and sulfur sauce, bedazzling the cab as it went. As suddenly as the floods came, they receded. Amazingly, not one drop made it outside the van.

"Are you okay?"

Oddly, besides having the worst breath ever, being covered head to toe in ick, and feeling inside out, Melvin felt pretty good. "I think so."

"You don't need to go to the hospital? I better call your mom and check." Petro looked scared.

"I'm fine. Don't do that. If you tell her I'm puking in a van full of alligators, she'll drive down here, pick me up, and kill you. If you absolutely have to call someone, call Dad."

Petro mulled for a moment. They pulled off the first exit, which happened to be a truck stop. There was almost always a hose around back truckers used to do truck stuff with. Melvin hopped out and shook like a Labrador coming out of a pond. Petro hosed him off, clothes and all. Melvin went inside to change while Petro sprayed and cleaned out the rest of the van, carefully avoiding luggage and electronics. Luckily it was plastic-lined, which made for easy hosing. The gators weren't affected in the back of the van, so they, thankfully, stayed quiet and calm.

The boy returned with two Sprites to settle their stomachs and a handful of car fresheners in the shape of pine trees. Any time his stomach was upset, his mom gave him a Sprite. The bubbles and burps seemed to calm the churning.

Petro called Briar on the speaker phone. Petro was probably worried and needed reassurance from his brother. He wouldn't admit failure with Melvin, but really didn't want anything bad to happen to him under his care. He would never forgive himself.

Petro blurted out his confession fast, like Melvin blurted out his lunch. After the pukefest, he seemed overly worried he might have taken on too much responsibility with a kid for the summer.

"Hey, Briar, it's Petro. Look, Melvin just got really sick and threw up all over the van. He seems okay now. I just wanted to call and check in. Do you think I did something wrong? Should I take him to the hospital? Should I bring him back to you guys?" There were a few long, quiet seconds after Petro's confession.

Melvin chimed in, "I'm fine, Dad. I just got carsick."

Briar didn't say anything. Instead, he broke into a fit of laughter. It lasted several minutes. He sounded like he was going to hyperventilate. Petro had no idea why he was laughing. He was almost scared to find out.

"I finally got you back, and I didn't even have to puke," Briar gasped through a fit of giggles.

Petro was beyond confused. "What are you talking about?"

"Don't you remember when you threw up in my cowboy boots? We were on a road trip and you got carsick. Dad handed you the first thing he saw, which was my brand new cowboy boot. I swore I would get you back for that. Well, there you go. We're even."

Petro couldn't see the tears rolling down his brother's face, but knew they were there. He might have been in shock at Briar's reaction. "Aren't you worried about Melvin?"

"Nope. Kids puke all the time. When we first had him, I thought there was something wrong with him. He leaked from everywhere. Kids are gross. It's nothing to worry about. If he were really sick, he wouldn't stop whining."

Melvin rolled his eyes. "Thanks, Dad. You always know how to make me feel better."

Petro's nerves calmed. "Glad you find this so funny. I was scared to death." He couldn't help but smile about the time he upchucked in his brother's boot. He mentioned the onion ring and chili incident, only to get another round of belly laughter from his older brother.

"I almost wish I was there with you guys. Almost."

After a few more minutes of needling from Briar, Petro looked more confident about taking care of his nephew.

Melvin almost felt sorry for his uncle after having to clean up puke and being made fun of. "Sorry I spewed hurl all over the van."

"That's okay. It's my fault. I was cursed long ago by a cowboy boot."

Petro gassed up and they resumed their trek. Loki reminded them of the true power of a Chinese alligator by pooping out a huge, fishy mess in the back of the van before they left the parking lot. Petro completed another round of hosing, with the back of the van parked facing a wall to block people from seeing the gators. He wouldn't make that mistake again. The travelers found their way back to I-81 south. What the group collectively lost in bodily fluids, Melvin thought Petro gained in confidence as leader of the strange little posse.

CHAPTER ELEVEN
Slug-Bug Democracy

"Stupid Virginia," Melvin pouted.

"What are you talking about?"

A few hundred miles of tedious, billboard-littered Interstate had crawled by since Melvin's eruption and he was beyond bored. "Virginia is stupid and boring and so freaking big," Melvin huffed. "How much farther?" He unfortunately knew exactly how much farther. Mr. T, the GPS unit, ticked off every tenth of a mile. Igor, Melvin's laptop with satellite feed, displayed nearly the same distance, give or take a mile depending on the route. Even Renfield, Melvin's phone, had a GPS application that confirmed the light-years between where they were and where they were going. They had been in the car for an agonizing ten hours and had over nine hours remaining until Montgomery.

"We're at least halfway there," Petro said hopefully, though his butt had begun hurting four hours into the trip.

Melvin punched Petro in the arm with his boney fist. "Slug-bug, green! Ha!"

Petro didn't show pain or surprise. He was a punch-bug veteran, having served an entire life of duty. His brother, Melvin's father, introduced him to the warfare as children.

"I bet I can find more slug-bugs than you. I'll win." Melvin was confident with energy to spare. Petro had to keep his eyes on the road; granted that was where most Volkswagens were, but it was the parking lots that gave the advantage to the passenger. Petro couldn't pause driving to scan rows of cars in the zillions of lots they passed.

Petro's eyes narrowed and his voice sounded deep and scary. "You may find more, but I'll win."

"Not if I hit you more times." Melvin's confidence waivered. "How could you possibly beat me if I find more than you?"

Petro continued as if possessed by Chuck Norris. "I just need one."

Melvin gulped. "Truce. I'm hungry."

They pulled off the road for a pit stop, grabbing some grub from one of a thousand places with a value menu. "I'll go get us some food. You run circles in the lot over there." Petro pointed at a small patch of grass off the side of the lot.

"But I wanna go in. Why do I have to run around in the grass?" Melvin didn't say no, but didn't see any reason to do everything his uncle said.

"I need you to watch the van. You're the sentinel to guard the gators and our stuff."

Melvin thought it might be time to start pushing boundaries. He needed to know how much he could get away with over the summer. "Just because you make it sound cool, doesn't mean I'll magically go along with it. And don't bring out the 'because I'm your elder and you have to do what I say' reason, either." He hated getting that reason and tried to cut it off before Petro added it to his arsenal.

"You have way too much energy and need to burn some. It'll make for a more tolerable ride," mumbled Petro.

Melvin's arms folded, eyes squinted, and he leaned back on one foot, which was the universal stance for arguing; just like a boxer would circle his opponent with his hands up, or a sprinter would get into a crouch in preparation for the starting gun. "I think the gators can guard the van better than I." There was a pause as the two stared.

"Don't you mean better than me?" Petro pounced on the chance to throw off Melvin's game plan.

They both knew a frustrating little distraction always helped in an argument. "Whatever, you know what I mean." Melvin dodged Petro's first jab and returned with a 'Whatever' roundhouse.

Petro squinted, peering over Melvin's shoulder. The corner of his mouth lifted into an evil sneer. "Slug-bug, blue."

"But we have a truce." Melvin spun for verification of the sighting. The car was there, the same color as the bruise that was coming. Petro got him fair and square according to his father's rules. He wasn't excited about dodging an actual punch.

"You can only call a truce if it's even or the one calling the truce just got hit. You can't hit someone, then call a truce. You know the rules of the game. The same person taught them to us. I never called a truce." It was a long standing law that couldn't be broken, like the result of a rock-paper-scissors game.

Melvin swore he heard an eerie whistle far in the distance.

"I'll call a truce when I get back with the food, after you've run circles in the grass. Or I could just hit you." Melvin's mental gears grinded, spun, and sputtered for a painless solution as Petro popped all the knuckles in his right hand.

"Fine, I'll run circles, but I really have to pee." He couldn't let Petro win completely.

"Well, go pee then, and get back out here."

As Melvin left for the bathroom, Petro turned to the van, pretending to rummage through one of his bags. Melvin knew he was hiding a smile. He won this round, but the battle was far from over.

It was considerate of his opponent not to brag after the tiny victory. Trash talking was always fine, even expected, in some wins, like the outcome of a board game or a college football rivalry. However, the first mini-battle over the alpha male position in a pack of two was not something to brag about. Bragging could produce a seed of resentment which could blossom into disobedience, or worse, a lack of trust, which would make a long hard summer for both of them.

Petro worked around wildlife, some of it dangerous if not handled carefully and respectfully. Melvin needed to have faith in what he said. He needed motivation to do what his uncle told him to do.

He needed to trust Petro and know he did things for a reason. Melvin hated being ordered around by adults without good cause. He felt like they just wanted him to do things to keep him occupied, which brought on disputes. Constant arguing would not lead to trust, nor would the old 'do what I say because I said so' reasoning.

"I'm getting a headache. I'm not used to being mature. I really hate giving up on a slug bug game, too," Petro said as Melvin walked back across the parking lot intentionally slow.

Petro pulled a metal whistle on a string from around his neck, handing it to Melvin. "Here, keep this. If you get in trouble, blow it and I'll come running."

Melvin tested it with a shrill toot.

"It's only for emergencies," Petro said as he pulled Melvin's hand down. The whistle seemed like a good idea, but the shrieking sound couldn't help his headache.

"I don't need it." Melvin pulled another whistle from around his own neck. It was plastic and looked high quality and expensive. "I've had this thing since I could walk. Take a guess at who gave it to me."

"Had to be your mom," Petro replied, smiling.

"Yup."

"It's good to know I'm on her wavelength, at least about some stuff. Now get to running." He nodded towards the grass patch.

Melvin watched Petro leave to get a couple value meals, hopefully avoiding anything with onions, pickles, or chili. The trip was already becoming a huge learning process and that was one lesson driven home. Melvin obediently ran big dusty circles on the dry grass patch until Petro returned.

They drove on into the night, finally stopping past Knoxville, Tennessee. Petro pulled into a rest stop for a few hours of sleep. Melvin passed out a couple of hours back and continued to sleep contentedly. The circles must have helped. They slept in their seats, doors locked under a street lamp in the van. Carrying two alligators into a motel room wouldn't work out well, and it was too hot to leave them in the van without the air conditioner running.

Petro leaned his seat back, rubbing the tunnel vision from his eyes. A few minutes later he was asleep. A couple quiet hours went by. The occupants of the van woke from the occasional big rig truck rolling by or someone's high beams rolling over their faces. Clouds slowly formed and a thick layer of dew covered everything stationary. Slowly, a few sprinkles of rain tapped on the roof and windows. It was enough rain to lull them into a deep sleep.

At precisely three-seventeen a.m., a boom rattled the van, making the water puddle on the roof vibrate. The passengers couldn't have been more shocked out of their sleep if a S.W.A.T unit busted in using flash bang grenades. It sounded as if a train hit a truck full of balloons.

Melvin leapt forward, tangled in his seatbelt while attempting to cover his head. He hit his knee on the dash and yelped as his heart kicked into overdrive. His head swung back and forth in wide-eyed panic.

Had the steering wheel not folded him in half on his way up, Petro would have been stuck to the ceiling like a cartoon cat in a room full of bulldogs. He beeped the horn accidentally, adding to the confusion.

Ten seconds of pain and confusion passed before everyone settled down and realized where they were and what was going on. Avalanche had released one of his sonic booms, probably inspired by rain tapping on the roof. Lights in a few cabs of parked trucks came on, only to go out minutes later.

Petro stretched and got out of the van mumbling something that sounded like coffee. Melvin took his turn when Petro came back with a huge, steaming cup from the vending machine. A few minutes later, they drove south again on I-75 towards Chattanooga, tired, alert, and a little rattled.

CHAPTER TWELVE
High-Five

Melvin and Petro made good time early Sunday morning. Mr. T estimated a six-and-a-half-hour drive, but the lack of traffic cut it by nearly an hour. The travelers didn't talk much over the remainder of the journey, still recovering from the previous day. The gators seldom stirred from their air conditioned-induced slumber. The Interstates flowed through Chattanooga, across the northwest sliver of Georgia, and deep into Alabama.

The red-clay soil wore kudzu like a blanket. The only things prospering besides the highway ivy were churches. They were everywhere, like Starbucks in the city. There seemed to be more places of worship than houses. The only things Melvin could tell people spent money on was church and huge truck tires. Maybe they need the big tires to cross the kudzu to get to Sunday school.

Petro sat up at the wheel and put on his 'professional' face. "We're about half an hour from the zoo. I need to stop and get cleaned up a bit."

Melvin thought Petro was being odd, considering they just hit a rest stop forty-five minutes earlier. Maybe he needed to get some paperwork together for the zoo people or something. They pulled off north of Montgomery. He didn't just change his clothes, he changed everything. He returned in clean, pressed khaki pants, a tucked-in button-up with a shiny belt, clean boots, hair combed and gelled, teeth sparkling, and Melvin thought he may have even smelled tolerable. He looked like the Crocodile Hunter on a job interview. There was definitely something up.

Melvin had to know. "Why'd you get so dressed up to drop off the gators?"

"What, this?" Petro asked, glancing down at his ensemble. "I'm going in to work and need to look professional around my colleagues."

Melvin let it go for the moment. "All right. I was just wondering. I don't have to wear a belt, and tuck in my shirt, do I?"

"No, but you may want to wipe the jelly off your chin. It's been riding along since breakfast."

Melvin scrubbed at his face with the sleeve of his hoodie. His mother's spit-covered thumb was probably itching somewhere. He pulled on his new 'Bronx Zoo' hat so he wouldn't have to comb his hair. The Fitzpatrick males all had the same light brown mane that looked like a cow's favorite flavor of lollipop. Gel could hold it down for a short while, but the finger-in-the- light-socket look always fought its way back.

Petro looked at Melvin several times as if he was building up to something important. "When we get there, I need you on your best behavior. Don't touch anything and watch where you're going. It's a zoo and it can be dangerous. We need to present ourselves as professional to my colleagues, since this is work."

Melvin wondered why his uncle gave him the speech now, but didn't yesterday before they went to the Bronx Zoo. He smelled a rat, and it was wearing cologne. He would never do anything to get in the way of Petro's work. His dad taught him better. Work is not something to take lightly. Maybe Melvin was being paranoid and Petro performed his job more professionally than he thought. It was funny to hear his uncle say the word *colleagues* so seriously. He had mentioned them twice in the past few minutes. Then, being the eleven-year-old kid he was, he started thinking about the elephants and tigers he might encounter and forgot all about his uncle's strange professionalism.

"Hey, Jonesy," Petro said to the guard at the back entrance to the zoo. The smiling, pauch-bellied man swaggered over to the van window.

"Hey there, Petro. How goes it?"

Petro replied, "Fine, fine. I've got these two gators from the Bronx. I assume they're going to the quarantine building. Who's the vet today?"

"That would be Dr. Gillam. I'll get her on the radio and have her meet you over there. Want me to get a keeper, too?"

Petro smiled. "I think we can handle them. Besides, I've got my nephew with me and he's an experienced gator wrestler." Petro leaned back in his seat as Jonesy waved to Melvin.

"Hello there, young man. Okay. You know, since he's not on our official payroll, he's not supposed to touch a gator. It's a class-one animal," Jonesy reminded.

"Oh, I know. See ya later, Jonesy," Petro said, driving past the gate, as if on a mission.

"Nice to meet you." Melvin and Jonesy both waved as the van zipped into the parking lot.

Petro backed the van to a clean-looking roll-up garage door with a huge 'Q' painted in blue. He checked his teeth in the mirror again and pasted down the hairs that had escaped the gel already. Melvin pulled off his hoodie and slid Renfield, also known as his multi-phone, into his pocket. He didn't get enough pictures while at the Bronx Zoo and wanted to make up for that.

Petro walked to the back of the van, brushing wrinkles out of his pants as he went. Then he waited. He looked like a game show contestant who didn't know what to do with his hands while on camera. He put them in his pockets, then on his hips, then back in his pockets. He was nervous about something, which made Melvin uneasy too. After a few minutes the garage door rolled up, making Petro jump. He quickly righted himself and turned to the door.

An attractive, friendly-looking lady walked out. "Hey, Petro. Sorry if I made you wait. Who's your friend?"

"Um, hello, Dr. Gillam. This is Melvin. He's my nephew. I'm watching him. For the summer." Petro's words came out stiffly in short bursts. He pointed robotically at Melvin as he introduced him, but his eyes never left Dr. Gillam's face.

Melvin looked at his uncle as if a turnip just grew out of his nose. Then he looked at Dr. Gillam. Then back at his uncle. "Oh …," he said aloud, realizing why Petro was acting so weird. He had the hots for Dr. Gillam.

"Nice to meet you, Melvin. You can call me Cassidy, and so can you, Petro. I feel old when people call me Dr. Gillam." She put her hand out to shake with Melvin.

"Um, sorry. You're not old." Petro spat. Along with the goofy hair, the Fitzpartick boys inherited a gene that made them act like blathering idiots around pretty girls.

"Nice to meet you, too," Melvin replied, shaking her hand.

Cassidy smiled at Petro, possibly catching on that something was weird. "So, you guys brought me some gators. Did they give you any trouble?"

"No, all was good." Petro opened the van door.

Loki's tail swung out, hitting Petro in the crotch, as if Babe Ruth's ghost had been coaching her swing for the past two days. Petro leaned over, one hand on the van door for balance. "Oof," was all he could get out. Loki trotted off to the other end of the van, happily.

"Homerun!" Melvin couldn't help but laugh.

"Ouch, are you okay?" Cassidy stifled a giggle, but let it out when she met Melvin's eyes.

"I'm fine," Petro gasped, his face red with pain and embarrassment. He picked up Avalanche and carried him through the door into a clean exam room, trying to ignore the ache.

Cassidy fought the smile off her face. "Set him on the table. I need to examine him before we put him in his pool. Do you have time to help me get them situated, or do you need to get going? I can get a keeper to help if need be."

"I've got plenty time. Sorry, plenty of time, whatever you need." Petro's smoothness rivaled a cactus.

"Can you weigh him for me?" Cassidy put on rubber gloves while looking over the transfer paperwork.

"Eighty-six pounds." Petro carried him over to the stainless steel exam table and leaned across Avalanche, securing his head in one arm and his tail in the other. Avalanche didn't seem to mind; he still had his snout taped shut. The vet ran a metal-detector-looking device over Avalanche's back. It beeped and flashed a number on the screen. Cassidy scribbled something on a chart. She poked and prodded the gator in just about every soft spot Melvin could think of. Then Petro leaned back, exposing the alligator's belly. Avalanche struggled but calmed down after a moment, until Cassidy put her thumb up the gator's butt. That's right, her thumb went right up in there. Avalanche let out a wide-eyed grunt.

"Yup, he's a boy," was all Cassidy said upon pulling her thumb out. She looked at Melvin, who was slack-jawed. She held up the hand that had just been in the gator bum. "High-five?"

Melvin shook his head. She laughed while changing gloves. She proceeded to draw blood from the middle of Avalanche's skull. "There's a great vein right here in the head of crocodilians for getting blood. It's usually the easiest place to draw from."

Melvin's eyes became the size of Avalanche's as he watched the syringe fill with a thick red stream. She took the blood over to a counter and divided it among slides and tubes and other things Melvin wasn't familiar with. She wrote more on the chart, then gestured for Petro. He followed, carrying Avalanche like a stack of firewood. Once they got to the gator's room, Petro held him tight as Cassidy took the tape off his mouth. Petro released him into a sloped pool, slightly bigger than the one at the Bronx Zoo.

They did the same with Loki. She put up more of a fight, but was smaller and easier to deal with. She swam fast to the corner of the pool, splashing all three with a fast swipe of her tail.

"Crap," Cassidy said. "Sorry about that. I've got some towels in my office.

"No problem," Petro grunted, now back to staring at the young doctor's face. "No more glasses?"

Cassidy smiled. "Nope, I got eyeball surgery, so I don't need them anymore. Thanks for noticing."

Petro blushed. "Um, you're welcome." He exhaled, shaking his head in shy frustration. "Looks good," he continued in all his Shakespearean glory.

Strangely enough, Cassidy blushed.

Melvin stood there, not wanting to ruin his uncle's groove, but really wanted that towel. "Did you say you had a towel?"

"Oh, yeah, sorry. They're in my office here." She stepped through a door and Petro followed, almost knocking Melvin out of the way. She handed out towels from a stack on a shelf. The office was small and blue. It had an L-shaped desk in one corner and a large fish tank. There was a sign on the front of the tank with pictures identifying yellow tangs, a lion fish, and a couple of clown trigger fish. There was a shelf above the tank with several trophies. One was a chrome dodgeball reading 'Best Out of the Match,' another was a girl throwing a ball. The plaque on that one read 'First Place – Auburn Ball Smashers.'

"What's an Auburn Ball Smasher?" Melvin asked.

"That's my dodgeball team. We play every week or so."

"That's cool. I didn't know you were a dodgeballer." Petro seemed to get his words back finally. "I've heard of you guys, but never had a chance to come watch."

"You should come by sometime. We play in Auburn. Unfortunately, this week's bout was canceled due to injuries."

"I, uh, we'd love to come sometime. We couldn't come this week, though. I've got a reptile lecture at the nature center this Saturday. Melvin's going to help me with it." Petro probably made a mental note to cancel whatever he had to do on any Saturday, ever.

Melvin's eyes widened. "News to me."

Cassidy walked out of her office door, "That sounds fun. I sponsor a girl that comes with me to the games. It's a big sister, little sister thing. I was wondering what we could do this week since the match was canceled. I'll bring her to your lecture."

"Good plan." Petro went back to single syllables at the thought of seeing Cassidy outside of the zoo.

"We can make it a date," she said so matter-of-factly that she could have been ordering extra sugar in her coffee. "Now, can you help me with one more thing?"

Melvin looked up at Petro, who seemed to be looking at everything and nothing at the same time. He was probably rechecking what Cassidy just said to make sure it was what she actually said.

"You're catching flies," Melvin said, but not loud enough for Cassidy to hear. Petro abruptly closed his mouth into a proud grin. Melvin realized there was an opportunity to be annoying. "Ewwww, Petro's got a daaate," began Melvin, pointing and shaking his head and shoulders at his uncle.

Petro instantly smacked his nephew in the back of the head while giving him the 'I will kill you dead' look. Melvin stopped making the noise but continued the annoying dance.

"I'd be happy to help," Petro said out the door, giving Melvin one last warning glare.

CHAPTER THIRTEEN
Friend, Not Baby

Cassidy led them down a long hallway lined with heavy fire doors. Each door had a chart hanging below a safety-glass window. The charts had medical information on whatever animal occupied the room. Stickers on the windows at eye level warned what could happen if that particular door were to open. They passed a room full of rainbow-colored birds flying around, squawking at each other. Every time one landed, another chased it away. Another room had two huge porcupines in a corner. They could have been cuddling, but Melvin didn't think that was possible, considering the hundreds of two-foot spines sticking out in all directions. One room had Red river hogs. They were little, punk-rock pigs with yellow Mohawks. They ran around making a mess and head-butting each other, like most punk rockers. Finally, they reached the end of the hall. The big door read 'Primates.'

"Melvin, have you been tested for tuberculosis?" Cassidy asked. "It's the test where they put the little needle under the skin of your arm, then check it three days later."

Melvin's eyes widened and he felt a code red pout alert growing. "Yes, I had to do that on Christmas break so I could go back to school. I don't have to do it again, do I?"

Cassidy reassured him. "No, no. To go into the primate wing, you have to be negative for tuberculosis. It's a quarantine thing."

"I can't catch it from them, can I?"

"Nope, they are negative. We just want to keep it that way. You have to be very careful in here, though. Don't get next to any cages. These guys are fast, strong, and smart. They will trick you if they can."

Melvin lied. "No worries."

Cassidy continued as they went in the door, "Matilda may be pregnant, so I need to run some blood work. She's been trained extensively by her keepers, but her hormones are a bit wacky right now. She can be unpredictable, but she really likes men. So it would be a humongous help if you could come in to distract her while I draw blood from her arm," Cassidy said to Petro with a coy smile.

Petro's chest puffed up. "I'd be happy to help. I haven't had much experience with primates. What is Matilda, a spider monkey or something?"

"She's a Sumatran Orangutan. She knows some sign language and will let me draw blood in exchange for a treat. This should go smoothly. It's zoo policy to have backup whenever dealing with a primate this big. So, you're my backup."

If Petro was nervous, he didn't show it. "Should be fun. I got to help with a baby orangutan once. She was a handful."

"They are about eight times stronger than humans, so don't underestimate her," Cassidy warned.

In the room with Matilda was a large rolling barred door connected to the floor and ceiling. It was kind of like a jail. Then Matilda's cage was built behind that, with another heavy rolling set of bars. She had access to a huge outdoor exhibit, not to mention all the fun jungle-gym type toys that could be stuffed into her huge room. Tractor tires hung from the ceiling by cut-up fire hoses. Plastic fifty-gallon drums scattered on the floor, along with more oversized tractor tires not tied to anything. Huge telephone poles criss-crossed the room at different angles, all connected with more fire-hose and rope as thick as a soda pop can.

Matilda sat watching TV on one of the tires, as if it were a couch. The TV, out of reach on the other side of the cage bars, played cartoons. Matilda had long orange hair covering her entire body, except for a round face. She had a pink blanket draped across her head and held a cabbage patch doll in her arms, like a baby. She was the cutest thing Melvin had ever seen. If a tiger came across her in the jungle, Melvin thought the tiger would bring fresh fruits in exchange for cuddling privileges, instead of eating her. Her big intelligent eyes widened as the three entered the room.

Cassidy leaned over and whispered, "She loves Spongebob Squarepants." She continued, addressing Matilda using a high-pitched, friendly voice as if talking to a puppy or someone really old. "Hey, Matilda. How are you doing today?"

Matilda's eyes got bigger as she chewed on a fingernail. She poked herself in the chest several times, then crossed her arms in an X and folded her arms as if still holding the doll she had just set down. She did the same movements several times in the same order.

"She's signing, isn't she?" Petro asked.

Cassidy nodded. "She's saying, 'I love baby'."

Melvin pulled out his phone, switching to video camera mode. "Cool," Melvin said, focusing on her.

Melvin was considering video-blogging over the summer. That way, if he gets eaten by a giant python or trampled to death by a water buffalo, the followers of his blog will hopefully look into his demise. Melvin figured his only followers, being his mom and Chucky, would miss him if he suddenly disappeared.

Cassidy and Petro moved in through the first rolling door, pulling it closed behind them. Melvin stayed outside, filming the interaction.

One set of bars stood between where Petro and Cassidy stood and where Matilda sat on her tire. She didn't seem very large, probably about the same height as Melvin, but a lot rounder.

Cassidy talked to her again, using the squeaky, cute voice. "Is that your baby, Matilda?"

Matilda hugged the cabbage patch doll tight.

"What if your baby is hungry?" Cassidy asked.

The orangutan released the doll from her hug and placed it on her breast as if feeding it.

"That's right, Matilda. You feed your baby if it's hungry. What else does your baby need?" Cassidy seemed to have a great rapport with the sweet ape.

Matilda crossed her arms again in the same X pattern.

"Yes, your baby needs love. Show your baby love."

Matilda held the baby out, giving it a kiss with lips that stretched farther than seemed possible. Then she smiled, showing her crooked teeth while holding the doll, and rocked back and forth.

Cassidy continued, easing Matilda into a comfort zone so the procedure would go smoothly. "Good job, Matilda. Is your baby's diaper dirty?"

Matilda turned the doll around, putting one finger in the back of the doll's pants, checking for poo. She shook her head in a 'no' gesture.

"You are such a good mom. Now fix your baby's hair."

Matilda sat the doll on her lap, brushing hair away from its face. There was a rhythm to their interactions. Cassidy and Matilda must have practiced this many times.

"What if your baby misbehaves? What do you do then?"

The proud mother turned the doll on her knee, giving it several swats to the butt. Then she turned it back, fixed its hair again, and shook one of her long fingers at the baby.

"Okay, now give it more love."

She kissed the baby and pulled it into another hug.

"Okay, Matilda. We're going to come in now. It's shot time. Is that okay?"

Unlike most humans, Matilda didn't seem nervous at shot time. She had obviously been worked with often.

Cassidy rolled the inner door back. "This is Petro. He's a friend. You can show him your baby if you want. If you don't want to, that's fine."

Petro followed Cassidy in to meet Matilda, who made another sign with her hands after pointing at Petro.

"That's right, Matilda. Petro's a friend. I'm going to give you a shot, so hold still. Okay?"

Matilda held out her right arm on cue. She stretched her other arm out, plopping her hand on Petro's head. Petro smiled as she rubbed his hair into its normal messy state.

"Ha, I guess you like my hair the way it usually is," Petro said nervously. He didn't move his arms or back away. In less than a minute, Cassidy finished drawing blood.

"Thank you Matilda. I forgot to bring in your treat. We'll get it for you right now."

Matilda made the 'friend' sign at Petro.

Petro said, "That's right, we're friends," as he made the same motion with his fingers.

Then Matilda did a funny thing. She pointed at Petro and made the 'baby' sign.

Petro shook his head. "No, I'm a friend, not a baby."

Matilda made the baby sign and again pointed at Petro.

"Friend, not baby," Petro repeated, somewhat nervously.

Matilda made up her mind. She grabbed Petro, who was a few feet taller, pulling him into a hug. Petro had no choice. Matilda could have hugged him in half if she wanted.

"Friend, not baby!" Petro yelled, frightened by Matilda's overwhelming strength.

"Release, Matilda!" Cassidy yelled. But the great ape had her new baby and wasn't letting go. Cassidy tugged at Matilda's huge arms in an attempt to free Petro, but the jaws of life would have had little effect at that point.

Melvin, still taping, couldn't let such a perfect opportunity go by. "Hey, Matilda, what does a baby need?" he asked, mimicking Cassidy's voice earlier.

Matilda looked at Melvin excitedly, ignoring Cassidy as if she were a fly. Having found a new baby doll and someone to encourage her, Matilda played along. She pushed Petro back from her hug with both hands, then planted a huge, sloppy, giant-lipped kiss in the middle of his face.

Petro yelled, "Friend, not baby!" several more times as Matilda lathered his face with monkey spit.

Cassidy turned around, laughing, "What are you doing to your uncle? I'm going to go out and get her treat for a trade. I don't think she's going to hurt you." She came through the first door, leaving Petro alone with his new mom.

Melvin wasn't done yet. "How do you feed your baby?"

Petro shot a look at Melvin between smooches, but that's all he could do before Matilda shoved his face into her chest. She cradled him for a few seconds, while he struggled in vain.

Melvin laughed so hard he could barely hold the camera still. "Is your baby's diaper dirty, Matilda?"

"Friend, not baby!" Petro screamed again, but he might as well be talking to a stump.

"You are too much," Cassidy said, coming back in the outer door. She had an orange-vanilla ice cream pop for Matilda in one hand, which made opening the doors a bit slower.

That was fine with Melvin. This was priceless.

Matilda flipped Petro over like a pancake. She put one finger in the back of his pants, pulling them out to check for poo, giving Petro a wedgie in the process. She put her nose back there and gave it a good sniff, just to be sure. She looked at Melvin, excitedly. 'No' she shook her head, eagerly awaiting her next instruction.

"Friend, friend, friend, not baby!" Petro's voice was getting scratchy from all the yelling. He grabbed at whatever he could reach to pull himself away from the amorous ape. She was way too strong to let him get away.

Cassidy closed the first door and was working on the second.

Melvin was almost out of time. He was hyperventilating with laughter. "What if your baby's bad?" he choked out.

Matilda turned Petro over her knee with one muscled arm, shaking a long finger at him with the other.

"Friend, not baby!"

She proceeded to spank him several times. The angle was perfect. Matilda was gleefully facing Melvin's camera, with Petro bent over her pot-bellied lap screaming, "Friend,"-whack-"not,"-whack-"baby,"-whack, over and over with no effect.

Cassidy got through the second door. "Okay, Matilda, I've got your treat. Put your new friend down and you can have it."

Matilda picked Petro up by the back of the pants with one arm, moved his entire body off her lap and dropped him, face first onto the straw-covered floor. She reached for the orange cream pop with the other.

Petro got up, covered in slobber, bruises, straw, and orange hair. He dazedly walked out of the door with Cassidy mumbling, "Friend, not baby."

Melvin recorded the whole thing, and emailed the video to himself and put his phone away before his uncle got through the second door. He already had big plans for the video and had to keep it safe.

"Oh, you are SO dead," is all Petro could say to Melvin, though there may have been a hint of pride in his voice.

Cassidy cleaned Petro with another towel. "Thanks for helping. You made it a lot easier for me. I think you got a new friend out of it, too."

"I think she got a new baby out of it, if you ask me," Melvin snickered.

"I know where there's a Volkswagen dealership on the way home," Petro said through a slow sneer.

Melvin swallowed. Retaliation would be brutal for this, but somehow, Melvin knew it was well worth it.

"Thanks again. I've got to get some rounds done. Donald the Penguin swallowed his fourth penny this month."

"It was no problem. Thanks for the experience." Petro beamed.

"Yah, thanks," Melvin added.

"So, I'll see you two on Saturday, right?"

"Yes, Saturday good." Petro smiled.

Petro's Field Notes
Orangutan

Orangutan *(Pongo pygmaeus)* is an orange ape with several human-like characteristics. They have been witnessed using many tools, and live in close-knit communities. They can also be incredibly sneaky! There was an orangutan at a zoo that would escape from its enclosure on nice sunny days. After several escapes, the zookeepers put up a camera to see how he was getting out. He had been picking the lock of the outside door with a piece of wire he hid in his mouth. Though they are intelligent and incredibly strong, they are in serious danger of extinction. Much of the forest they inhabit is being destroyed by people collecting palm oil. So, one of the things you can do to help insure they stay around is avoid cooking with palm oil. If you must cook, I recommend booger oil.

CHAPTER FOURTEEN
Warm Wet Stupid Honor

Melvin followed his slightly disheveled uncle back to the van. Petro's once neat and professional appearance was now ripped, scuffed, and coated with a thin layer of orangutan drool. To Melvin's surprise, Petro didn't seem angry or even annoyed. He wore a distant but gleeful smile. "You have the slack-jaw of bliss," Melvin told Petro.

Briar often made fun of Melvin for getting that same look on his face when working on a new gadget or getting sucked into a good Warriors Apprentice video game session. His eyes drooped, mouth hung open, and still managed to smile, hence the slack jaw of bliss.

Much like Melvin, Petro paid no attention to the statement. He kept smiling like a zombie after his third trip to a brains buffet, where Einstein was the special of the day.

"I've got a date with Cassidy," Petro exhaled as they moved their equipment from the zoo's rental van into Petro's vehicle.

Melvin didn't have a word for his uncle's machine. It might have been an SUV many years ago, but evolved into a motorized toolbox with every gadget ever invented for traveling through any terrain. A huge snorkel-looking tube sprouted from the front passenger side. An elephant could use the tires as flotation devices. It was festooned with antennas, racks, fog lights, spot lights, winches, and hitches of all shapes and sizes. The paint was faded red, under a generous coating of mud, leaves, sap, pine needles, and bird poo. 'Only Trash Litters,' 'I Brake for *Ambystoma cingulatum*,' and 'My Truck Could Eat Your Truck' were a few of the stickers plastered on the bumper and rear window. The windshield had its own collection. All the way across the top and bottom were parking decals for various state and national parks, universities, and zoos. Petro never removed the old ones, just slapped new ones on top.

The interior looked like a space shuttle cockpit designed by John Deere. There were gauges for things Melvin didn't think could be gauged. They were lined up on the dash, neatly labeled via Sharpie marker and built into several custom plywood boxes. There were no less than three gear shifters sprouting from the floor of the cab between worn bucket seats. The radio had a built-in cassette deck and a C.B. radio hung from the ceiling, explaining one of the antennas. Petro almost made up for the tape deck by having two different GPS units mounted to the dash.

The rear of the truck was one big drawer system built in with nooks for everything from a chainsaw to rock-climbing gear to hand-held radios. There was a big red cooler and a bigger blue cooler. The blue one was curiously labeled 'Steve' while the other was labeled 'Not Steve'. Melvin loaded his gear into the back seat, which was the only open spot.

Petro started the beast with a few lever twists, gear shifts, pedal pumps, and button mashes.

"Who's Steve?" Melvin wondered.

"Just a friend; you'll meet him in a little while," Petro dodged the question, then quickly changed the subject. "My truck runs on a mixture of batteries, vegetable oil, gasoline, and luck," He announced, finally losing the vacant grin.

Fine, if Petro can change the subject, so could Melvin. "So, you got all dressed up fancy to look good for Cassidy, didn't you?"

If Melvin had a question, he asked it. He'd never felt odd about satisfying his curiosity, which his mother encouraged every chance she got. "If someone doesn't want to answer a question, then maybe they shouldn't be doing what you're asking about," Shea said at least three times a week, usually in reference to a politician or celebrity.

Petro couldn't keep the dull grin off his mug. "Well, Melvin, I may have looked funny back there, but it was all part of a plan. I wanted to ask her out, but sometimes that's not how it's done. Sometimes, you have to get the girl to ask you out."

Melvin didn't believe a word of it. "If you liked her, why didn't you tell her?"

"Have you ever told a girl you like her?" Petro replied.

"No, but I've never really liked a girl. I'm sure if I did, I would just tell her."

"Well, let's wait until you like a girl and tell her, then we can discuss my strategies at getting dates."

Melvin knew it was luck and not Petro's ridiculous 'comb your hair and act like an idiot' plan that got a date with Cassidy, but decided to drop it. Petro obviously didn't know what he was talking about.

The truck rumbled, squeaked, and moaned. The hum of the giant tires on pavement could drown out a fog horn blown through a megaphone. Every time Petro changed from third to fourth gear, the engine backfired hard enough to make Melvin's teeth clack together.

A loud forty-five minutes later, Petro pulled off of I-85 north onto the Wire Road exit. "I ate squirrel brains there once," he said matter-of-factly as they drove past a truck stop.

Melvin didn't ask. He was afraid to pursue the story because Petro might try to make him eat squirrel brains. They drove for what could have been five miles, but might only have been three. Pine trees grew out of red dirt on both sides of the road. Small fields appeared and disappeared as they coasted through gentle curves.

Big black vultures walked awkwardly around on the ground, about ten yards off Melvin's side of the road. Petro pulled over. Maybe he wanted to show Melvin something about the huge creatures.

"Steve will love this," Petro said as he hopped out, walking to the rear of the vehicle. He opened the back, pulling out a small shovel, and opened the cooler marked 'Steve.' An awful stench boiled out, but Petro didn't seem to notice. "Come on, kid."

Melvin got out, expecting anything. He didn't think his uncle would pay him back this quickly for the orangutan incident. That was one he would plan and plot. Mostly he wanted to get out of the truck because it smelled like a doo doo pie after Petro opened Steve's cooler.

"What are you doing?" he asked, following his uncle toward the flock of huge birds with a shovel in the middle of nowhere. Nervousness pecked at Melvin like the vultures pecked at the disgusting mound they stalked.

"Steve loves them at this stage of decomp," was all he said, making Melvin more twitchy. The birds took off with wing-beats strong enough to make dust devils come up from the red, sun-dried soil. The gust of hot air hit him like a mummy fart.

A pile of stinky fur, meat, and bones was left behind. Gross. He had never seen vultures close up, only drifting in the far-off sky.

Petro tried to pick up the carcass in one shovel-load, but it was too far gone and broke in half with a nauseating, stretching splat.

"That's foul," was all Melvin could say. He already didn't like whoever this Steve guy was, and quickly covered his nose and mouth with his T-shirt.

"Nope, it's not a bird. It was a deer, but now it's chow for Steve."

Melvin already didn't like Steve. Maybe he was one of those one-eyed, inbred kids with hair growing out of his misshapen head in clumps, and lived under someone's porch, just like in the movie he wasn't supposed to watch. This was Alabama, after all. He imagined having to share a dirt pile under a porch with 'Steve' all summer, sucking maggots out of eye sockets of road kill.

Before Melvin could blow chunks, Petro walked past him with the deer half that fit on the shovel. He plopped it in Steve's cooler and came back for the second half. Melvin would have had his mouth open in a dumbfounded look if he wasn't worried about something flying in, or out of it for that matter.

Petro maneuvered the other half onto the shovel. This side had the fly-covered head throwing it off balance. Petro had to scrape it out of the dirt a few times before it finally flopped into the disgusting box of death. He closed the lid, wiped the shovel off in the grass and climbed back into the driver's seat. "Let's go. We're almost home."

"Great." Melvin rolled his window down to disperse the stench, and just in case Ralph decided to make another sudden visit from his bubbling belly.

Petro turned onto a gravel path and handed Melvin a key from the visor. Melvin was happy to climb out to open the blue-painted metal gate. It was dummy-locked, so he didn't need the key.

"Twitch must be here. You can leave it dummy-locked," Petro offered as he drove past.

The driveway could have been a mile long, following a small stream through a thick mix of pine and hardwood trees. The gravel turned to dusty clay after a few hundred yards. The trees opened into a large clearing. A huge pole with dozens of hanging gourds was the first thing they encountered. Each gourd had a hole cut in it for birds to use as a nest. It was an apartment complex for tweeters.

"Those are Purple Martins. They eat mosquitoes and other bugs that fly around my house," Petro said when he saw Melvin looking. They turned another bend to see a mobile home with big porches on the front and back. The backyard had a huge pond surrounded by a six-foot chain link fence. Other utility buildings scattered about the clearing. A big fire pit surrounded by logs for sitting, and a small barn with another fenced area occupied one end. Melvin heard chickens squawking from that direction. A beat-up purple sedan sat parked near there.

The squawking got louder as they parked. The second Melvin's feet touched the ground and closed the door, a monstrous, four-legged creature slinked from behind the truck and pinned him to the door. Melvin didn't see the animal when they drove in and was too scared to move. It must have been two-hundred pounds of muscle. The beast looked like a greyhound ran into radioactive swamp gas and mutated into this thing. It sniffed his crotch, showing a set of teeth Shark Week would have a day of shows dedicated to. The foot-long nose probed Melvin, while fierce steel-blue eyes pinned him as effectively as his black-furred, stone-cut body had. *Wolf? Hyena?* Melvin squeaked nervously in hopes of catching his uncle's attention, still on the other side of the truck. Finally he stuttered, "Big doggy," loud enough for Petro to hear.

Stupid Alabama by Michael P. Wines

"Oh, sorry, I forgot to tell you about Choopy." Choopy sounds like Snoopy but with a chew instead of a snew. "He lives here, too. I can't really call him my dog though, seeing as he doesn't do what I tell him and I don't feed him. He's wild. I'm not sure what he eats, probably road-kill, like Steve."

"Is he going to eat me?" Melvin whimpered.

"Hope not. Your mom would be pissed."

Choopy finished his sniff-down and released the boy, but not before thoroughly peeing on his leg.

"Aw, gross! I'd almost rather be eaten." Melvin felt the warm wetness soaking through his jeans and into his shoe.

"That means he likes you, or maybe he claims you. I'm not sure which. He only does that to things he wants to keep," Petro smirked.

"I'm honored," Melvin pouted.

CHAPTER FIFTEEN
The Road-Kill Less Traveled

"Where can I change?" Melvin asked, still freaked from meeting the devil's horse.

"I'll clear out my office. You can stay in there. Give me a minute. I wasn't expecting a summer guest. First, let me introduce you to Twitch." Petro ignored the fact that Melvin had monster pee squishing between his toes.

"Glad I don't have to sleep under the porch," Melvin muttered.

"Well, of course not, that's where Steve lives," Petro said in a 'duh' tone as he walked to the barn.

The image of a clumpy haired, snaggle-toothed, lump-headed Cyclops boy came back into Melvin's mind, almost distracting him from his wet leg. He followed, wondering what kind of creature would befoul him next.

Petro turned a corner. As barns go, this was a tidy one. Well-kept tools hung from the walls, all in designated places. A bicycle dangled upside down next to a couple of canoes on a rack, sharing space with red plastic kayaks. Oars, paddles, and life preservers hung from the ceiling. Fishing equipment and nets of all kinds leaned against one wall. Several blue barrels of chicken feed sat at the far end of the barn with access to the outside fenced area.

Melvin saw a short, red-headed girl in the coop muttering to herself. She wore blue jeans and an oversized purple t-shirt, folded up in the front and loaded with fresh eggs. Most of the chickens were outside, avoiding the intruder.

The girl held up an egg as if it were the new Egg King of the Coop, talking to it. She hadn't realized Petro and Melvin were behind her. "Yes! I got eleven eggs without breaking one. That's a new record."

Petro's evil smile flashed at Melvin conspiratorially. "Hey, Twitch, I'm back," he said, louder and faster than needed.

Twitch jumped like a rabbit being electrocuted. Eggs flew in all directions, breaking on the walls and against the chicken wire. The one she was holding popped, sending yolky slime all over her face and glasses. The few chickens still in the barn squawked in protest, or maybe that was just how birds laughed. The girl turned around, slowly, covered in goo and shaking. Her face reddened in anger and embarrassment.

"Every single time!" she yelled, growling. "This is my favorite shirt!" An airbrushed wolf's head, howling at the moon, was decaled on the shirt. The word *Twitch* scrolled across the sky in a font made of fangs. "Oh, who's th … Periwinkle!" she yelled, mid-word. She came through the screen door, pointing intently at Melvin. Twitch moved fast for such a small person. She was about Melvin's size and height, but in her late teens or early twenties.

Twitch poked Melvin in the chest, leaving a gooey print. "That's periwinkle!" she said, referring to his shirt. "It's both my favorite color and favorite word. I want one just like this," pointing to her wolf decal, "but like that," pointing to the color on Melvin's shirt. She talked and moved very fast. Neither her words nor movements made much sense.

"Who's the little boy?" she asked, not concerned about the egg snot dangling from the corner of her glasses.

Melvin was put off by being called a little boy, especially considering she was the same size.

"This is my nephew, Melvin. He's staying with me for the summer. Melvin, this is Missy McCalister, but everyone calls her Twitch. She's a biology student at the university and helps me in the lab and with some of my field projects."

"I'm his minion," Twitch said proudly. Her brow furrowed and her eyes narrowed, looking at Melvin. "You're not going to be one of his minions, too, are you?"

"No," Melvin started.

Petro interrupted. "You get a promotion, Missy. I now dub you the Queen Minion Esquire and Melvin is now your very own assistant." Petro raised his right hand in a 'stop' motion, in time to plant it on Twitch's forehead as she assaulted him with a hug.

Missy blurted, "My very own minion!"

"What have I told you about personal boundaries and being professional?" Petro asked while she flailed her arms in an attempt to grasp him. "You can't go hugging your coworkers, professors, or just anybody. I know that's a stupid rule, but some people get freaked out about it, and I'm one of them."

"I'm so excited! Thank you, thank you, thank you!" Twitch pulled back, wild-eyed but grinning. She crouched over with slumping shoulders. Her head sank into her neck, like a turtle, while her hands came up to her face. The girl touched one index finger to her mouth as if pondering life, then seemed to figure out the answer. Her eyes somehow managed to widen more than before. Melvin thought her eyeballs might come out and squish against the inside of her glasses if they opened any farther. The girl did all that in about three quarters of a second. It was a bit of a blur, like watching a hummingbird blink.

"Are you on the caffeine again?" Petro asked, seriously.

"How can you tell? Woo hoo! I've always wanted a minion. My stupid boyfriend refuses, even though I call him that sometimes, anyway. How was your trip? Was it fun? Did you get to play with the Chinese alligators? They are so cool. Did you know they can bark like a dog, but louder?" The words sputtered out of Twitch like a machine gun on full auto. As she spoke, her eyes bounced between Petro and Melvin as if she were watching ping pong in fast forward.

Twitch's eyes stopped on Melvin. He wondered if she was going to start yelling periwinkle again.

"Hey, did Choopy pee on your leg?" she asked.

"Yes."

"Lucky!" Twitch moaned. "I've been trying to befriend that dog for six weeks and he won't so much as sneeze on me."

Melvin didn't know how to respond. "Um, sorry?"

Petro turned to Twitch, breaking up the awkwardness as much as possible with road kill, "I've got a deer in the cooler for Steve. You want to feed him?"

"Oh, heck yeah!" Twitch exploded with way too much enthusiasm and volume. "That can be your first duty as my minion. Help me feed Steve. I love Steve."

"Wait just a freaking minute. Who is Steve?" Melvin asked, harshly enough for his mom to send him to his room, had she been there. Melvin had had enough. He was still covered in dog pee. He was promised into a crazy person's miniondom without agreeing to it, and still had no idea who or what Steve was.

Both Petro and Twitch looked at Melvin as if he just farted at a funeral.

Petro turned to the girl. "Please excuse my nephew. He's been in the car for two days and must be out of sorts. He's from New York and has never been down south before. New Yorkers aren't generally this rude."

"Oh, he's a newb," Twitch said, looking down her glasses, still dripping with chicken ectoplasm.

Melvin knew a newb to be a new and inexperienced person at a particular activity. It is most often used by online video gamers as an insult. He took great offense, considering his gaming experience and his familiarity with the word. No one, but no one, ever called him a newb and played long enough to tell the tale.

However, feeding a rotten deer to a thing or person named Steve, who lived under the porch of a mobile home in Alabama was definitely something he was new to, so he decided not to make another snotty comment.

Twitch pointed to a gate in the chain link fence that could open on the top or bottom half. A heavy cable ran between two poles a foot above the top of the gate to the far side of the pond in the backyard, inside the fenced area. The pond was large enough to cover most of the fenced-in yard, including under the large wooden porch. She looked to Melvin. "Minion, as your queen, I command you to get Steve's cooler out of the truck and bring it over to the gate. I'll help, seeing as you are puny."

Melvin gave up with a gasp. "Fine."

"That's fine, my 'Queen', my 'Minion Empress', or 'Majesty Missy'. You can call me Twitch, like most people do, once you've earned it. For now, I am a royal to you."

Petro smiled, holding back a laugh, or perhaps tears.

Melvin thought she was a royal something, but decided not to say it, seeing as they just met. "Whatever," Melvin replied. He could tell she had prepared that speech long ago and was excited to finally use it.

They dragged Steve's cooler to the gate. Twitch put on two thick rubber gloves that went well past her elbows. She opened the cooler, with little reaction to the pungent odor.

Melvin stepped back, not knowing what Twitch was about to do with the stinky deer and not wanting to be close enough to find out.

Twitch lifted half of the carcass to a hook on the line leading over the pond. She moved the cable to put the other deer half on another hook. The wire was on a pulley system attached to both poles, so the hooks could be wheeled over the pond. Twitch hung out the meat, like clothes on a line between apartment high-rises in the city, until it hung a few feet above the water. Then she closed the top half of the gate.

"Steve loves deer," she said, watching the grossness dangle twenty feet away with mystified eyes.

Before Melvin could think about what was happening, and why anyone would want to eat that, Steve showed up. He exploded from the calm water, grabbing the front half of the deer-ka-bob.

Steve was an alligator that made Loki and Avalanche look like a shrimp's pet Chihuahua. Steve's head was four-feet long and two feet wide. He easily grabbed the offering, without more than his head and two front feet leaving the water. The disgusting deer haunch stretched and finally popped off the hook with a crunching of bone and snapping of tendons. He shook the deer violently once to the left splashing water twenty feet out of the pond on the far side. Then back, snapping his head toward Melvin and Twitch. The lulling head flung off the deer, rocketing over the fence, finally landing near the far barn. A wave of pond water followed the decapitation. It hit them as if they stood next to a puddle during rush hour. Neither Melvin nor Twitch moved as the swamp tsunami overtook them.

Steve opened his huge maw, tossed the meat back and swallowed. Then he gobbled the second chunk off the wire. It was gone with a gulp. Steve disappeared under the calming water as if preparing for his next attack.

Melvin turned to look at the head as if it were a home run hit out of the park. It was gone, but he saw Choopy's tail lurk around the corner.

"That was the coolest thing I've ever seen," Melvin said, not caring that he was soaked head to toe in a number of smelly liquids.

"I love Steve," said Twitch.

Petro's Field Notes

AMERICAN ALLIGATOR

American Alligator *(Alligator mississippiensis)* is Alabama's largest reptile. They build huge mound nests for their eggs, eat all kinds of creatures, and generally freak the holy crap out of most people in close proximity. Gators are easily spotted at night by shining a flashlight across an open lake. Their eyes reflect the beam with a creepy red glow. So if you ever find yourself in the bayou after dark, be sure to carry a flashlight and enjoy the bloody sparkle while you can … Okay, in reality gators aren't really anything to worry about but scaring people is fun. The eye shine is freaking cool though. A nifty sciencey fact about gators is that their sex is determined by the temperature their eggs incubate. Some hot years the eggs all hatch out as boys, and some cold years the eggs become girls. If the temperature is optimal for egg incubation in the nest, then half will turn into boys and the other half girls. Then there is usually less fighting over who gets to wear the blue sweaters and who gets stuck with the pink ones come winter.

CHAPTER SIXTEEN
The Epically Challenged

Petro wasn't the cleanest person, but wouldn't allow Melvin in his house sopped in runoff and whiz. So he took great care in spraying pond scum and dog pee off his nephew with the hose in the front yard.

Twitch helped by pointing out dry spots and occasionally yelling "Turn, minion," while giggling and attempting to look authoritative at the same time.

After a few minutes of standing in the hot Alabama sun, Melvin's clothes dried enough to gain access to Petro's house and shower. He enjoyed the time drying by watching Petro hose the egg and mud off Twitch while she protested. Choopy helped out by herding her back to within hose range every time she ran, once grabbing one of her pants legs and dragging her back. Melvin almost forgave him for the fire hydrant treatment earlier.

Twitch shook off most of the wet grass and squeezed as much water out of her clothes as four seconds would allow. "See you in the lab tomorrow?" she asked Petro.

"We'll be there."

"Good, make sure my minion gets plenty of sleep. I've got lots of jobs for him in the morning," Twitch said through a toothy grin.

"Yes, your Royal Majesty of Miniondom," Petro replied with an eye-roll.

Twitch opened her car door while texting what could have been a novel, only pausing to reply. "Ooh. I like that one. Remember it, lackey." With that she backed into a shrub and shot down the driveway in a zig-zag, leaving a wake of red clay plumes and flying grass chunks, texting and driving into the distance. Melvin and Petro heard several branches snap and saw the needles of more than one pine tree shake as she managed her way to the main road.

"You are never, ever allowed to ride in any vehicle while Twitch is driving," Petro said.

"Not a problem," Melvin agreed. He grabbed his bags from the truck.

Other than having a foundation of stacked cinderblocks and a trailer hitch on the front, Petro's house was surprisingly nice. It wasn't what Melvin imagined a mobile home to be. Inside were three bedrooms, only one used for its intended purpose. One was an office, which was about to be turned into sleeping quarters for Melvin. The other was a library of books, magazines, field journals, pinned bugs, jarred fish, frogs, and reptiles, and the occasional stuffed bat. In the middle of the house, the living room (with a huge flat-screen) connected to the kitchen (with a dishwasher) by a fireplace. A door off the kitchen opened to the back porch, next to the washer and dryer. There was an amazing view of Steve's pond and the lush pine forest surrounding Petro's home. Past the kitchen was Petro's bedroom with a bathroom attached.

Melvin was granted the bathroom at the other end of the house. He only recently moved into an apartment with his own room. Before, he slept on a pull-out couch and always shared a bathroom with his parents. He'd always had to carry his laundry at least three blocks to clean it, only to find he forgot his bag of quarters and had to go back. Petro's house had its benefits, though he still wasn't going to tell anybody from home he was staying in a trailer.

He dropped his bags in front of the door to his soon-to-be bedroom, and headed for the shower. Petro cleared a spot in his office by the time he was clean, dry, and had clothes to match. Journal articles and notebooks were piled everywhere, like the computer magazines in Melvin's room back home. The walls were plastered with 'Salamanders of the Cahaba', 'Frogs of the Red Hills', and several other posters featuring rodents, bats, bugs, fish, snakes, lizards, and fresh-water mussels from some river, valley, park, or county.

Melvin could sleep on the office's pull-out sofa and had most of Petro's desk to set up shop. Once he had his laptop running, and a bag full of gadgets unpacked and charging, he felt like the summer was possibly doable. He was way out of his element, but knew he could get back to it anytime with a few keystrokes and button clicks.

Thinking of that, he opened the email he sent to himself earlier with the video of Petro being befouled by the orangutan. He started to forward the video to his dad and Chucky, but decided to cut it into several smaller clips for easier download. They didn't have nearly the speed or power in their computers as Melvin did in his laptop. The whole video was over three minutes long. He cut the introduction to Matilda into one clip, the talking and signing into another, and saved the best for last, with his uncle being pillaged and plundered.

Melvin watched the video of Matilda kissing, spanking, and generally abusing Petro over and over. It was funnier every time he watched it. He eventually broke that video into several small clips. Each segment had Matilda excitedly kissing, nursing, checking his diaper, or spanking Petro, who frantically screamed, "Friend, not baby," through the entire ordeal. It was Internet gold.

Melvin had to be smart. He knew once this video was sent anywhere, to anyone, it would get posted on YouTube. He wasn't sure what he wanted to do with it, but thought he should hold on to it for a while. He did forward it to his dad, with a message telling him not to show it to anyone yet. He knew Briar wouldn't repost it without permission. It was too good not to share with his dad, who could truly appreciate it. Melvin felt like an evil genius with a shiny new army of laser-wielding, flying monkey robots.

Late afternoon turned into early evening. Melvin came out of his room only when he smelled pizza, and to tell Petro, "Nothing much," when asked what he was doing.

He barely noticed Melvin. Petro was busy in his own world with his own project. One thing about the Fitzpatrick boys, when they were focused, there was no distracting them.

Petro had been busy on his Red Hills salamander grant proposals. Melvin watched as Petro moved the piles on his desk to the table in the living room. He read through articles, arranging them in piles, and made notes in a spiral notebook labeled *Red Hills salamander*.

Melvin had heard his uncle tell his parents about his latest project. It required grants, research, government approvals, and organizational skills he didn't have. It was a massive project, maybe too big for him. Petro seemed to be up for the challenge. Mainly because no one else would do it and without help the rare amphibian would disappear forever.

Melvin returned to slicing and editing the video, as a plan began to form in his head. He hadn't seen anyone do it before and thought if he did it right, it could be huge. If he did it wrong, however, no one would notice because no one would care. So he had to do it right the first time. He researched the web, watching videos and downloading trial software. Melvin's plan required development skills and programs he didn't have. Like Petro, Melvin was up for the challenge if only because no one else would do it. *This will be epic*, he thought.

Melvin's first night was a long one. After a call to his mom to assure her of his safe arrival, he was hit with a pang of loneliness, though he would never admit it. The fold-out couch was as comfortable as a pallet of bricks. Every move he made crunched or squeaked. It was a wonder Melvin could hear anything over the unbelievable noise of the country. Crickets chirped, cicadas whined, owls screeched, cows mooed, trees moaned, coyotes yipped, and frogs burped, bleeped, ribbited, or did whatever frogs did.

What are people thinking when they say they want to get out to the country for some peace and quiet? Melvin thought. Obviously they have never been here.

Stupid Alabama by Michael P. Wines

Melvin looked up *Sounds of the City* on his iPod and played it on a continuous loop through his headphones. Car horns, random shouting, dogs barking, sirens wailing, and garbage cans clanging eventually lulled the boy to dreamland.

CHAPTER SEVENTEEN
General Tso's Infantry

The morning hit Melvin like a mop dipped in glue. At seven it was already hot enough to fry a chicken along with her eggs. Melvin, like the other Fitzpatrick males, sported a few cowlicks, but in this humidity his head looked like the whole herd got a taste. Ragweed made his eyes red and his nose run, as if he were a teenage girl meeting her favorite pop idol.

"Wow, looks like you've got some allergies. Maybe later I can send you through a field of poison ivy," Petro smirked from behind a huge mug of coffee. "Didn't your mom send you with some medicine?"

"Probably," Melvin grumbled, trudging back to his room to look. A few minutes later, Pop-Tarted, orange-juiced, and armed with his trusty inhaler, Melvin was ready for the day.

Petro showed Melvin how to feed chickens and collect eggs. It wasn't as hard or dramatic as Twitch made it out to be. "I think these eggs are bad," Melvin said, picking up a brown one half the size of the white eggs he was used to. They weren't just brown, though. Some of them were yellowish or greenish. There wasn't a single big white one in the bunch.

"They're fine. Not the same kind of chicken," Petro muttered. Apparently the seventeen gallons of coffee hadn't kicked in yet. "Bring them with us; makes great lizard food."

"The chickens?" Melvin asked, imagining what kind of lizard could eat an entire chicken. Even Melvin's dad couldn't eat a whole chicken.

"No, dummy, the eggs. Come on. Let's go up to the lab."

A fifteen-minute ride led by horse and cow pastures, a spattering of trailer parks, and even a few real houses. The university came into view over a hill. It had the biggest football stadium Melvin had ever seen, surrounded by blocks of new looking, clean, well-kept buildings and one small old one.

Students bustled down the sidewalks in groups. The gaggles were mostly made up of girls, all dressed in shorts and nearly matching t-shirts. They wore ponytails and giant sunglasses. Some brave girls ventured brightly colored flip-flops, but most wore black. The groups of boys uniformed themselves in cowboy boots, jeans, and polo shirts. A few boy-girl pairs walked together, but were the target of both groups' snickers.

Petro pulled in behind the one small old building. The sign over the front door would have read 'Physiology' but was missing the P. Inside, Petro led Melvin past closed doors and a creepily dark staircase to a room full of dead stuff. Jars full of snakes, frogs, lizards, and salamanders lined shelves, organized like a library. Instead of coming here to check out books, people got a jar full of putrid foulness. Under each set of shelves were large metal boxes, presumably to hold things that couldn't be stuffed into jars. It smelled like an armpit soaked in butt juice. The stink wasn't only due to the dead stuff, but the chemicals they were stored in. Melvin almost wished for his allergies to return.

"Aw! Crab Rangoon!" someone shouted from an open door in the back of the room.

Petro sighed, shaking his head in a 'what now' gesture as they walked to the source of whoever was angry at their lunch.

Through the door, Twitch was prying a tiny turtle off the finger of a tall, skinny guy who kept yelling things off a Chinese menu. "Let go, you little egg-roll! Ow! Mandarin chicken!"

"Would you quit whining, ya giant baby? I've almost got it off and you're making me hungry," Twitch scolded the guy, who had to lean way over to match her height.

"What's all the yelling about?" Petro asked through a giggle.

Twitch, until now focused on pulling the turtle off slowly and carefully, yanked it off in a startled, well, twitch.

"Holy-Hot-and-Sour-Soup, that hurt!" hissed the giant, rubbing his now turtle-free finger.

"See, good thing I came up with a special code for you to use," Twitch snooted. "I told you there would be a little boy here today. He's my minion."

"This is my boyfriend, Eric. One of his talents is the ability to cuss in seven languages. I told him it wasn't appropriate around a little boy. So, he uses Chinese food instead. It was my idea." Twitch talked like she could run out of words any second and had to use as many as she could while they were still available.

"Hey, Petro, and uh, little dude," Eric said with a wave.

"Aw, da cute wittle pudding wants to eat my arm off," Twitch broke into baby talk to the turtle, now happily attached to one of her fingers. "I told you it didn't hurt."

"It was chomping on my cuticle," said Eric, attempting to save face.

The room was loaded with dozens of reptiles and amphibians. These were alive, unlike the last room. Tubs with turtles, tanks with frogs, and cages with lizards lined the walls. It was set up like the zoo. A sink, fridge, desk, and chest-freezer huddled together on one wall, while the other walls shelved live animals. Petro took the eggs Melvin brought from home and put them in the fridge. In the back of the room was yet another door. *Danger: Venomous Reptiles, Do Not Enter*, a sign on the door said.

"You aren't allowed in that room, ever. I promised your mother, no rattlesnakes," Petro said, gesturing to the back room.

"He won't let us go in there, either," Twitch pouted.

"What are all these animals for?" Melvin asked.

"We use them for teaching tools. People pay attention better if you're teaching them about snakes and you actually have one to show them. You can help Twitch and Eric in here this summer," Petro added.

"All ri …," Melvin began.

"I've got a present for you!" Twitch blurted, cutting Melvin off. "Wait right here."

"Sweet," Eric mumbled. "I don't have to wear it."

Melvin gulped nervously as Twitch produced an orange tent of a t-shirt. "Put it on. Put it on. Put it on," she repeated seventy-eight times until he did. The shirt hung below his knees and the short sleeves went past his elbows. In block letters across the front were the words *Twitch's Minion.*

"It's a little big, but it will shrink in the wash," she said hopefully.

"It's a dress and it smells awful," Melvin sputtered.

"I got it for Eric, but he refuses to wear it after the water snake soiled it. So, since you are my first official minion, the right belongs to you. Wear it well, Young Sir."

"Great," Melvin said. His face scrunched in a 'Do I have to?' grimace.

"Think of it as a lab coat, to protect you from reptile poop and frog whiz," Petro helped through a smile.

"It's a uniform and I expect you to wear it at all times in the lab," Twitch said.

"General Tso's Chicken!" said Eric. "That looks good on you, kid."

Melvin felt ridiculous, and hungry.

Petro's Field Notes
EASTERN INDIGO SNAKE

Eastern Indigo Snake (*Drymarchon couperi*) is the biggest native snake in the United States. It's so big it eats Eastern Diamondback rattlesnakes (the biggest rattlesnake in the world) for dinner. Despite its size and ability to take down a rattlesnake, it is a gentle creature. One of the reasons the Indigo snake has become so rare is because people can walk right up to them, pick them up, and take them home. They are like big, black, scaly dogs. If you're ever lucky enough to see one, be sure to leave it alone. They are impossible to house train. The biggest snake in the country makes the biggest poops, too.

CHAPTER EIGHTEEN
Jail Break and the Gunslinger

"Oh, yah, um, Petro," Twitch stammered, looking in every direction except his. "A6 escaped."

"What! When?"

"I'm not exactly sure. I was cleaning the indigos and found a clip on the floor. It took me a minute to figure out which cage it went to. When I did, there was no snake."

"Have you started looking?"

"I just realized she was missing and was about to text you when the girly oaf got pinched by the turtle." Eric sank into the background as much as a baby giraffe on roller-skates could. Awkwardness was his one true talent.

"Sorry. I was the last one to clean them. I really stepped in a pile of Pu Pu Platter this time," Eric whimpered while studying his feet.

"When was that?"

"Three days ago."

"Wow, okay. You guys start searching the building. Tear the place apart if you have to. Melvin and I are going to get the receiver and try to pick up a signal."

"Wait, what?" Melvin asked. "Does the snake have a walkie-talkie or something? What exactly are we looking for?"

"It's an Eastern Indigo snake. We implant transmitters into the snakes so when we release them we can track their movements. There are thirty of these snakes set to be released in a few weeks. Each one is extremely important for the native population. Actually, these will be the native population."

Melvin looked puzzled.

"Basically, the thirty snakes we release will be the first Eastern Indigos in Conecuh National Forest in over fifty years. We've been raising these guys for nearly three years, leading up to this." Petro paused as Melvin began to comprehend. "They are rarer than pandas, and have little radio transmitters implanted under their skin."

That last part Melvin understood. Gadgetry was his language. He knew his uncle worked on saving wild snakes, but didn't know any details. Eric feverishly searched the room while Twitch attempted to force him in several directions at once. With a tilt of his head, Petro motioned for Melvin to follow him.

Melvin was led to yet another room full of cages. These were set up more uniformly than in the other room. All the cages had the same clear, sliding, plastic front held in tracks with large binder clips. The snakes inside were a solid bluish-black with an orange chin. They ranged from about three feet long to almost six. When they got to the cage marked A6, three of the four clips were on. The bottom right clip lay on the floor. The snake must have pushed her way between the flexible cage front and the side where the clip should have been. Melvin thought he heard his uncle growling, but couldn't be sure and didn't want to ask.

Petro stomped to a closet, mumbling words that would have made a sailor blush. He pulled out a folded antenna with a cord attached to a digital receiver. Melvin was excited, getting to work with an electronic device he had never fiddled with before.

"Read me the frequency number on the tag on A6's cage. It's taped to the top right."

Melvin hurried over, standing on his tippy-toes to read the number. There were several bits of information on the card: P.I.T number (whatever that was), snake ID, date of birth, sex, transmitter serial number, and finally, the frequency, *99.19*.

Petro punched in the number, only getting static from the small speaker in return. He turned the unfolded antenna in several directions, getting the same. He typed in the number of a snake near to him, B7. The transmitter beeped loudly. He typed another number, presumably 99.19, back into the receiver. Beepless static returned, followed by several words not on a Chinese menu.

Melvin followed Petro, who was clearly annoyed, upstairs. He paused every few steps hoping for a beep. They climbed out a window onto a fire escape, then to the roof. The roof seemed to sway with heat haze. Petro went to each edge, holding the antenna as high as he could and pointing to the horizon. Only static answered. Getting back to the side they entered, he set the antenna down. His head hung low as he muttered another string of unspeakables.

Then the receiver whispered a beep. Petro lifted his head in time to hear another barely audible chirp. He twisted a few knobs on the receiver. The beep was steady every four or five seconds. He picked up the antenna and it disappeared. He moved it around in angles he thought the antenna should point. No reply.

More frustrated than ever, Petro set the antenna back down. The beep returned as before. Melvin figured it out. The antenna rested on the metal fire escape, adding its mass to the search.

"Too bad we can't turn the fire escape," Melvin said, revealing the mystery to his uncle.

"Oh, the fire escape, good call. The transmitters have a three-mile radius. So, the snake must be close to the end of it. We can't tell exactly which direction, but we can narrow it down to north and northwest." Petro hopped over the wall back onto the metal stairs. Melvin followed, getting his shirt-dress tangled on something every few steps.

Petro hurried toward the front door and paused to lean his head in the room his minions were searching. "Did you find it yet?"

"No, not yet."

"Keep looking. Look everywhere but the venomous room. Leave no stone unturned." Petro used his authoritative voice.

"But the signal was ..." Melvin started.

Petro gave Melvin a 'shut up or I'll melt your brain' look, then continued. "Don't stop until you find it."

"We will. We're so sorry, Petro." Their apologies dripped with guilt.

Melvin followed Petro to the truck, slightly confused. "They will never leave a clip off of another cage again," his uncle explained with a vindictive smirk.

"How long are you going to make them keep looking?"

"Until we find it or whatever's left of it." With that ominous statement, Petro drove north, then pulled over to find the beep again. It was stronger. Petro narrowed the direction. "I have no idea how the snake got this far across all these streets. I hope it didn't get caught by a hawk once it made it out of the building."

Melvin thought of this as a cool way to learn how to use a new gadget until he heard the worry in his uncle's voice. To Melvin this was a way to kill time until he could get back to his computer. Melvin realized, to Petro, it was three years worth of hard work and a genuine care for an animal most people would rather see dead. His uncle had raised these animals from eggs, fed them every meal, cleaned and cared for them. One careless moment by a well-meaning volunteer could ruin this snake's chance at freedom. It might even set back the species' chance at reestablishment.

Melvin felt guilty for not taking the situation as seriously as he should have. Twitch and Eric seemed as if they would have given up their left legs to find the snake. They passed a field of man-made ponds on one side of the road. It looked like a commercial fish farm. The ponds were rectangles in a massive grid with enough room between them for a one-way road.

Melvin decided to help as much as he could. He held the antenna out the window, searching for a beep. It came back, stronger than before. They were getting closer. The direction was slightly clearer as well. It was north by northwest, which translated as straight and to the left.

Petro followed the beeps until they veered more drastically. He turned off the street onto a side road, past the ponds and into a wooded area. Once they went left for a few hundred yards the beep switched back to the north. They crunched onto a gravel road with a large swinging gate, thankfully open.

"I've done work out here before and have a few students still working on this site. It's university property, thankfully. I think I have a key to the gate, somewhere." They followed the ever-increasing beeps down the road for a quarter mile, until the beeps turned to the right. Trees surrounded a natural pond. A white pickup was parked on the road leading to it. They'd have to continue on foot.

"That looks like Jimmy's truck. He's the head of the fisheries department. He's a little odd, but knows more about fresh-water fish than anyone on the planet."

Petro pulled a long snake hook and a pillow case from behind his seat. They walked past the truck to the edge of the large pond. The man Melvin presumed was the owner of the truck stood knee deep in the pond struggling with a large net in the water.

"Hey there, Jimmy."

The man looked up, startled, but recognized Petro at once. "Howdy, Petro. This one of your students? I swear they get younger every year." His voice sounded like a Southerner imitating an old western movie. The voice was not the strangest thing about him, however, not by far. He wore a big cowboy hat, an American flag-colored swimsuit that had to be three sizes too small, the bushiest beard Melvin had ever seen, and a serious-looking revolver in a holster. The gun-belt was strapped on high over his potbelly, so the gun wouldn't get wet, which made the outfit look even more ridiculous. Melvin couldn't see his feet, but would be surprised if there weren't cowboy boots on under the water.

Jimmy dropped the net and walked up the bank with his hand held out for a shake. Sure enough, cowboy boots. "The name's Jimmy. Nice-ta-meetcha." He had sun-reddened skin and sun-bleached blond hair tied in a long braid down his back, covering most of the parts Melvin unfortunately saw. He could have been mistaken for an albino Sasquatch, dressed up for Halloween. He shook Melvin's hand with a grip that could crush walnuts.

"This is my nephew, Melvin. He's hanging out with me this summer."

"Well met, young man. Where ya from?"

"Uh, Brooklyn, sir."

"New York City! I'll try not to hold it against ya. It does me right to meet a kid nowadays that uses the word *sir* in reference to his elders, and not only to police officers. So, what brings you boys down to my pond?"

Petro explained, "There's an escapee we've trailed here. Transmittered indigo snake."

"Jail break, ya say. Need another in your posse?" Jimmy winked as if he was out here waiting on them to show up.

"We can always use another pair of eyes."

With that, Melvin turned the volume up on the receiver, glad to get out of the awkward meeting. The beeps were loud and seemed to be coming from the other side of the pond. Petro followed Melvin around the bank. Jimmy waded along the edge, sloshing mud in and out of his boots.

Melvin wondered why he had the gun. If he was in the city, he would surely go to jail on multiple charges, but here he was one of the top guys. Finally, he couldn't help himself. "Why do you have a gun, Mr. Jimmy?"

"Snakes and Yankees," he replied with a wink. Melvin was sure he'd answered the question the same way for years. "Present Yankees and snakes excluded, of course."

The beeps grew louder and louder. On the other side of the pond, a few yards in, the beeps quieted again. Melvin had never operated a receiver like this, but assumed he had just passed the snake. He turned around, guiding the antenna until the beep returned to its former strength. He walked a few steps back in that direction. It happened again. He looked to Petro, who, with more experience, tried his hand. The same thing happened.

"It must be underground. These guys live in gopher tortoise burrows and spend most of their time in deep holes."

When Petro turned the antenna toward the ground, it quieted once more. He was officially confused again, as demonstrated by scratching his head with the antenna. The beep got louder.

"I think it's under your hat," Jimmy said.

Melvin followed the direction of the antenna, straight up into the trees, where he found the snake. "There."

The men looked up. The snake was about twenty-five feet up, sitting on a couple of crossing branches. "Good find, Melvin!" Petro exclaimed. "I've never seen an Indigo in a tree, nor has there been a recording of one. This is truly bizarre and unusual behavior."

Melvin watched as his uncle's behavior turned bizarre, but maybe not unusual. He had a feeling this would be another moment to be remembered, so he pulled out his phone and started recording.

"You want me to shoot it down?" Jimmy asked, nudging Melvin as if everything he said was a long-time joke between them.

"No, thanks," Petro replied. With that, Melvin's uncle shimmied up the pine closest to the snake.

The snake, in turn, moved across to the interlocking branch away from Petro. He climbed down, moved over a tree and repeated. This went on for several minutes. Melvin recorded the whole thing while Jimmy called out obvious directions like, "It's right there," or "She moved again." The snake moved closer and closer to the pond through the canopy.

Finally, the forest opened to the water. A6 was still close to twenty-five feet up, but in smaller branches. Petro climbed onto the limb of a large pine, ten feet up. He grasped a branch of the thin sapling the snake was on, and began bending the tree over, using his weight on the trunk. If he were to let go, the snake might catapult off to the next county. Petro bent the stick down to where the snake was about three feet away. It had nowhere to go, but was still out of arm's reach.

So Petro jumped. His left hand held onto the bent tree, while his right hand flew out and clutched the snake around two of its coils. The second he had a grip on the reptile, he let go of the sapling pine. Every leaf and needle in a ten-yard radius shook. Both Petro and A6 fell, like turds from a pigeon, into the pond.

Petro found his footing. He arose from the mud holding A6 as if it were the baby lion king. The snake, in turn, had his thumb firmly clasped in his jaws, but Petro didn't seem to notice. He stomped around the muddy water like a professional wrestler who just won the title.

"I got it! Who's the freaking biologist, now? Who's the biologist? That's right! I'm the freaking biologist! I caught the freaking snake! Check it out, Scotty! Everything's okay!" He continued splashing around grunting, actually flexing his muscles, as if he had any.

Something at the side of the pond was startled by the commotion and squealed off into the woods. In his celebratory seizure, Petro didn't notice, and Melvin assumed stuff ran through the woods squealing all the time. Luckily, Jimmy recognized the sound. A second later there was more leaf stomping and branch-breaking. This time something bigger came toward them, instead of running away.

The underbrush ten feet away exploded, sending leaves, dirt, and rocks in all directions. A black pig the size of a school bus charged the closest target, Melvin.

Jimmy pulled his pistol as if he practiced for this moment all his life. He probably grabbed a fistful of chest hair along with his iron, but it didn't slow him. He shot four evenly timed bullets from his hip, using his left hand to cock the hammer each time. The pig, hit by all four in a spot the size of a baseball on its chest, died mid-charge. Its legs stopped running, but the force and weight behind the rush made it slide the rest of the way to Melvin like a 747 coming down in a field with no landing gear. It came to a stop on top of Melvin, its six-inch long, yellow tusks dripping slimy, frothy spit inches from his throat. It smelled as if the whole boar was made of fart.

Melvin fell backward, covered in dead pig. He somehow managed not to drop his phone in the mud. Some things were more important than life and limb. The hog weighed close to three hundred pounds and two hundred of that must have been stink. The beast smelled like a dead skunk's butt had a baby with the world's largest armpit. Petro rushed forward, pale with fear. He pulled the pig off Melvin with the hand not being chewed on by A6.

Petro patted Melvin down, checking for injuries. They were both in shock over how close Melvin came to becoming monster meat. They looked to Jimmy, who had a grin stretching across his sun-cooked face.

Jimmy began his own wrestler's rant. He threw his hat down on the ground and danced around it. "Wee hoo! How ya like that, little piggy? We's a gonna have a roast tonight! Who's the gunslinger? Jimmy is, that's who! Sir Jimmy the Gunslinger of Ala-freakin-Bama! Ha Ha! Yes, Sir, I got me a momma hog, toooday! Waaar Damn Eagle! Yeah! Try whistling Dixie now, Pig!" He fired his last two shots into the air in celebration. One round sent splinters raining down on them from the overhanging tree, while the other might have landed on Mars.

Melvin thought it would be safer back under the boar, involuntarily ducking with each blast of the gun. Jimmy holstered his shooting iron. It was so hot from firing that it left a burn on his round belly in the shape of the gun's cylinder. With a yelp, he cooled the burn with pond water. Jimmy would show that scar off to everyone he came across for the next few weeks while retelling the story of his boar-slaying glory. Melvin didn't mention he had it on video.

Melvin and Jimmy shared an awkward 'thanks for saving my life and not shooting me' hug as they separated.

"I guess that boar explains why the snake was up in the trees," Petro muttered on the way to the truck, still with A6 firmly attached to his knuckle. A small trickle of blood dripped down his hand to his wrist. Petro didn't seem to notice the snake, much less the blood.

"Gas-man, you're bleeding," Melvin offered.

"Oh, yah, thanks." Petro hadn't snapped out of his haze. Oddly, he seemed sad. It was strange after what had transpired. The relief of finding the snake alive and Melvin not being eaten to death seemed like enough to cheer up anybody. But Petro sulked to the back of the truck. He pulled the snake off his hand, and placed it into a pillowcase and tied it closed.

Melvin poured water over his uncle's hand to rinse the blood off. Petro barely noticed. Before they got into the truck, Petro pulled Melvin into a firm hug. He pushed him back to arm's length, looking him in the eyes. "I'm glad you're okay."

Melvin squirmed. "I'm fine, Mom. Can we go now?"

Petro held him in place, looking him over one last time to be sure he wasn't impaled on any hidden pig tusks. He patted Melvin on the head and climbed into the truck. All the way back to the lab, Petro seemed preoccupied and sad. Melvin couldn't believe a little boar attack could dampen his spirits so much, especially since he caught his escapee. Hopefully, his mood wouldn't last.

Once A6 was back in her cage with all four clips on, Petro lightened up a bit. Twitch and Eric were still in the next room, tearing things apart, frantically looking for the snake. Petro let them off the hook, but made them clean up the mess they made while searching.

"What did you do to your lab shirt?" Twitch demanded upon seeing Melvin. His huge orange shirt, now covered in any number of fluids from a dead boar and a couple gallons of mud, actually looked as bad as it smelled.

"Um, sorry. I was tackled by a dead, three-hundred pound wild boar. It was his fault," Melvin said pointing at Petro. He peeled the slimy t-shirt off, and let it drop to the floor with a wet slap. "I'll, uh, wash it."

"Egg foo young happens," Eric shrugged.

Petro's Field Notes
WILD BOAR

Wild Boar *(Sus scrofa)* is a feral pig. It was introduced to the Americas by none other than Christopher Columbus. It is also known as a razorback and has been known to grow up to 700 freaking pounds! You would think people would love them because, hey, free bacon. But no, they multiply so fast and eat so much that park rangers and farmers have to trap them so they don't destroy our local forests and farms. They will eat anything, including snakes, turtles, ground-nesting birds, ground-nesting bird's nests, tree roots, and even leprechauns.

CHAPTER NINETEEN
Scotty

Over the next few days Melvin and Petro worked out a loose schedule. Melvin got up in the morning, took care of the chickens, and ate breakfast. Then the two went to Petro's lab. Melvin cleaned cages with Twitch and Eric until lunch, which went by fast.

Eric turned out to be quite the tech geek. He even helped on the university website over the summer for extra credit hours. So Twitch's minions talked about all things geek most of the morning. It was fun for both to annoy Twitch. She didn't care much about fourth-generation cell phones versus third, or how many satellite connections it took to pinpoint a GPS signal in three dimensions. Once she got so worked up by being left out of the conversation that she stopped paying attention to what she was doing, which led to spilling soiled lizard litter all over herself.

After lunch Melvin worked in what Petro called the Museum. There were no mummies or dinosaurs or anything cool like that, however. Melvin got a list of jars of dead salamanders to open and sort through. He had to pull the dead critters preserved in alcohol out of jars and read the number tied to one of their legs, if they had legs. Once he checked the numbers off the list, he changed the alcohol and put the jar back.

Stupid Alabama by Michael P. Wines

The first few million salamanders Melvin went through were absolutely disgusting. Eventually he got pretty good at recognizing the different species. He had no idea how to pronounce some of the names, like *Pseudotriton ruber vioscai*, but could point one out in a salamander lineup. On a few occasions, he found salamanders in the wrong jars. He couldn't put them in the correct jars, though. He had to change it in the database and go back in the old, handwritten record books to figure out if it was misidentified originally or misplaced. Some of the books went back to the 1920s. Melvin imagined cavemen collecting salamanders in jars. That might explain some of their weird names.

In the evenings, after Melvin washed off all sorts of reptile funk and salamander slime, he and Petro would either cook out on the grill or go out for dinner. Then the two Fitzpatrick boys went to their separate rooms to work on their individual projects.

Petro continued going through boxes of old scientific papers and journals, collecting a pile of data on the Red Hills salamander.

Melvin went through the video and pictures he had compiled so far. He caught something on the video of Petro catching A6 and falling into the pond.

When Petro was doing his victory dance in the water with the snake, before the boar attacked, he said something strange. Petro yelled, "Check it out, Scotty! Everything's okay!"

Who was Scotty? Maybe Petro had an imaginary friend he hadn't told Melvin about.

Melvin skyped his parents every night before bed. He told them about his day, leaving out some parts like the boar attack. Melvin decided to keep quiet about some things until he got home. His mother would never get any sleep worrying about him. His dad would feel horrible about not telling her if he knew. Melvin, however, had no such guilt.

"Petro said something odd the other day, after he fell out of the tree with the indigo snake," Melvin said to his dad via his laptop. He tried to keep his voice down so Petro couldn't hear in the next room. "I think he called me Scotty."

Briar paused for a moment. The same sad look Petro had a few days before washed over Briar's face. "Scotty was Petro's best friend when he was about your age. They ran around in the woods all day, chasing lizards and building tree forts. They were inseparable. They camped out most nights. The nights that were too hot, they mostly stayed at our house.

"Scotty's family didn't seem to notice when he wasn't there. His dad wasn't around much and his mom had five other kids to take care of. So we sort of adopted the boy during the summers." Briar paused, either not wanting to say the words or not being able.

"After a while, the two boys became like brothers. They were around each other morning, noon, and night. They pestered the heck out of me. They were always putting a frog in my shoes or drawing on my face when I was asleep. Being around each other night and day, they had a few pretty good fights, though they never lasted long."

Melvin could relate to that. He and Chucky got into fights all the time. Sometimes they didn't talk for days.

Briar continued, "One day Petro and Scotty got into an argument over a lost pocket knife. It was misplaced and they blamed each other. It was no big deal, just another spat between friends. Scotty stomped off in a huff and Petro trod the opposite way. That was how things usually happened. Scotty went home, got bored or annoyed, and came back with a great new idea he needed help with, and all was forgiven. Then the two boys were back in the woods again as if nothing happened.

"Scotty didn't come back this time. After a couple of hours, Petro walked over to Scotty's to apologize. He figured it was probably his turn to make up first and Scotty was being stubborn. But Scotty hadn't come home."

Briar took a deep breath. "Scotty went down to the creek. He had been swinging on an old rope above a deep spot in the creek. Petro, Scotty, and I had done it countless times. The rope swing was there since before I could remember. It was a twenty-foot drop from the peak of the swing to the water below. We used to try to see who could get the highest over the water before letting go and splashing into the creek. However, our mother forbade us from going alone. We had to use the buddy system.

"That day Scotty went alone, even though he knew better. There was a storm the day before and a big log washed downstream and into the deep spot. It was only a foot or so under the surface and couldn't be seen from above. Scotty swung out and let go. He must have hit his head on the log. It knocked him out and had no buddy to help him …" Briar swallowed hard.

"Petro found him, but it was too late. I think he still blames himself. He won't talk about Scotty, but it's obvious he still thinks about him all the time."

Both Melvin and Briar were crying at this point, but neither felt embarrassed.

"So, if he calls you Scotty again, let it go and think of it as a compliment. You must be reminding him of those summer days chasing lizards with his best friend.

"Okay, change of subject," Briar said, sitting up and swallowing back his tears. "What are you doing with all the video you've been collecting? I see an epic prank in the making."

"I've got some ideas," Melvin said in a froggy voice. He was glad to know the story but wanted to get off the topic. He cleared his throat before resuming. "I was thinking of making a video blog. But instead, I think I'm going to turn it into a cell phone game. You know, one of those games you can download on your phone. I've been doing some research and figured they aren't that hard to make." Melvin would have gotten more into the technical speak of it with his father, but knew he couldn't follow. He was excited to talk about the idea with his dad, even if Briar couldn't help much technically.

"That sounds like a great idea. I'm sorry again about not being able to send you to computer camp, but it sounds like you're learning more without it."

"I already know it all," Melvin said through a grin. "Oh, and did I tell you, Petro has a date on Saturday?"

"Really?" Briar's smile came back. "I hope you embarrass him thoroughly, like he did to me on every date I ever went on."

"Oh, you can count on me." Melvin schemed, trying to ignore the thought of his dad on dates. *Ech.*

CHAPTER TWENTY
An Off Day

"Earthquake!"

Melvin awoke to find the world shaking. His bearings and balance were off. Every time he tried to sit up, the house shook, pitching him from one side of the fold-out to the other. Adrenaline flooded through his body.

Think! What am I supposed to do in an earthquake? But all Melvin could concentrate on was the overwhelming size of his bladder. The roof could cave in any second. The ground could open up and swallow the house whole. Melvin didn't want to die in a trailer in Ala-freaking-bama having to pee so badly.

"Earthquake!" Petro yelled again from somewhere nearby.

Then it happened. The old couch mattress began folding up on him. The springs and railings rattled violently. A fissure must have opened in the floor. Melvin was getting sucked in. He reached for the end of the cushion as it collapsed in on him. He was being swallowed by the rickety couch. Melvin sacrificed his balance to grab at the edge of the bed, now above his head. His body jerked to the side, but his right hand caught the bed before it sucked him into the earth. He pulled himself out. He felt like a bug in a flushing toilet, grabbing onto a poo log just to stay afloat.

Petro appeared at the end of Melvin's bed as he climbed atop it. He had one leg of the fold-out in each hand. He must have been pulling the couch along with Melvin from the sinkhole.

But why was he laughing? Melvin realized the rest of the room wasn't sinking or rocking. Pictures would have fallen from the walls and books off shelves. It was only the couch.

"Good morning, Sunshine. How'd ya sleep?"

Realization dawned on Melvin. Petro had awakened him by shaking his bed.

"Ugh, that was not cool! Move! I really have to pee," Melvin spat as he stomped past his uncle.

"It's emergency preparedness month. I was just being full of preparedness," Petro said through a long belly laugh.

Melvin had lost the first battle of the day, but he swore to win the war. "You're full of something. Alabama doesn't have stupid earthquakes." Melvin pouted to himself as he brushed his teeth. "Today he's got a date and I'm going to be there for the whole thing. Watch out, Petro. I'm coming for you."

Melvin was still sleepy but had enough adrenaline in his system to jump-start the space shuttle. He stumbled through his morning bathroom ritual too quickly. *Pee, check. Teeth brushed, check. Hair combed, check, well, as checked as it ever gets. Allergy medicine, check. Wait. Was that last check correct?* He washed his face as he thought about it. Something wasn't right. Splashing water on his face woke him up enough to realize he took the wrong allergy pill. He took the night-time version instead of the day. *Crap.* It was shaping up to be a stellar Saturday. He'd already been punked and could now look forward to being a zombie at the one time he really needed to have his game face on. *Fabulous.*

He dragged himself to the kitchen, inhaled a Pop-tart and guzzled an energy drink. Hopefully, the caffeine and sugar would counteract the sloth-inducing effects of the medicine.

"We've got to get going, Melvin. I've already been to the lab to get the critters for my talk. We need to get down to the nature center and set up for the show."

Stupid Alabama by Michael P. Wines

"Okay, Mom. I'm coming. Just let me get dressed. Gah."
Melvin threw on his favorite blue T-shirt and a pair of cargo shorts.

"Your shirt's on inside out, buddy. Awake much? I considered letting it go, but figured I already had enough fun with you this morning." Petro smirked.

"Crap." Melvin tugged off his shirt, turning it inside out with an effort. He felt as if he were moving through caramel. Every step slowed by cobwebs and weights attached to his hands and feet. This was going to be a long day.

Melvin took a power-nap in the truck on the way to the nature center. It didn't help. Grog the grump-master had taken over and was running things for Melvin.

Dug out of the ground and nestled among several massive shade trees was the amphitheatre. Large stone steps radiated around the center stage hollowed out of the earth. Melvin unloaded cages and pillowcases full of all manner of reptiles and amphibians, placing them wherever his uncle instructed.

Petro paced as people started to trickle in. A lady who worked for the nature center brought a microphone for him. A wire attached the mouthpiece to the transmitter clipped to his belt. As he tested it, Cassidy showed up. She wore a blue and white sundress. Her curly brown hair hung past her shoulders in highlighted ringlets. She looked much different than she did in her zoo uniform.

"Hey, Petro. This is Sasha. She's my little," Cassidy said, gesturing to a girl about Melvin's age. Sasha sported a blue and orange T-shirt over shorts. She had caramel skin, black hair, and the biggest, prettiest eyes Melvin had ever seen.

"Wow, you look beautiful," Petro said to Cassidy through the microphone. His face instantly reddened as the crowd snickered. He fumbled to turn down the volume. "Woops. I've got something for you." He turned around quickly, banging his shin on a tub containing a huge turtle.

"I guess he's kind of cute," Sasha said to Cassidy. "And he's just as smooth as you described."

Cassidy gave Sasha a secretive smile. "Sasha, this is Melvin. He's Petro's nephew. He's staying for the summer."

Melvin stared, open-mouthed, at the girl, knowing he was supposed to say something, but had no idea what.

"Uh, hey," Sasha said. After an uncomfortable pause, "Okay, what are you looking at?"

Melvin tried to think of something, anything to say. He wanted to make fun of his uncle or talk about the weather, sports, politics, religion, whatever. Anything at this point would be fine, except for what came out. "You have humongous eyeballs." Apparently, smoothness ran in the family.

Cassidy and Sasha stared at him, not sure how to react. Petro rescued Melvin by returning with a handful of flowers for Cassidy and a small box of chocolates for Sasha. "For you," he said. "And it's nice to meet you, Miss Sasha."

"Oh, thank you. That's so sweet," Cassidy said, pecking Petro on the cheek.

"Cool. Thanks, dude," Sasha said as she took a step away from Melvin. "Chocolate might buy my loyalty with Petro, but that Melvin kid is creeping me out."

Petro glazed over, stunned by the kiss as much as Melvin was fogged by the drugs. Luckily, music began playing through the sound system, signaling the beginning of Petro's show. The audience, mostly families with pre-teen kids, settled down, nearly filling the amphitheater to capacity. Cassidy and Sasha took spots in the front row.

Petro pulled Melvin to the side, instructing him. "Okay, I've done this before. Just bring me the cages when I tell you."

"Okay." The sluggishness began lifting from Melvin's mind, bit by bit. He realized at the last second that he forgot to record Petro's show. This was a great opportunity for more footage. He pulled out his cell and switched it to video mode.

"Will you record his show for me? I'm sort of keeping a video diary of my summer," Melvin whispered to Cassidy. She nodded, taking his phone.

Stupid Alabama by Michael P. Wines

The music faded and the crowd watched expectantly. "Welcome to the Auburn Nature Center and For …" Petro began, but realized his microphone was still turned down. A quick fiddling with the headset and he began again. "Sorry, everybody, let's start over. Welcome to the Auburn Nature Center and Forest Preserve. My name is Petro Fitzpatrick and this is my ever-so-lovely assistant, Melvin."

The audience laughed as Melvin gave his uncle the stink eye. Surprisingly, Petro had good stage presence. He started off telling the crowd about amphibians. Melvin brought cages and took them away as requested by his uncle. Then he moved to reptiles. He told them about each animal, their basic life cycle and some interesting facts concerning their defense mechanisms. It was enough information to teach the crowd while keeping them entertained and interested.

"I promised Melvin's mom 'no rattlesnakes' so he can't help me with this part. There is somebody with venomous experience that can help me out. Cassidy, would you mind giving me a hand?"

Cassidy handed Melvin's phone to Sasha. "Sure, I guess." She stepped down onto the stage as Petro pulled a large bucket from behind a table. Then he blew up a balloon, tied it off and handed it to Cassidy along with a four-foot-long set of snake tongs. She seemed to know where this was going and held the balloon with the clamping end of the tongs. As she did so, Petro coaxed out the largest rattlesnake Melvin could imagine, even from TV. It had to be six-feet-long and bigger around than a two-liter pop bottle. Petro held a long snake hook in each hand, never getting into striking range of the serpent. It coiled in the center of the stage, head risen. Its tail sat up in the middle of its coil. Petro gave it a light nudge and it began to rattle.

Several gasps came from the crowd. Melvin noticed many parents in the audience moved back, while the kids moved forward, trying to get the best view possible.

Petro made a big show of getting the rattlesnake to rattle. He held a microphone on a stick up close so the crowd could hear. Then he demonstrated how the rattlesnake wouldn't strike at just anything. He held out the balloon on the long set of tongs, giving the snake a target. It continued to rattle, but didn't strike.

"The rattlesnake knows the balloon isn't alive, and there's no reason to bite it. It can sense the heat of mammals with the pits in its face, between the eyes and nostrils. That's why they are called pit-vipers. Now, if I add a little heat to the balloon, from my lovely and hot assistant," he held the balloon up to Cassidy's face, smiling at her nervously.

She blushed as the crowd snickered. Sasha and Melvin both let out a "gah," and rolled their eyes in response to Petro's flirting.

After a few seconds, Petro put the balloon back on the end of the tongs and moved it in front of the serpent. The second the warm side of the balloon got within range, the snake struck, faster than lightning. The balloon popped with a loud bang. The three first rows of people, including Melvin and Sasha, jumped.

Petro went on to show off a couple more local venomous snakes. He then thanked Cassidy, and urged the crowd to applaud for her a little too dramatically, if you asked his nephew. Sasha and Melvin were then asked to come on stage for the final snake. Melvin handed his phone to a friendly looking old lady next to him and showed her how to point it to record.

Slowly coming out of his night-time medicine-induced fog, he climbed back onstage. It took him a few seconds to find the stairs. Sasha had to point them out as she walked up.

Petro pulled out a huge trunk and opened the latches slowly for dramatic effect. Sasha and Melvin faced the crowd, fidgeting with each latch.

Finally, Petro opened the trunk. Inside was a huge snake. It was possibly eight feet long, slender and fast as a bullet. He held the snake up for the crowd to see.

"This is a coach-whip. It is a non-venomous snake that lives around this area. Melvin, do you want the tail end or the pointy end?" he asked.

"Uh, the tail," Melvin said, looking at Sasha guiltily.

"How very chivalrous of you," Petro said as he stretched the tail end out to Melvin. "Sasha, don't worry. I'll hold the pointy end. As I have mentioned, snakes have several defense mechanisms. If they are startled by a predator, they can bite, run away, act big and tough to bluff. There's one other, very effective way of dealing with a potential threat. Can anyone guess what it is?"

The crowd began yelling all kinds of ridiculous answers to Petro's question. Some kids said it would squeeze like a python; others thought it might somehow sting. They were all wrong.

"The best defense mechanism a non-venomous snake has is not its bite, or its hiss. Cassidy, will you hold up the viscious predator I left in the trunk for the snake to see, please?"

Cassidy looked into the trunk. She reached down and picked up a stuffed animal that looked like a dog. She wiggled it in front of the snake.

The crowd chorused "Aww," upon seeing the toy. But once Cassidy moved it toward the coach-whip, the snake reacted. Petro let its head have about a foot of wiggle room. It hissed and struck several times at the stuffed dog.

"Now, the snake is biting and hissing and acting mean in an attempt to scare the doggy and get away. Once the wicked coyote actually touches the snake, the real fireworks begin. Cassidy, will you bring the stuffed animal close enough to touch the snake, please?"

Melvin didn't like the sound of that, and neither, it seemed, did the snake. As soon as the decoy touched him, it was bitten several times. The serpent was so fast the crowd could barely tell when it was striking. Unfortunately for Melvin, the coach-whip released its last defense mechanism in a slimy surprising fashion. The tail end of the snake erupted with a geyser of horrendous, stinking, snotty poo.

The first few hundred gallons hit Melvin squarely on the chest. Some came out so fast it deflected onto his bare neck and arms. The sickening splat got quite a reaction from the crowd. Sasha dropped the middle of the snake and ran to stand next to Cassidy, out of the drop zone. Melvin held on to the snake like a fireman battling a sewage plant fire. He had enough wits about him not to point the horrible hose at the crowd.

Once the dookie rocket finally stopped and the crowd calmed down, Petro explained how it was a great defense mechanism. "If the animal has the snake in its mouth and the snake does that, what do you think the fearsome canine is going to do next?" he asked the audience.

"Spit it out!"

Melvin stood on stage, dripping top to bottom in musky awful. He held out his arms so they didn't touch his shirt and stick. He was mortified. He was onstage being laughed at by five hundred people in front of the girl he kind of could one day think was possibly pretty. He may as well have swan-dived into a port-a-potty.

"That's right. So, don't pick up snakes, even if you know they are non-venomous." Petro returned the snake to its container. "Let's have one more round of applause for our lovely, and not so lovely, assistants, everybody."

Camera flashes went off in the crowd. Melvin knew they would want to show their friends the gross little boy covered in green apple splatter. An idea came to him. Finally his wits were coming back. Maybe the force of the snake's butt squirt knocked some sense into him. He picked up the microphone attached to the stick Petro used earlier on the rattlesnake.

"Hey, everybody," Melvin began awkwardly. "I'd like to thank my Uncle Petro for teaching me all about snakes. I've only been in Alabama about a week and have learned lots of things about animals. I was worried this was going to be a horrible trip."

Melvin walked slowly across the stage with a toothy grin towards his uncle as he talked. Everyone, including Petro, listened, wondering what he was doing.

"Did I mention that my Uncle Petro is on a date? How about a round of applause for the two lovebirds, everybody?" Melvin inched closer as the crowd awkwardly applauded a blushing Cassidy and Petro.

"One more time, I'd like to thank him for all he's done to me over the past few days." Melvin turned to Petro, a couple of feet away. "I'll thank him with a great big hug!" Melvin launched at his uncle, slimy arms wide and favorite blue T-shirt soaked to the skin in bile. He grabbed Petro around the waist and chest in a bear-hug, rubbing off as much ick as he could. The crowd roared with laughter.

The little old woman gave Melvin his phone back, assuring him it was all on video.

The date was cut short due to Petro's newly acquired offensive odor. "How about we call this one a draw? You're lucky she agreed to go out with me again," he said on the way back to the lab to drop off the animals.

Melvin agreed with a nod and a smile.

Petro's Field Notes
COACH-WHIP SNAKE

Coach-whip Snake (*Masticophis flagellum*) gets its name from speed. They are long, thin, whip-shaped snakes with a legendary behavior of chasing people. Upon catching a human, they constrict with muscular coils like a python, then insert the tip of their tail into the fallen person's nose to make sure their breathing has stopped. Once the person is dead, they tap-dance until BoBo the God of Shrink-Wrap comes and replaces the human offering with huge piles of cottage cheese. Well, maybe that's not how coach-whips really are. Mostly they are fast for the purposes of retreat from predators, like us. They have no reason to attack anyone, ever. If picked up by a person (which they consider a predator), they defend themselves with a steady stream of vile musk-soaked poo. They are not a fun animal to study in the field or the lab for that reason.

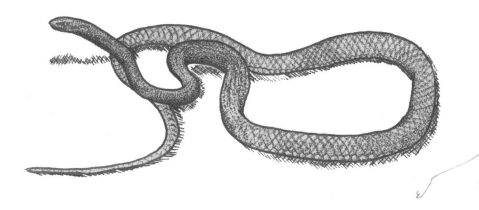

CHAPTER TWENTY ONE
Stupid Swarm

After scrubbing his skin raw with every type of soap he could find, Melvin finally excised the smell, or maybe just got used to it. With his chores complete for the day, he downloaded the new video and began his nightly ritual of cutting and editing footage into something he could work with. He wasn't sure how his embarrassing stage show would fit into the game, but saved it anyway.

Later that night a noise awoke him, originating from outside his window. He couldn't be sure, but it sounded like a scream. Still half asleep, he parted the curtains to investigate. He couldn't hear anything, no frogs calling or crickets chirping. All was silent and black as a graveyard in a cave. Nothing let out a peep, possibly for fear of whatever made that inhuman noise.

Melvin's imagination took control of reality as he peered into the darkness. He'd seen too many scary movies at Chucky's house. The boys acted like they weren't scared, but would never watch the films alone.

He recalled one particularly gory scene where a group of teens were spending the weekend in a cabin. The killer was a monster with hooks for hands. The victim knew when he was coming because he would scrape his curved metal appendages across doors or windows before he attacked. The beast ripped out their intestines and strung them across the ceiling fan while the helpless victim watched. Then he turned the fan on, which pulled out the rest of their guts, like spaghetti on a fork.

Melvin backed away from the window feeling foolish, but nevertheless scared. He grabbed the headlamp Petro gave him to find chicken eggs in the nest boxes. He looked out the window again, this time with illumination. As he parted the curtains he found himself face to face with a pair of yellow glowing eyes staring back at him. The creature let out a scream that sounded like ten thousand knives scraping across the world's biggest chalkboard.

Melvin jumped back involuntarily, blurting out his own scream. He landed awkwardly, catching his elbow on the corner of the desk. He yelped again from pain. The light from his headlamp chaotically flashed all over the room.

Melvin finally got to his feet and flipped the light switch. The room lit up to show the rickety old ceiling fan slowly start turning. His wits left him as he threw open the door to run for safety, still screaming his alarm.

As he turned the corner at full speed into the hallway, he ran into Petro's chest and bounced onto the floor.

His uncle had come to see what the fuss was about. Melvin pointed at his room, babbling incoherently about claws and guts on a fork. His elbow ached and his nerves were tuned tighter than a banjo string.

"What's wrong, kid?" Petro asked, looking freaked out himself.

Then the beast screamed again. It was longer this time and made all the hairs on Melvin's neck stand at attention.

Petro pulled the headlamp off his hysterical nephew's noggin. He strode to the window and pulled back the curtains.

Fear-stricken, Melvin watched in horror. He expected a bloody hook-tipped stump to crash through the glass, catching Petro in the stomach. The fan creaked ominously as his uncle looked out at what would surely be his last glimpse.

"Oh, what a cute little guy! Come here, Melvin. You've got to see this," Petro said, thoroughly confusing his nephew.

"Who, what is it? I don't want to see it, whatever it is," Melvin spat.

Petro looked at him as if he pooped in a swimming pool. "Just get over here and look. It's nothing to be scared of, you little sissy pants."

Melvin slowly climbed to his feet and worked his way over to the window, being sure to stay out of reach if a claw came crashing through. On a thin tree branch sat the most freakishly cute creature. It was an owl the size of a softball. It had massive yellow eyes and a tiny beak nestled just below them. It shook its wings out and ruffled its feathers, making it look a bit bigger. Then it let out another scream, this time not so bloodcurdling.

"It's a screech owl," Petro said. "They're fairly common around here. I don't see them often because they're nocturnal. Though, I do hear them once in a while."

"Well, it freaked me out. I thought owls hooted. I wasn't expecting something to scream at my window in the middle of the night. I'm not used to stupid Alabama yet," Melvin said with a hint of pout and a touch of whine in his voice.

Petro laughed. "There's nothing around here to be worried about as long as you keep your wits about you."

"Are you kidding? I almost got eaten by a bus-sized mama hogzilla," Melvin ranted. "There's a four million pound alligator named Steve just outside the back door. On top of that, a humongous horse-dog-thing called Choopy claimed me for his own. I'm not sure if he plans on eating me or feeding me rotten deer brains. So I have no idea what's going to get me next. When I wake up to a pair of yellow eyes screaming at me through my bedroom window, I have the right to be jumpy!"

Petro giggled through his nephew's tirade. "Okay, calm down. The pig was a freak happening. I've never heard of one doing that before and it won't happen again. Steve is contained in his pond behind a fence and Choopy loves you. I can't think of any creatures that would come after you to inflict harm unless you do something to provoke it."

Petro paused, as if considering what he said.

"What about coyotes, or bears, or rattlesnakes?"

"There's nothing to worry about. The coyotes are more scared of us than we are of them. If there were bears around, Choopy would chase them off, and rattlesnakes are nice enough to warn you when you're getting too close," Petro said, pausing again. "The only thing around here to worry about is trespassing on the wrong land and, well, that's just about all."

"What do you mean just about?" Melvin asked.

"Well, there's one thing, but it's so rare that to find it would be kind of cool, unless you got bit," Petro said, leaning closer.

"What is it? A cougar?"

Petro shrugged. "Nah, it's really nothing to worry about. Go back to sleep."

Melvin's sense of curiosity jumped up and down, screaming. "Just tell me what it is!"

"If you must know, the only thing that's worrisome around here is the fiddle beetle, but they're so rare that no one has seen a swarm in years."

Melvin gulped. "They swarm?"

Petro continued. "Yeah, but they really aren't anything to worry about. The good thing about them is if they do swarm, it's kind of like a rattlesnake. They let out a weird warning hum that sounds like an out-of-tune harmonica. Their prey knows to run and has a chance to jump in water or get into serious shelter. They are persistent little boogers, though."

Melvin was enthralled. "Why's a bug so scary? It's not a spider or scorpion or anything like that?"

Petro leaned closer, speaking quietly. Melvin listened intently to every word.

"They have huge poison-tipped mandibles. The venom won't kill, but evolved to paralyze the victim with pain. The beetles like to eat their meat fresh and don't want it to die until the swarm's thousands of bellies are full.

"I knew an entomologist who was bitten by just one beetle about ten years ago. He said it felt like his hand was being slammed in a car door while on fire, and that was only one bite. He cut off the pinky finger that was bitten with a pair of garden shears to stop the pain. Luckily, he lopped it off before the toxin spread to the rest of his body."

Melvin's eyes were as wide as dinner plates as he inspected his own pinky, imagining the pain.

Petro finished his story. "After that, the professor only studied butterflies. To this day every time he hears a harmonica he runs out the door like a bunny on the first day of hunting season. But like I said, nothing to worry about. If you hear them coming, find shelter they can't chew through, or jump in a lake."

Melvin exhaled heavily, knowing he wouldn't get back to sleep that night.

"Now go back to bed. There's nothing to be scared of," Petro said with a smile as he walked back into the hall, closing the door behind him.

"Easy for you to say," Melvin gasped. The dumb owl had flown off during their conversation. He closed the curtains. Then he flipped off the light and, more importantly, the creepy ceiling fan. As he climbed back in bed, he grabbed the headlamp and placed it on the bedside table, just in case. Slowly, the noises of nature came back, slightly reassuring him.

Melvin lay there for what seemed like hours, not able to get the freaky beetle out of his mind. Eventually, he considered the source. He'd never heard of a fiddle beetle before and realized his evil uncle may have been making the whole thing up. It was easy to check. He grabbed his phone, not wanting to leave the safety of his comforter.

He typed 'fiddle beetle' into the browser. *Wikipedia* popped up instantly with a page all about the scary little critters. The picture was horrifying. The bug must have been four inches long; half the length was a monstrous pair of pinchers. There were even pictures of skeletonized cattle that had the bad luck of being swarmed. Most of what Petro said about the creature was correct. They were found from central Georgia all the way over to Mississippi. Stupid Alabama was right in the middle of their range. Melvin wished his uncle was only messing with him for once.

CHAPTER TWENTY TWO
Stupid Alabama

Melvin woke up homesick and in desperate need of a Mom hug, though he would never admit it. He tried Skyping. Nobody answered. Then he called. No luck. Finally he sent her a text saying, "Hi, Mom," in hopes of a tiny acknowledgment that she still remembered her only son. Her baby boy sent to wallow forever in a place that could have been made of farts and snot, not the funny ones, but the gross kind.

Fifteen minutes later, she responded with a lousy, "Hi, Koo Koo Butt." It only made him feel worse. Though he hated the nickname, it made him miss her more.

His dad was busy; so was Chucky. Nobody had time for him. Melvin felt like a huge bother and always in the way. "Stupid Alabama, and stupid chickens, and stupid heat, and stupid everything else stupid," Melvin pouted to himself through his morning chores.

Petro barely spoke at breakfast. He was deep in research mode. Melvin knew there was no way to break his uncle's focus unless a bus full of Dallas Cowboy Cheerleaders broke down in their front yard.

He turned to the one thing that would never let him down, video games. Ranger's Assassin, it is! He warmed up Igor and plugged in his headphones. Stupid chickens and stupid crickets couldn't distract him if the sound blared straight into his ear holes. Upon opening, the game asked if he wanted to update. Of course he did; it shouldn't be a question. Melvin had been slacking on his duties with all the programming and stupid Alabama stuff. *Update, click …*

The progress bar popped up. "Thirty-five seconds to install. Sixty seconds to install. Four minutes to install. Twenty-seven minutes to install. Forty-eight minutes to install."

"Ah, crap!" He usually does all his updating with the help of Frankenstein, his desk top computer. It ate updates for breakfast, whereas Igor had to write a freaking cookbook about them.

It was unthinkable, but Melvin had to actually go outside and play. There was no basketball court or skate park around. If there was it would probably be made of stupid Alabama farts and snot like everything else!

"I'm going outside."

Petro grunted as Melvin walked past.

"Stupid outside," he pouted.

"What was that, buddy?" Petro asked.

"Nothing. I'm going out."

Petro grunted again without looking up.

Sunlight hit the boy like a wave. He felt millions of droplets of sweat bubbling out of his skin after only a few seconds. A slight breeze came by, coating him in a light layer of red dust. *Stupid Alabama.* Melvin wandered over to Steve's fence.

Even the alligator was hiding from the sun. Choopy was nowhere to be found. *Some dog. He doesn't even play.* He wandered around the yard for a while, poking things with sticks, as is the custom of boredom. Eventually he found himself in the barn again, because he'd already cleaned the chickens that morning. He had never spent any time exploring the rest of the barn, though.

Petro had some weird stuff. There were piles of wire box traps, boat equipment, yard tools, stacks of buckets, and a curious chest he found in a corner covered with a tarp, years of dirt, and blankets of spider webs. Maybe it held a treasure map, a magical sword, or a door to a mysterious land. He ran over, knowing it wouldn't be anything as cool, but needed to fight off the boredom somehow.

It took some work to pop the latch and lift the lid, but when the hinges squeaked open he was greeted by something valuable, pictures. There were hundreds of old pictures of his dad and Uncle Petro as kids. They had real life, no joke, extra-long, business-in-the-front, party-in-the-back, mullet haircuts! It was a blackmail goldmine.

Melvin quickly pocketed some of the best pics in case Petro came looking for him. Once he felt safe he scanned the albums more closely. Briar and Petro looked a lot like Melvin. They all had upturned cowlicks in about the same places. Melvin didn't have rat-tails growing out the back, thankfully. A lot of the photos had a third kid in them. He was shorter than Petro and usually dirtier.

It must have been the famous Scotty. Melvin flipped the photos over. "Scotty Zimmerman, Briar, and Petro," was written on the backs of several. All three looked happy. They smiled, sometimes holding up fish they caught. Petro usually had a frog in his hand or a lizard clamped onto his ear. *Weirdo.*

Melvin found one good picture of Scotty in the middle of the other two boys. He held out a salamander to the camera. Melvin pocketed it as well. Maybe his dad could frame it as a present for Petro later.

Melvin checked his phone. It had to have been an hour since he left the house. Surely Ranger's Assassin was done downloading by now. Twelve minutes had passed. *Stupid Alabama time!*

He went inside. He could scan the pictures with his phone and download them to Frankenstein remotely.

Petro looked up from his sadly insufficient computer. "There you are. Get your boots on. We've got a snake call over at the Weaver's place."

Melvin couldn't help being difficult. His uncle made it way too easy for him. "How does a snake use the phone?"

"The snake didn't call; Mrs. Weaver did. She's a sweet lady who can bake anything. It's always smart to stay on her good side."

"Does that mean she has a snake, or wants one?"

"She has one in her quail coop. It's probably just a rat snake. I'm glad she called me before she called someone else over to shoot it. Maybe I'm getting through to my neighbors after all."

Melvin ran to his room, slipped the pictures into his backpack and grabbed a snake stick from the pile leaning behind the door. A quick glance showed Ranger's Assassin still had almost thirty minutes to go. "Gah, I'm ready."

They hopped into Petro's truck and drove a few miles down the road. It was funny to Melvin that Petro considered the Weavers his neighbors. He didn't know anybody in New York that lived more than five blocks away, much less three whole miles.

They pulled up to a small, well kept brick house with rocking chairs on the front porch and a large barn in the back. A woman, shorter but much wider than Melvin, came out the front door to greet them. "Hello, Petro. I'm glad you're here. There's a copper-bellied moccasin trying to eat my button quail. You better get that thing out of here before I send Mr. Weaver out back with a scatter gun. Here, these are for you and your little helper."

She handed Petro a basket of steaming hot cornbread muffins. Melvin instantly liked her.

"Oh, nobody wants Mr. Weaver to carry a gun anywhere. I don't think he'd be too accurate." Petro laughed. "He'd probably shoot your quail or who knows what else. I'm happy to come by. Glad you called. Is it in the barn?"

"Yes, it is. Go get it and take it out of here, please. How am I supposed to make my famous quail-pot-pie if that dang old serpent eats my main ingredient? Henry's back there somewhere, probably playing in his shop."

Melvin and Petro gobbled a muffin as they walked to the barn. It was unexpectedly sweet and melted in Melvin's mouth. He really liked Mrs. Weaver.

They walked through the open garage door. Things were stacked neatly. Chickens squawked in the large front coop, half in and half out of the barn, like Petro's. The quail were farther back. They were brown birds, shaped like pigeons but smaller. A little orange and black snake was stuck in the wire with the front half of its body in the cage and the other half hanging out. It didn't look comfortable.

"Cool. It's a corn snake," Petro said. He wiggled the little guy out gently as it squirmed. "They're harmless. It was probably eating the mice that eat the seed around here."

The snake was checkered on the belly and about a foot and a half long. It was as thick as a marker and way too small to eat one of the birds. Melvin was surprised one of the quail didn't eat it. Petro handed the snake to him. It instantly bit his thumb.

Melvin jumped as if he backed into a barbed wire fence. "I thought you said it was harmless!"

Petro looked at the boy as if he just bought magic beans. "They are, doofus. Does it hurt?"

Melvin thought for a second. It really didn't. The cute little guy munched on his thumb as if it were wrapped in bacon. "It doesn't hurt at all."

Petro smiled. "See, nothing to worry about."

"I want to keep him. I've never had a snake before," Melvin interrupted, imagining a new best friend in the fight against boredom. Besides, he could send cool pictures of a snake biting him to his friends. It would make him look tough.

"I think it's best if we let this little guy go. Besides, you don't have a permit to keep him in New York."

A door at the back of the barn opened. A deep voice boomed from the dark room behind it. "I smell muffins and trouble. Now, which is it? It better be muffins 'cause I ain't got time for trouble today."

Petro smiled. "Hey, Henry. It's Petro Fitzpatrick and my nephew Melvin. We came to get the snake out of your barn."

"Well, it sounds like you boys got it. I appreciate it."

Petro put the snake into a pillow case he pulled from his cargo pants, tied a knot in the bag, and handed it to Melvin.

They walked back to Henry's shop. The room was dark. Melvin didn't know how anyone would be able to see in there.

"This is my nephew, Melvin. This is Mr. Weaver. He's a sculptor. He's been making booger jugs since before I was born."

Melvin didn't know what a booger jug was but hoped it wasn't what it sounded like. He held out his hand like his dad taught whenever he met an elder. "Uh, nice to meet you, sir." Mr. Weaver just sat there on his chair in the dark. After a second, Melvin put his hand down, feeling awkward.

"Well, you sound like a fine young man. Are you Briar's boy? Come here and let me have a look at you," he said, grabbing Melvin by the shoulder with deceptively strong hands and pulling him closer.

Mr. Weaver wore sunglasses. Either he was too cool for school or was blind. Melvin felt dumb for holding his hand out earlier.

Mr. Weaver's rough hands felt Melvin's head and worked his fingers over his face. "You are a fine looking boy. Briar must have married somebody pretty, because you came out all right."

"Sorry, Mr. Weaver. I didn't know you were blind," Melvin said.

"It's okay, boy. I've been blind all my life. Did you try to shake my hand a minute ago? Ha, that one gets them every time." He smiled. "You know what else gets them?"

"No, what?" Melvin asked, thoroughly entranced by the old man.

"This!" He pulled his sunglasses up and leaned close to Melvin into the light. He was missing one eye completely, with a hole where it should have been. The other eye was yellowed, crooked, and sort of wrong.

Melvin jumped back, expelling a girly squeak.

Petro and Mr. Weaver laughed long and hard.

"It gets them every time. I got your uncle and your dad like that when they were about your age. Briar fell backward into a watering trough. I bet he peed on his self a little."

"He got me pretty good, too," Petro said, laughing. "I ran into a wall trying to get away. I thought he was going to eat me or something."

During the laughter, Mr. Weaver reached over and grabbed one of the muffins from the basket. "Thanks for bringing these. Delilah usually waits until I'm working to make them. She knows they're my favorite and hides them from me. This old nose knows better, though."

"Well, actually Mrs. Weaver made those for us, for taking care of the snake," Melvin said, still dripping in awkward.

"Really. Well, I guess I have to pay you back for that lovely treat. How about I make a jug for you? I was just working on a new one. I'll make this one look just like you. You can take it back to your daddy and show him how handsome you are."

Melvin got excited. "That would be great! But I would have given you some cornbread anyhow, that is until you scared me with your eyes and laughed at me."

"Ha ha. Well, I'm sorry for that, young man. Let me repay your kindness with one of my world famous booger jugs. I've already made the bottle, now I just have to add your face. Stand over here so I can get a better look at you. I want to get all the details perfect."

Mr. Weaver swiveled in his chair and moved Melvin to one side of his potter's wheel. He felt the shape of Melvin's face again. There was an assortment of sculpting tools and bits of broken tile, buttons, and even a few bottle caps on a table on the other side of the wheel.

He cut slices out of some places and added clay to others. He reached and picked out the right tool by touch, replacing them each time into the same spot. Melvin's eyes were getting used to the low light. The jug faced away from Melvin so he couldn't see the progress. Every few minutes Mr. Weaver felt his face again, leaving behind some sticky wet clay. He picked up pieces of tile, feeling for shape, sometimes breaking off an edge to form it just the way he wanted.

Melvin wondered about the almost super-human ability blind people have with their other senses. *How could he feel a face and replicate it perfectly?* Melvin couldn't do that even if he were staring at a picture.

Mr. Weaver gave Melvin's face a final pat-down, virtually covering it in a layer of clay. "There, now. I believe we have an exact match." He turned the jug to face Melvin and Petro.

The image had huge hollow eyes too far apart, a scrunched pointy pig nose, crooked broken teeth in a mouth too far to one side, and ears shaped differently and in the wrong place.

"It looks just like him." Petro said, giggling.

"I don't look like that!" Melvin spat.

Mr. Weaver leaned back in his chair with a broad smile. "My mama, rest her soul, always told me beauty is in the eye of the beholder.

I think that was her way of telling me I'm ugly without hurting my feelings. Now, boy, I ain't got eyes. So, this is just how you look to me."

Petro and Mr. Weaver laughed like drunken hyenas.

Melvin flushed, knowing the two men had gotten him pretty good. He'd be scraping dried clay off his face for hours. It was a pretty cool jug, the more he looked at it.

Petro flipped on the light switch. The shop lit up. Shelves of booger jugs lined the walls. They were all different colors and each had a different ugly face. Once Melvin got over the embarrassment of being tricked, he had a good look at the collection. They were amazing.

"Do I really get to keep this one?" Melvin didn't know what to believe any more.

"You sure do. I bet your daddy would appreciate it. I've still got to glaze and fire it. You can come pick it up in a few days."

"Thanks," Melvin said. That would take care of the present for his dad, now he just needed something for his mom. Maybe he'd get to keep the fifty bucks they each gave him and spend it on something for himself.

They returned to the house with a snake and an empty biscuit basket. Melvin spent the next few hours finding the perfect place to release the snake. He didn't even notice that Ranger's Assassin was done updating.

CHAPTER TWENTY THREE
Stupid Change of Plans

For the next few days Melvin and Petro busied themselves with work. Petro researched his Red Hills salamander project, while Melvin developed the first level of his game from the video he had been collecting and editing. It was tedious, mind-numbing work. The only breaks they took were to run to Petro's office. Summer classes had started on campus, so it took forever to find a parking spot. Melvin cleaned cages while Petro looked through more journals and dead pickled salamanders. *Yuck.*

"I've still got to get some field work done. Which means we get to go camping next week. My deadline is coming up for the grant proposal. It's got to be perfect and I need more data and samples from the colony. In the process, I can teach you some field techniques," Petro said on the way back to the house.

Melvin was still worried about fiddle beetles, but knew not to get in the way of his uncle's work. "Whoopee," he said. Petro's attempts at teaching him things mostly ended up as boring daydream-inducing lectures.

When they got back, there was a handwritten note and a business card attached to the screen door of Petro's trailer. "Oh, this is bad," Petro said while reading it. "I thought if I ignored him, he'd go away. Pack up your stuff. We're going camping right now."

Stupid Alabama by Michael P. Wines

Melvin had no idea what to think. He wrestled the paper from Petro's hand. The business card was from Mitch Mitchum-Investigative Reporter. Melvin gulped. He read the note.

> *Mr. Fitzpatrick (if that is your real name)- I am following up on a story I broke a few weeks ago in New York. I did some digging and expertly discovered you were transporting alligators through the city on the day terrorists viciously attacked a group of pedestrians. There are questions that need answers. I have repeatedly emailed and phoned. You have ignored every communication. If you want to play hardball, believe me, Mr. Fitzpatrick, I am a professional and ALWAYS get my story. I am staying at the Best Western in Auburn. I am not leaving until I get a statement.*
> *-Mitch Mitchum – Investigative Reporter - Channel 5 News*
>
> *P.S. I noticed the excessively large crocodile in your backyard. How convenient.*

Melvin could almost smell hair gel and teeth whitener on the note. This was bad. Thoughts started whizzing around Melvin's brain. *What if they got sent to one of those terrorist prison camps? They surely wouldn't have Internet access. What if he had to be in a cell full of criminals and had to poop in front of everyone? Horrifying!*

"Are we going to jail?" Melvin asked. He tried to hold himself together, but the idea of dropping the kids off at the pool while a room full of thugs watched was too much. "I don't want to poop in front of strangers!"

Petro looked at his nephew as if he just did. "What? We're not going to jail. We didn't do anything illegal. There is something scarier than jail, though."

Melvin couldn't get past the toilet bowl of shame. "What could possibly be scarier than prison?"

Petro spoke quietly, as if saying it might make it actually happen. "What if your mom finds out I drove you here in a van full of alligators?"

156

Melvin knew Petro was right. There was no explaining that one away. Mom would kill him so dead even Steve wouldn't want to eat him. "Let's go camping."

Petro always had his truck packed and ready for anything. He added food, water, a couple of long climbing ropes, and harnesses. Melvin packed clothes he wouldn't mind getting dirty (which was any and all). He grabbed his headlamp and extra battery packs for all his gadgets. The two wayward adventurers were out the door in less than five minutes.

They drove for hours. The site they needed to reach lay to the southwest. Melvin couldn't believe there was anywhere more country than his uncle's house until they entered the Red Hills of Alabama. The only people they saw were truck drivers delivering loads of timber to sawmills.

Petro had an annoying habit of stopping for every bump, stick, chunk of tire, rock, and bit of debris to make sure it wasn't a dead reptile or amphibian. When he found a flattened snake, frog, or turtle, he took a picture of it. Then he got a GPS point and checked repeatedly which county they were in. Truckers honked and waved as they drove by at nine thousand miles an hour.

Melvin was in charge of watching the right side of the road while Petro kept an eye on the left. What could have been a stick or bit of tire moved on the right. Melvin didn't realize he had been watching excitedly for the past few miles. Anything was better than not paying attention, and possibly upchucking like he did on the way to Alabama. "There's a snake!" Melvin blurted.

Petro slowed and pulled to the side of the road. The two Fitzpatricks jumped out to see what it was. Melvin eventually found the serpent, about two feet long and thick as a hotdog. It was black with a white belly. Petro may have hit it with the truck when he pulled over. It was coiled, upside down with its tongue dangling out the side of its open mouth. The poor little thing was even starting to smell.

"Freaking cool!" Petro said. "Do you know what that is?"

"A snake we just ran over." Melvin felt guilty. If he hadn't pointed it out, Petro wouldn't have accidentally killed the poor guy.

"Ah, but I didn't run it over," Petro said, smiling.

"Well, then how did it die? It was alive a second ago when I saw it crawling for the grass. For someone who loves these animals so much, you sure don't seem upset that we killed this one."

"We didn't. In fact, it's not dead." Petro reached over, and flipped the snake right side up. It immediately rolled back over, sticking its tongue out again. It was acting!

"What? Do that again!" Melvin couldn't believe his eyes. He pulled out his phone for a video.

Petro turned the snake over. It was solid black and had an upturned pig-nose. It flipped over again, the same way, this time expelling an awful odor. It even made itself smell dead. "It's an eastern hognose snake. She's playing dead. They evolved the behavior to trick predators. They are rare around here."

"She deserves an Oscar. I thought we killed her. How do you know it's a girl?" Melvin asked.

"Easy, the boys don't get this big. The girls have to be big to carry eggs. The boys don't. It's called sexual dimorphism."

"Gross."

Petro recorded a GPS point, took a few detailed photos with a serious camera he had hiding in one of the nooks of his truck. Then he referred to a book, *The Reptiles and Amphibians of Alabama*, which was so well used it looked as though it had been through a washing machine, then rinsed in mud. "What county are we in?" Petro looked feverish with excitement.

Melvin checked his satellite position on Google Maps, still continuing to film. "Wilcox County."

Petro grabbed his nephew by the shoulders, jumping up and down as if he'd been the next contestant on *The Price is Right*. "It's a county record! It's a county record!"

"So, what does that mean?"

Petro talked as if he had a brand new pocket protector and fresh tape to hold his glasses together. "That means I get to publish a note in a journal saying I found one here. Nobody has recorded one in this county ever, officially. It'll go into the record books for future study."

CHAPTER TWENTY THREE

"Actually, I found it," Melvin said, expecting to see his uncle deflate.

"Good point. You better write the note and send it in then. I'll show you how when we get back. It'll be your first publication." Petro smiled with what looked like pride in his eyes.

"Sounds like homework," Melvin pouted.

They continued, stopping four more times for various bits of ick-jerky. Petro pulled off the quiet highway onto a gravel path that looked like a billion other dirt roads they'd passed. He drove into a meadow, not far from the road.

A fire pit nestled down into the center of the clearing, surrounded by four log benches. A worn footpath led back toward the road, while another snaked deeper into the woods. Petro unloaded boxes and tubs while Melvin worked on setting up the tent where his uncle directed. After a frustrating ten minutes, the dome-tent went from a tightly rolled sack to a jumbled mess of poles and inside-out canvas. Melvin had botched it up soundly.

Petro walked over, shaking his head. "Rookie." He had the structure up and staked within two minutes. "I hope you cook better than you set up camp. I've got a few more things to work on. How about making us some dinner?"

"I can do that," Melvin replied. He ran over to the truck while Petro sat on a log, checking a box of equipment. Melvin returned ten seconds later with two Pop-tarts and a couple cans of Coke. "Dinner is served."

"You should drop out of school to become a full-time chef," Petro moaned as he scarfed down the untoasted strawberry pastry.

"I'm really good at cooking breakfast, too," Melvin said after an earthshaking burp.

"Come on, kid. I want to show you something." Petro picked up a net attached to the end of a broom handle and walked down the trail heading away from the main road.

Melvin followed, carrying a snake stick. He wasn't sure why he brought it. It just made him feel more official.

Stupid Alabama by Michael P. Wines

The path ended at a small pond about a hundred feet from camp. Petro walked the perimeter, through mud, stopping at the spot it seemed to be the thickest. He scooped out a big pile of leaves and muck with the net and flopped it onto a grassy patch behind him. Then he looked through it, as if mining for precious gems.

"Come here. Look at this," he said, not turning away from the pile of swampy gunk.

Melvin reluctantly leaned down. It smelled like a giant turtle ate a dead skunk and turned itself inside out via explosive diarrhea. "Gross!"

"Quit being a baby and look."

Melvin held his breath and looked, half expecting his uncle to rub a handful of awful in his face. In the muck a couple of yellow dots separated themselves from the dull brown color. A big black salamander with yellow and orange spots strutted to the top of the pile, then another.

He began seeing all kinds of creatures wiggling around. There were two other types of salamanders. One tiny one with a copper stripe on its back came into view and another short thick guy the same color as the mud. Then other creatures began appearing.

Melvin didn't notice the smell after a couple minutes of marveling at the living sludge. He found a total of six salamanders, nine tadpoles of various sizes, three crayfish, and a ton of random bugs in just one scoop of muck.

"This is actually kind of cool," he marveled, now up to his elbows in the stinky mess.

Petro expounded about temporary ponds and ecosystems as Melvin searched through a couple more piles. The boy stopped his uncle only to identify new critters he found, but mostly let the lesson go in one ear and out the other.

Melvin rinsed off as much as he could with pond water, and cleaned himself up back at camp. The sun set, and the creatures of the forest turned the volume up. Some of the frogs and insects were deafening. The stars and moon lit up the night sky like frozen fireworks. For just a minute, Melvin didn't miss the city.

Petro's Field Notes

EASTERN HOGNOSE SNAKE

Eastern Hognose Snake *(Heterodon platyrhinos)* is far and away my favorite snake. They aren't big. They aren't even dangerous unless you're a toad (their favorite food). But they are one of the best actors in the animal kingdom, including humans. For one thing, they can pretend to be a cobra! Hognose snakes can flatten the skin around the neck making them look ginormous and intimidating. If that doesn't work, they play dead! They flip themselves over, open their mouths, lull out their tongues, and squirt a dead-smelling musk out of their butts. Who wants to eat a stinky, rotten, old dead snake? Once the predator loses interest and moves on, the hognose rights itself and slithers away. I don't see Johnny Depp pooping his pants for a death scene.

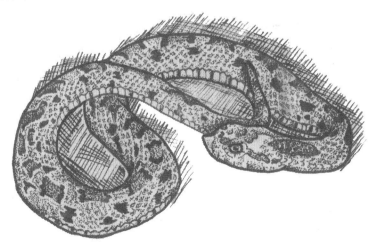

CHAPTER TWENTY FOUR
Sacrificing Marshmallows to Save the World

Melvin was ready for the festivities to begin. His dad's friends had a cabin in upstate New York they visited a few times a year. Roasting marshmallows was always one of the highlights of the trip. It's what he did every time he went camping. He could almost taste them. He wanted the skin burnt to sweet, bubbly, flaky blackness only to gobble it so he could burn the next sticky layer.

Melvin and his dad had a rivalry going to see who could carve the best marshmallow stick. Briar won last time by getting one that forked at the end. That way he could cook two at once. His dad wasn't around now, so he wouldn't mind if Melvin stole his idea. He put on his headlamp and searched the nearby ground for a suitable branch.

"Hey, Uncle Petro, when are you going to start the campfire?"

"I'm not. There's not going to be a fire tonight. We've got work to do."

Melvin broke the first candidate for ultimate cooking tool over his knee. It had three-pronged promise, too. "You know what camping is without marshmallows?"

Petro looked up from sorting through a bag of equipment on the tailgate of his truck. "What?"

"Being homeless," Melvin pouted.

Petro laughed and tossed him a wad of what looked like seat belts. "Put that on. We've got to catch some Red Hills salamanders tonight."

He picked up the straps. Buckles and metal rings looped though the jumbled mess. "What is it?"

"It's a mountain-climbing harness. These guys don't live in ponds like the ones we found earlier." Petro expertly put on his own gear as Melvin struggled to untangle his.

After a frustrating few minutes, his uncle helped him. He had to step in, pull it up to his waist, and fasten the belt. Then he tightened all the straps to fit. It felt like the world's tightest diaper.

Melvin's stomach lurched at the thought of climbing a sheer rock face to a dizzying height. If that weren't scary enough, he had to do it in pitch dark. "I didn't know there were mountains around here." Melvin's voice went up an octave. It might have been from fear or the harness was too tight. He wasn't sure which.

"No mountains, just one really big cliff. We have to rappel down. The salamanders are in burrows dug into the side. We have to catch them on fishing hooks. It's fun. You'll love it." Petro piled mounds of gear onto his nephew.

"What's all this for?"

"You can't rappel without a rope, carabineers, helmet, rope brake …" His uncle continued as he stacked gear on the sagging kid.

"Well, at least if I fall, all this crap will pad my landing," Melvin said, wobbling and jangling under the weight.

Petro tapped Melvin's helmet, causing the headlamp to wobble and almost knocking the boy over. "That's the spirit, kid. Now, let's go."

They walked down the trail leading closer to the road. The hike took twenty minutes of walking up and down slopes, carrying the equivalent of an elephant driving a steamroller. Melvin's armpits grew new armpits to sweat extra. By the time they arrived, he smelled like it, too.

The trail disappeared into open air and darkness. They would only need to take two more steps to the edge. A hundred feet of gravity would welcome them with open arms and jagged rocks.

Melvin had always been told if he was lost and alone in the woods to hug a tree. Now he had found a new situation to do just that. He had been up in the tallest skyscrapers. He even rode in glass elevators over a hundred stories in the air. This was different. There were no guard rails or Watch Your Step signs. One wrong move and over the side he would go at a million miles an hour to a dirty old pile of rocks and kudzu.

Even if he survived the fall, he would break bones or suffer internal bleeding. He could spend the rest of his life in a wheelchair, or worse yet, pooping in a bag because he couldn't do it on his own.

Petro tied two ropes off to closely growing trees a few yards from the edge. Once secure, he threw each coil of rope into the waiting darkness.

Melvin clung to the trunk of a tree, looking away from the clutches of oblivion.

Petro turned around to find his nephew latched to the tree as if he were stranded in the ocean, clinging to a buoy during a hurricane. "Come on, I'll get you hooked up," he said, hopefully.

Melvin shook his head. "I'm not going to do it! I don't want to poop in a bag for the rest of my life."

"What is it with you and pooping in weird places? Come on. I wouldn't let you get hurt. Here, watch me." He latched carabineers and twisted ropes into loops. He checked straps and tugged on his harness.

Melvin turned around to see, but wouldn't release his life-preserving oak.

Petro gave him one last smile, then jumped. He held the attached end of the rope in his right hand. The left clutched the loose end behind his back. He faced the wall, so the last thing Melvin saw was the headlamp disappearing from view, like throwing a flashlight down a well. The line pulled tight. He heard the sound of his uncle smacking against the side of the cliff.

From below came a sudden, "Woo hoo! You've got to try this, kid. It's a blast."

Melvin reluctantly let go and crawled to the end of the world on his belly. The line attached to his uncle was as tight as a guitar string and made for a good handhold. He wriggled his body so he could see Petro smiling up at him.

"See, it's not so bad. I wouldn't put you in a situation where you'd get hurt. Your mom would kill me. I'm coming back up. Watch how I do it."

That made sense. The threat of death and dismemberment from his mom was convincing enough to give it a try. Plus, it did sound fun. He would just have to get the pooping in a bag image out of his mind.

Petro attached the brake (another dangly metal thing with a handle) to the rope. He released completely, relying entirely on the gear to hold him up. "Look, no hands."

He put one hand on the brake and the other on the rope. As he stepped up he slid up the line. His weight was put alternately on the brake and his feet as he worked his way back to the top. It looked simple enough.

"If I fall, and have to poop in a bag the rest of my life, I'm going to mail you every sack!" With that warning, Melvin worked up enough courage to let Petro hook him up. He listened as his uncle showed him where to put his hands and how to maneuver up and down the line. They both checked his gear several times to make sure everything was snug and attached correctly. Petro was on a parallel line a few feet away.

Petro backed to the edge and slowly leaned back this time, instead of jumping. Melvin followed, keeping an eye on his feet, his hands, the rope, his uncle, and everything else around but the huge space between himself and the bone-breaking, skull-fracturing rocks below. He got to the ledge and took a slow step backward, just like he had been shown. His toes pushed against the wall a few inches below the edge. Then he slid his other foot down.

He suddenly slipped several feet, the rope catching him. Panic would have set in had the harness not put all the weight of his body and gear directly on his crotch. He let out a gasp as his body stuck flat to the wall.

"Lean back like you're sitting in a chair," Petro said.

Melvin did, not caring if he fell, anything to get the crushing weight off his aching marbles. The pressure lifted as he sat back, putting his feet between himself and the vertical bluff. He hung for a few seconds to catch his breath and let his grapes re-inflate.

Once fully recovered, Melvin looked down. He expected to see a mile-long drop to waiting rocks. At this angle, however, the cliff looked more like a hill. The fun part of his brain was slowly kicking the sissy wimpy part's butt. He wondered, with a giggle, *Does that mean I have butts in my head?*

Petro pushed off with his legs, as if jumping sideways. Melvin watched and mimicked. It really was fun.

"Okay, now as you push back, let the rope go with your left hand, like I showed you. Just grab it and pull to slow yourself down."

Melvin did what he said and dropped a few feet as he pushed outward. It was scary but lots of fun. He imagined the S.W.A.T team hopping down a building to crash through a window to shoot the bad guys. This is exactly how they would do it.

He pushed off for two more good jumps and found himself at the bottom. "That was so cool!"

"I told you. Now, we've got to catch some salamanders." Petro put the brake on his rope and climbed back up about ten feet.

Melvin followed. He looked around at the side of the hill, slowly noticing dozens of tiny purple faces looking back at him. They were everywhere. He watched as his uncle showed him how to lure the little salamanders out of their burrows with a worm on a hook. They didn't seem to be scared of the light from their headlamps. Once they had their heads poking out, he let them bite the worm. Petro pulled the wiggling, slimy creatures out and grabbed them. Once in hand, he placed them in a plastic sandwich bag, wrote a number on it, and put the bag in his backpack. He then labeled the burrow with a red reflective flag. The number on each salamander's bag matched the flag so he would know where to return them.

Melvin looked past his uncle. The hillside lit up with reflective flags. "Wow, how many have you caught here?"

"This is number seven hundred eighty-four. They live in this whole area but the density of the population on this slope is higher than anywhere else. The department of transportation wants to straighten the road right through this hill to make it faster for truckers to get through. If they do, most of this species will be displaced and will probably end in extinction. So, each of these salamanders will be one more reason not to destroy the hill. I'm trying to keep that from happening."

"Why can't the truckers just slow down, or build another road somewhere else?" Melvin thought it sounded rational.

"I wish it were that easy. Drivers get paid for each load of logs they deliver. If they can go fast and deliver one more load per day, they make more money to take home for their families. So, it's hard to blame the truckers. They're just doing their jobs. This is the shortest route between the mill and the trees being logged, so building a new road is out of the question. Plus, where would the money come from to build a whole new road? I certainly don't have it."

They continued talking and fishing for salamanders as they slowly worked their way back to the top. Petro moved the ropes to a couple of trees a few yards over and they zipped down the hill again.

The only time Melvin got scared was when a pterodactyl-sized moth flew up his nose. He had to hold on to the rope with one hand to dig it out. Before he knew it, they had caught twenty eight salamanders. He was having fun, but also felt good because he was doing something helpful and useful.

He videoed Petro fishing out a couple of the squirmy amphibians, then he made his uncle take pictures of him hanging on the rope. He figured no one would believe him without proof.

It was well past midnight when they got back to camp. Melvin managed to take off his boots and attach his phone to a portable charger before passing out in a heap on top of his sleeping bag. He didn't even have the energy to pout about no marshmallows. *Who knew saving the world, or at least a tiny part of it, was so exhausting?*

Petro's Field Notes
RED HILLS SALAMANDER

Red Hills Salamander *(Phaeognathus hubrichti)* is the state amphibian of Alabama. They are long, skinny critters with short legs. Despite the name, they are grayish-purple and called Red Hills salamanders because they live in the Red Hills of central Alabama. They dig long burrows in the side of steep hills and only poke their heads out at night. The best way to catch them is with a fishing hook! If a bug is wiggled in front of their holes, they shoot out like a jack-in-the-box. They will try to eat anything that can fit in their mouths. I once caught one on the end of my pinkie finger.

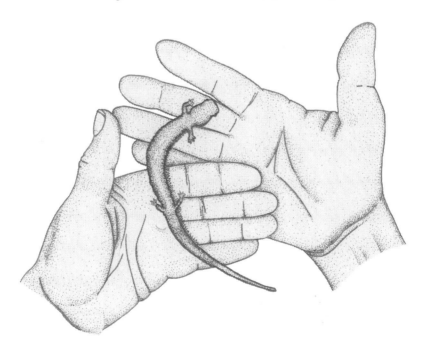

CHAPTER TWENTY FIVE

Never Disturb the Devil When He's Pooping

Melvin wandered down a poorly lit hallway past lockers, dropped books, and ancient banners, reading every sign as he went. He passed countless empty classrooms, a deserted, dusty cafeteria, and the marching band practice room full of knocked-over chairs and long forgotten instruments. He walked faster, with a building panic, by the janitor's closet and several storage rooms. He leaned into a hard run past the lab equipment room, the principal's office, the front desk, and trophy cabinets with dozens of decrepit bronze statues mocking him.

He ran on, stumbling and panicking, with the gut-deep knowledge that something was going to happen, soon. Melvin tripped over another sign. It read *Restrooms* with arrows going every direction. *Which way!?* He realized his mission. He had to get to the boys' room.

Melvin stumbled on, turning everywhere at once. *There! There was the girls' room.* His destination must be close. The safety and privacy of his very own stall was just around the corner. He recognized the place. It was the clean bathroom on the third floor that no one ever went to.

Finally, the magical sign that brought hope, peace, and joy to his heart and bowels. It read Boys' Room. Melvin pushed into the door, crashing face-first. It was locked. *Who locked bathroom doors? Why?*

Melvin felt the powers of desperation and frustration imbibe his muscles with strength. He kicked the door with all his might. It gave way with an earth-shaking crash, swinging violently on its hinges.

He walked through as the door swung shut with a click. The lights were out, but he saw the toilet a little ways ahead. It was illuminated by a Jacob's Ladder from the heavens. Harps began to play as Melvin walked to the porcelain alter. He felt safe and relaxed, having fulfilled his quest. Almost.

He dropped his pants and sat upon his mighty throne. Just as he was about to satisfy his destiny he heard a giggle in the distance. Then another, though he couldn't tell from where. The harps got louder, followed by the loud clang sound of a switch being thrown.

Lights blinded him from all directions. He found himself in the middle of the basketball court, still on the toilet. To his horror, he realized the bleachers were full. The entire school pointed and laughed. Boys held their nose in mockery while girls giggled and pretended to look away, but didn't.

Amongst the crowd was everyone he had ever met and hundreds more. Chucky filmed him from floor seats. When they made eye-contact, his best friend gave him a thumbs-up from behind the camera. He said, "This is live on YouTube, bro! Pinch one out for the world!"

His mother was a few feet away being interviewed by Mitch Mitchum. "How do you feel about your son pooping in front of the entire planet?" he asked.

Melvin looked up to see a split screen on the jumbotron. One half was himself on the toilet, the other was his mother answering the reporter's question.

"Well, at least he made it to the toilet this time," she said into the echoing microphone. "I'm so proud of you, Koo-Koo Butt!"

Melvin shuddered in frozen embarrassment. He couldn't move. The band began playing fight songs, though they sounded funny. There were no drums, only a buzzing horn section. Then another band on the opposite side of the gymnasium began to buzz. They battled, out of tune and time. It almost sounded like they were all playing harmonicas.

Then his dad showed up, saying, "Wash your hands in the water. You've got to get to the water."

The whole crowd took up the chant, "Get to the water."

Melvin's horror was beginning to be replaced with confusion. *Why did he have to get to the water?* The harmonica band began marching toward him, becoming louder.

"Get to the water!" they chanted.

Then Petro took over. "Get to the water!"

The uniforms on the band members became clearer. They all had the same insignia – The Fighting Fiddle Beetles.

Petro shook him by the shoulders. "Get to the water!"

"I always wash my hands after I poop!" Melvin screamed.

"What? We've got to run. We've got to get to the water," his uncle insisted.

The lights turned off, finally. Somebody turned on the heat. His uncle continued with the chant. The toilet, crowd, and bleachers faded away, and he was yanked into reality.

"Melvin! Wake up. We've got to get to the water. The fiddle beetles are coming!" shouted Petro.

Melvin was totally confused. "From the bathroom?"

They were in a tent. The flap was open and Petro was shaking him. There was a buzzing outside. The swarm!

"Get to the pond, the water! I'm right behind you."

Melvin shot out of the tent as if he were a bullet from a gun. There were two trails. He remembered one led to the pond, the other to the cliff. The buzzing got louder and came from a couple of directions. It was dark, hot, and hard to see.

"Go left," Petro said, sprinting behind him with a flashlight.

Melvin ran. He stepped on sharp sticks and rocks in his sock-covered feet. He didn't bother to put on his shoes. The image of the skeletonized cow popped in his head as adrenaline kicked into gear. He went from sound asleep to a full sprint through the deep dark woods in two-point-three seconds. He fell twice, skinning the palm of his left hand.

The humming came from two directions behind them. For a second Melvin imagined Petro was messing with him. He thought better of it since the tuneless sounds emanated from somewhere else, plus there was more than one. Petro couldn't produce multiple sounds. He couldn't yell and play a harmonica at the same time. This was not a drill.

A couple deer crashed off the trail ahead of him. They must be running from the beetles, too. He could hear Petro falling behind. Melvin knew by the broad swipes from the flashlight he was still running, not caught yet. It couldn't be much farther. It wasn't a long walk from the tent to the pond and he was going warp speed.

What if he missed it or ran right past in the dark? The thought scared him as much as the swarm, but he couldn't stop to look. Finally, the trees opened into a meadow. The water in the center looked like black glass, reflecting moonlight.

He turned to find Petro. He saw the bouncing flashlight making its way through the woods with the sound of the swarm close behind.

"Get to the water!" Petro yelled, breaking into the clearing.

Melvin screamed like the hot girl from a horror movie as he ran in. As the pond got deeper, it slowed him down. Once into his knees, he had to dive or be caught wading through the muck. The safety of the slimy mess washed over him. He held his breath, fully submerged, waiting for the splash of his uncle diving in. The mud seemed to be alive. Everything wriggled on his skin. It was only waist deep, and half of that was sludge.

Petro was right behind him. Surely the beetles didn't catch him so close to shelter. Melvin lifted his head out of the water, cautiously exhaling. The flashlight sat still on the ground, shining a beam across the rippling pool. Melvin couldn't see past it. The buzzing had stopped. Perhaps they had caught his uncle and were feasting on his dying body.

Melvin was so scared every hair on his body stood up, which is pretty hard to do under water. "Uncle Petro?" he whispered, fearing the worst.

All he heard was panting. Someone or something was out of breath. Then there was more panting from another body, another. Then laughter.

"I've never seen anyone run so fast in my life," Petro said, while trying not to hyperventilate. "I'm glad you waited to jump in the water, or I wouldn't have gotten it on film. Wait until Briar sees this. He's going to pee himself."

Realization hit Melvin over the head with a wet brick. "You set this whole thing up? Who else is here? I can't see."

"You have the girliest scream I've ever heard," came from a snickering girl's voice somewhere behind Petro.

Melvin recognized it. "Sasha? Is that you?"

"Ha ha, yes. We got you so bad," she said, throwing a snort into the laugh for good measure.

"I'm sorry, Melvin. I wondered why Petro wanted me to bring my harmonicas," Cassidy said, almost done with her giggle fits.

"You guys came all the way out here just to mess with me?" Melvin wasn't quite as humiliated as he had been pooping for the planet in his nightmare, but close.

"No, we came to camp and help out. I thought it would be fun for Sasha," said Cassidy.

Sasha said, "It already is," between snorts.

"What time is it? Why are you here so late?"

Petro finally caught his breath. "It's a little after five. Cassidy worked the late shift at the emergency vet clinic and came out to meet us when she got off."

Melvin squished his way out of the pond, wringing awful from his shirt.

"You smell like the creature from the butt lagoon," Sasha smirked.

"You would know." Melvin's witty retort brought nothing but more giggles at his expense.

"Here you go," Cassidy said, wrapping a towel around him. At least she was thoughtful enough to bring one. They walked back to camp, retelling each other their favorite parts of the prank.

"You're going to be sorry if fiddle beetles really do show up," Melvin said, reliving the shame.

Petro laughed harder. "That's just it! I made the whole thing up. I used *Wikipedia* against you. The hardest part was not telling you to look it up. I had to let you get there on your own. If I had told you to Google it, you might have figured it out and checked the source."

That detail burned more than the rest. His uncle used the Internet against him. The web was his weapon. There would be payback.

Melvin crawled into the tent to change into something dry. As he removed his wet clothes, he discovered his pants pockets were full of mud. They must have filled up when he dove into the water. Each pocket's handful fit nicely into his uncle's dry boots. It was no mega-prank, but at least put a band-aid on the amputation. Evil Melvin was hatching and had lots to do.

Outside he smelled a campfire come to life. "We brought the fixin's for s'mores," Cassidy said.

Melvin decided to focus on being evil after marshmallows.

CHAPTER TWENTY SIX
The Sweet Smooch of Revenge

Every step Petro took made a farty squishing sound due to the mud Melvin put in his boots. He gave his nephew a squinty-eyed stare each time Cassidy or Sasha giggled.

The boy was slowly on his way to recovering some pride. It also helped when it came time to teach the girls how to rappel. He happily zipped up and down the cliff as Sasha whined and Cassidy whimpered throughout their lessons from Petro.

They couldn't do much work on Petro's salamander project during the day. The girls, however, did learn the ropes with plenty of morning sun.

"I had to learn last night in the dark," Melvin said as Sasha clung to the familiar tree.

She held on with both arms and legs. "I should sue for child abuse. I might if they make me let go of this tree." Her competitive side took over once she saw how much fun Melvin was having. She eventually got the hang of it.

After lunch, Melvin helped Sasha put up the girls' tent. Watching his uncle the night before gave him a slight advantage in know-how. It took them about twenty minutes. It was nowhere near Petro's five-minute miracle, but Melvin was pleased with himself all the same. One more thing he knew how to do that his nemesis/crush didn't was fine with him.

Melvin took Sasha to the pond with nets and a bucket. He instructed her on how to use the net and showed her all the critters wriggling around in the muck. Petro and Cassidy stayed behind to work on adult stuff, whatever that was.

After half filling a bucket with unidentifiable amphibians, they walked back to camp. Cassidy and Petro didn't notice their approach because they were kissing! Cassidy sat on the bumper of her truck as Petro leaned in close. Melvin felt devil horns trying to poke through the skin on his forehead. He had a bucket of slippery, wiggly frogs and newts, and two unsuspecting people that happened to deserve a good prank.

He put his finger to his lips in the universal sign for, "Be quiet, hijinks are about to ensue." He turned on the video mode to his phone and handed it to Sasha.

Melvin considered getting the biggest salamander from the bucket, but realized he might be discovered before he could catch it. So he grabbed a handful without looking. He snuck up behind his uncle like a cat in a room full of sleeping pit bulls. Melvin realized he could have been shooting off fireworks and playing the bassoon and they wouldn't have noticed.

One last look back at the camera for a conspiratorial thumbs-up almost ruined it. Sasha was doing all she could not to laugh. Tears poured from her eyes and she was doubled over, barely holding the phone steady.

Melvin kept it together, somehow. Cassidy sat low enough so he could reach the back of her collar. Realizing his luck, Melvin took half the slippery critters in each hand and slid them down Petro's and Cassidy's shirts simultaneously. Then he ran for his life while yelling, "Ooooh kissy kissy! Ooooh kissy kissy!"

Sasha burst into fits, still filming.

Cassidy and Petro danced around like two broken robots on fire. To make it even funnier, every panicked step Petro took sounded like a poot because of the mud still in his boots. Salamanders and frogs flew from the two robot tornadoes as if they were stuck on sprinkler mode.

Every time they believed themselves to be clear of wriggling beasts, another would find an armpit, belly button, or butt crack, and the dance started all over again.

Sasha began chanting, "Smoochy, smoochy! This is the dance of loooove!"

That made Melvin snort so hard he farted, which led to another round of belly laughs. Both conspirators rolled on the ground.

Petro and Cassidy were so embarrassed they couldn't look at each other for over an hour. Every time they started acting normal, Melvin or Sasha would make a kissing sound.

Melvin snickered. "If you two blush anymore, your heads might pop."

"Then it would be hard to smoooooch," Sasha added. The two kids made for an amazingly annoying team.

Though the footage might not be a good fit for the video game, he was still glad to have it, and immediately sent it to his dad.

Briar said, "LOL. I've never been so proud of you, son," in a response text a few minutes later.

It made Melvin feel almost as good as getting his evil groove back. Over the next couple of nights they caught almost a hundred Red Hills salamanders and recorded data on each one. There were no more frog-down-the-shirt freak outs.

Sasha lost it once when she walked through a spider web the size of a Volkswagen. As she pulled miles of web off her hair and face, she asked Melvin, "Is it on me! Where is it? Is it in my hair?"

He saw the spider get flung off in the initial spaz attack, but kept that information to himself. Instead he answered, "It's right there," several times without actually pointing anywhere.

"Where!?"

"Right there."

"Where's right there?" Her voice had gone up to an almost impossible pitch.

"Right there," is all he said, giggling.

She socked him on the arm when she figured out what he was doing.

With both Melvin and Petro happy with what they'd accomplished over the last few days, they went home. Cassidy gave Petro a goodbye kiss to a chorus of, "Kissy kissies and smoochy smoochies."

When Cassidy threatened to kiss Melvin, he stopped. The kids exchanged high-fives and knuckle bumps.

On the way home an afternoon storm blew in from the east just after Montgomery. It rained so hard Petro had to turn on his hazard lights and pull over. Hail the size of marbles fell from the sky, and lightning struck close enough to make the vehicle shake. There were always rain and snow storms in New York, but not like this. The wind got brutal there, but never to the point at which it could pick up heavy things like buildings. The gusts battered and threatened to flip the truck, but never did. Luckily, Petro found an underpass to wait out the worst of the storm. It didn't take long to go by. Melvin looked at the radar map on his phone. The front of the storm was the worst part, like a red sword moving across the countryside. It had already passed over Petro's house, and was heading east.

They drove home past bent signs and downed trees. A couple of places the power had been out and traffic lights were dead. Drivers treated them like four-way stop signs, or at least were supposed to. Melvin was worried about the condition of Petro's house as they drove down the old country road.

There didn't seem to be much damage upon first inspection. One of the poles holding the birdhouses had been knocked over, but were easily restored to normal. The birds seemed appreciative. Then they pulled up to the house; not much damage at first glance. A few branches had fallen from the trees. The view of the backyard seemed different, however.

Petro and Melvin walked around to check the barns and back side of the house. An old pine had fallen through the fence. It was fixable with a chainsaw and some elbow grease.

There was a slightly bigger problem, however. Twelve feet of alligator was out and walking around the backyard like he owned the place.

Petro didn't seem at all panicked; well, not until Mitch Mitchum, investigative reporter, pulled up in the driveway with a camera crew.

CHAPTER TWENTY SEVEN
Stupid Chickens

"Aw, crap!" Petro said, either in reference to the twelve-foot, stalking, free-range alligator or the six-foot, stalking, free-range reporter. Melvin wasn't sure which, but guessed both. "You keep an eye on Steve. Don't get near him. Just watch where he's going. Blow your whistle if you get in trouble. I'll try to deal with the butt-chinned reporter."

Melvin pulled out the pendant of safety his mom had him wearing since he could walk. It had a whistle, compass, and a magnifying glass, though it could only magnify a small ant to the size of a medium sized ant. "Okay, good luck," he said, clenching his teeth around the mouthpiece like someone trying to referee a stampede.

Petro stalked around front to meet Mitch before he brought his camera crew to the backyard. Four people crawled out of the van. Two men carried cameras, while a woman busily applied a dust cloud of makeup to the reporter.

Steve moped to the far side of the barn, the opposite direction from the drama unfolding in the front yard. The dinosaur lazily scratched at the chicken coop a few times with one massive claw, then settled on a sunny spot in the grass.

Melvin ran into the barn and climbed to the second floor. He could get a safe view of both Steve and Petro from the higher vantage point.

Steve sat still, content with his new basking spot.

Melvin saw Mitch poking his uncle in the chest with a microphone, while gesturing wildly with his arms as if trying to make a scene for the camera. Melvin thought it might be good time to film the action while no one was looking and Steve was resting easy. He zoomed in with his camera. He couldn't record audio from that distance, but got great resolution.

Petro stood still, with his arms crossed, not speaking much. Mitch continued with his antics for the camera as if he were a manager for a professional wrestler before a cage match. The two cameramen moved back and forth, one held his camera at hip height, the other on his shoulder, both focused on Petro and Mitch. The makeup lady was back in the van, painting her nails and looking bored.

Melvin turned to check on Steve, who was gone. He looked frantically. The gator was sitting in the sunny spot a second ago, and couldn't have gotten far. Melvin wasn't concerned for his own safety, as long as he stayed on the second floor of the building. He stepped out onto the top of the chicken coop for a better view of the woods and the back side of the shed. Steve was nowhere to be found. *Crap.*

Then he heard branches snap and saw the underbrush shake twenty yards around the far side of the barn. Choopy popped from the woods backward, wagging his tail excitedly. He leaned down on his front paws, with his butt up in the air, and bounced back and forth. His focus was on Steve, who he was slowly following out of the woods and into the open. Choopy was the only dog-beast that would think playtime when seeing a twelve-foot alligator.

No wonder he hangs around with Uncle Petro, Melvin thought.

Choopy darted back and forth in front of Steve, as if mocking him. He almost got close enough for a couple of nips to the gator's front claws before leaping out of the way.

Steve raised his head and opened his mouth, chomping down every time the annoying thing got near. The two were mesmerized with each other. However, every step Steve took toward Choopy led them closer to the cameras and Petro.

Melvin set his camera down, propping it against a board, while keeping a wide focus on the human drama. He ran downstairs and flung the chicken coop open. Most of the hens were inside, still hiding from Steve's earlier probing. He grabbed a squawker under each arm and ran back towards Choopy and Steve, holding the whistle between his teeth, just in case.

Once, while collecting eggs and feeding the chickens, Melvin had forgotten to close the door. A couple of hens escaped. They couldn't fly very far, but could really move when they wanted to. He discovered that while attempting to catch the feathery little jerks. Choopy showed up and the chickens ran right back to the safety of the coup.

Melvin hoped a chicken in front of both predators would distract them from each other. The bird would lead them back to the henhouse and away from the people. It seemed like a good plan ...

He ran out to find Choopy, the biggest fastest pork chop in the world, steadily annoying the lumbering dragon. Steve made lightning-quick dashes after the dog every minute or so. He couldn't get more than ten or twelve feet, the length of his body; but he covered those short distances like a toothy rocket.

The boy ran wide around the squabble. He didn't want to get anywhere near Steve, or to distract Choopy from his play, which would be dangerous for the dog. One wrong move and the barking horse would be a fuzzy funnel cake.

"Hey!" he yelled, once in position. It was hard to say more with the whistle in his teeth. Steve paid no attention, but Choopy maneuvered to the side of the gator to have a look, while not turning his back from his bloodthirsty new toy.

Melvin held the chickens up by their feet, one in each hand, as if directing a plane where to taxi. They flapped their wings with almost enough force to pick the boy off the ground. The movement attracted both predators.

He released the birds, expecting them to sprint for the safety of the barn again. This time they decided to flap up to the nearest high point and roost there for protection. That just happened to be Melvin's head. *Stupid chickens.*

He tried to swat them down, but they lifted off just high enough to come right back down on top. Melvin backed up a few steps, knowing the gator was coming, but remained distracted by wings beating him about the head and shoulders. Finally he smacked one off and grabbed the other by the leg. He turned around just in time to see a mouth open like a folding chair, full of pink gums and yellow teeth the size of stalagmites.

Melvin tried to blow his whistle. It was too late. There was nothing Petro could do from fifty yards away. He was about to be crushed, eaten, and pooped out. The wide-eyed boy was too slow to get out of Steve's way, as if he were a fresh steaming turd pile, waiting for an approaching lawnmower to ruin his birthday.

Steve was so close his breath blew Melvin's cowlick back. It smelled like a combination of fish-butt and asparagus pee. The alligator was so fast, Melvin only got a chirp out of the whistle before the impact knocked it from his mouth. Luckily, the hit was from Choopy and not Steve's massive jaws.

Melvin was smacked so hard, the chicken stayed floating in the air. Steve bit down on the place Melvin had been, happily finding the hen instead. He also got Choopy's back foot.

The dog yelped. It wasn't a game anymore. His leg was trapped in Steve's mouth. Choopy turned, biting Steve's face. The gator was so large and content with the fluttering chicken, he didn't notice, or at least didn't react.

Once Melvin's senses returned, all he could hear was the pathetic yelp of the dog. Choopy had just saved his life and was now paying for it. The kid had come to like the dog, even love him, though he wouldn't admit it to anyone. Choopy was the only thing always happy to see him, even if he showed it by peeing on Melvin's leg. The alligator wasn't just biting a dog. Steve was biting Melvin's dog!

Snapping and popping sounds came from Steve's mouth. Choopy yelped louder.

Adrenaline hit the boy harder than Choopy had. Tiny Hulk was mad! "Get off my dog!" He jumped on the back of Steve's head, wrapping his arms and legs around the gator's neck. He might as well have been a flea trying to tame a bronco.

Steve flipped his head back, swallowing the chicken in a mighty gulp. He didn't seem to notice the weight of the boy, or simply didn't care.

Choopy had a split second to retract his foot. He limped off to the side.

A few feet away the second chicken clucked on the ground. That really was a stupid chicken. Steve turned, going for squawky, feathery, tastiness number two.

The confused hen clucked once more, which Melvin thought roughly translated to, "I should consider fleeing from the crocodilian before he consumes me. I would prefer to not be consumed." Then she fluttered away from the scene.

Steve followed, slow and steady. He was too far from the chicken to make a lightning lunge.

Melvin held on as if his life depended on it, because, well, it did. He wasn't sure if Steve realized he had a passenger. As they went, Melvin reached for his whistle. He looked up as he bit down on the mouthpiece. He felt as if he were riding an enemy tank, heading straight for the chicken which had just flown between his uncle and a very confused Mitch Mitchum.

Melvin blew his whistle like a train conductor from hell.

CHAPTER TWENTY EIGHT
Butt-Chins Aren't Romantical

The chicken squawked as it flew between Petro and Mitch. It paused momentarily to loop one of the reporter's legs, then fluttered away toward Petro's truck.

Mitch looked down with a confused expression on his face. He hadn't planned to have a chicken interrupting his interview. He lifted the leg and the hen circled as if he had stepped in one of Choopy's awful lawn monuments.

Petro looked at the reporter, amused, until he heard the whistle, which blared only a few yards away.

Melvin saw it all from atop Steve. The gator was so large, the boy couldn't wrap his arms all the way around the thinnest part of its neck. He put his feet on Steve's front shoulders. Every step the beast took dangerously jostled the kid from side to side.

The scaly-armored death train was nearly upon the two men when Petro sensed danger. He tackled the reporter out of the way, much like Choopy did to Melvin seconds earlier.

Steve continued past the men, or the spot in which they had been. He had a fever for the flavor of fresh fowl.

The hen was several yards away and gaining ground. It ran under Petro's truck, slowing momentarily in the shade to look back. Seeing the beast was still charging, the chicken continued on.

Steve sprinted to shorten the gap between himself and his fast food. The truck in the way didn't seem to bother him at all. He ran straight for it meaning to slide under and out the other side. Unfortunately, he wouldn't quite fit.

Melvin continued to hold on like a tick on a wild stallion. He didn't know what else to do. If he let go, Steve could grab him and swallow him like a featherless chicken. At the very least, the twelve-foot behemoth might run him over and smash his bones to powder.

Petro's truck got closer and closer, until it met the boy's forehead. Melvin continued blowing the whistle hoping that the red wall of metal would jump out of the way. He felt like a bug meeting its end on a windshield. His head smacked the passenger door soundly enough to leave a noggin shaped dent. He bit down on the whistle so hard it cracked.

The stunned kid flipped over backward as the alligator wedged himself under the truck. Melvin was dazed after head-butting the vehicle. A flurry of movement buzzed around him. Dust and gravel flew in all directions as the truck shifted up and to the side. Melvin didn't know where Steve's pointy end was, so he grabbed onto whatever he could. It just happened to be halfway down the animal's tree trunk tail.

Steve's head and shoulders fit under the carriage, but his big belly wedged, stopping all forward progress. When the chicken-frenzied beast realized he was stuck, he flailed like live fish dropped on a hot griddle. The front tires lifted with each of Steve's attempts at freedom. Gravel flew behind as he pushed hard against the ground. He flailed from side to side, swinging his head, protruding from one side of the truck. The back half came out the other side, whipping like a willow in a tornado.

That tail happened to have one confused, bruised, gravel-sprayed, discombobulated, monkey named Melvin attached to it, still blowing a broken whistle. The stars he saw became blurred dots. Melvin thought he hit light-speed. On the third whip of Steve's tail, he lost his grip.

186

The earth and sky traded places three times before he collided with something solid. Melvin would have felt bad if he had landed on Petro, Choopy, or even one of the cameramen. Luckily, it was Captain Butt-Chin who got in the path of bullet-boy. As soon as Mitch got to his feet from Petro's tackle, Melvin hit him like a ninja-star octopus.

The reporter pushed the battered boy off and staggered to his feet. He didn't notice the truck riding an alligator a few feet away. Mitchum dusted himself off, screaming about lawsuits and terrorists. He yelled a few bizarre accusations as Petro pushed past the man to check on Melvin.

The kid sat up still trying to blow the broken whistle. He looked around to see Mitch spouting obscenities while one cameraman filmed. The other guy focused on Steve who wore the truck like a backpack and had dragged it several feet.

Mitch continued his rant, much of which Melvin couldn't understand, his perceptions still clouded. The reporter picked up his microphone and shoved it in Melvin's face to ask him a question.

All Melvin noticed was the dirt in the cleft of Mitchum's face, probably from his two tumbles to the ground.

The boy looked at Mitch and said into the outstretched mic, "You need to wipe the butt on your face. It's kind of gross."

Mitch looked both confused and annoyed at the kid's statement. The cameraman filming them let out a giggle.

Petro pushed the reporter back, giving him a menacing look. "Get away from my nephew and get out of my yard." He sounded like Chuck Norris in any movie ever.

Mitch, like a kicked puppy, got in the van. Steve seemed content with his position under the truck and stopped moving. The cameraman recording the gator-truck wrestling match realized the action was over and followed. The other guy put his camera away and climbed in, but not without a smile and wink at Melvin. The make-up lady continued working on her nails as they drove off.

A truck-shaped bruise formed on Melvin's forehead. It felt like he had transformed into a unicorn. Then he remembered. "Choopy's hurt!"

Petro picked the kid up, though Melvin could walk on his own. He carried him to the front porch (too high for Steve to get to, just in case).

The dog limped over and licked the boy's head. His foot was bleeding, but didn't look like it went into a garbage disposal. Melvin had worried he would lose it after hearing the crunching and popping noises during the fight.

Petro called Cassidy and explained the situation. He told Melvin to go inside while he kept on eye on Steve.

"I'm not going in without Choopy. What if Steve gets loose and Choopy can't get away because he's hurt? He saved me. I have to take care of him." Melvin pleaded his case as if still talking to Chuck Norris.

"Take the dog inside."

"Will you get my phone from the barn? I set it up on the second floor above the chicken coop." Melvin used his pathetic, sick voice that almost always worked on his mother. Most times he could at least get a grilled cheese sandwich out of her using the tone.

Petro didn't say anything, but returned with the phone a few minutes later. The battery was dead. It must have been recording the whole time and ran out of juice. He connected it to his charger.

An hour later Cassidy and Sasha showed up. The back of her truck contained dozens of bags of ice. Sasha was sent inside with Melvin, who felt fine by then. They watched out the window as Melvin told her what happened, and the two adults dealt with the gator.

Petro threw a strap around Steve's snout. The strap was one of the tie-downs he kept in his truck. He pulled it tight so the gator couldn't open his mouth.

Steve didn't seem to care, too tired from struggling under the vehicle.

Cassidy and Petro surrounded the animal with the bags of ice. They let him cool down for thirty minutes before attempting a rescue. While they waited, Cassidy bandaged Choopy's foot. She said it wasn't broken, but was probably sprained and he should keep off of it for a few days.

Petro jacked up the front of the truck. He ran more straps behind Steve's front legs. He hooked a long strap to the trailer hitch on Cassidy's truck and connected the other end to Steve. Then he jacked up his truck even farther, until it was off the exhausted reptile.

By now the alligator was completely out of energy and didn't struggle at all.

With Petro's direction, and slow but steady movement, Cassidy dragged the sleepy giant around to the backyard. It took some time and redneck engineering, but they finally got the big boy into his pond. Petro even got the strap off Steve's snout before he sank in. They cut the log with a chainsaw and wedged a piece of plywood against the fence as a temporary fix.

"What happened?" Sasha asked while Petro and Cassidy were outside working on Steve.

Melvin explained as well as he could. Then they looked at the video on his phone. It captured Melvin with the chickens at the bottom of the screen, trying to lure the gator away. It also caught Choopy saving Melvin.

"What a good dog! Poor Choopy got bit by mean old Steve!" Sasha threw her arms around the dog, who was comfortably lying on the couch. He enjoyed the attention, cushions, and air conditioning.

The video continued to show Melvin latch onto Steve's neck and run into the truck. There wasn't much in the way of sound, except Melvin yelling, "Get off my dog!"

"Wow, you jumped on Steve to save Choopy. I thought you made that up," Sasha said.

Then the spinning stars came back and Melvin felt dizzy all over again. It wasn't from the bump on his head this time, though. It was from the unexpected kiss Sasha planted on his lips!

"You're brave, but if you tell anyone I did that, I'll kill you. Dead."

Melvin discovered being hurled face-first into a truck by a monster, and then being tossed twenty feet into a guy twice his size, was not nearly as dumbfounding and bewildering as being kissed by a real live girl. He wanted to do it again. He should say something to convince her to do it again.

Stupid Alabama by Michael P. Wines

"I told Mitch Mitchum to wipe his butt-chin," was all he could think of to respond. Maybe she would give him another one of those electric smooches. "What do I get for that?"

She slugged him.

CHAPTER TWENTY NINE
Jim laddie Walks the Plank

Cassidy and Sasha left once Steve was secure. Petro's girlfriend ruffled Melvin's hair, saying, "Be more careful next time, Danger Boy. I've never seen Petro so concerned. You gave him a real scare."

Sasha gave him another arm punch, accompanied by a knowing look that made his cheeks flush.

Melvin hadn't thought about how Petro felt about the ordeal. He was so distracted by the events it didn't cross his mind. It must have been scary for him to see his nephew riding an alligator into a truck.

Petro sat down at the kitchen table after the girls left and drank a glass of sweet tea.

"I'm sorry I scared you with Steve," Melvin said. He didn't know what to expect. Maybe Petro would send him back to Brooklyn for the rest of the summer. Maybe he would get grounded or yelled at. Melvin wasn't sure. He knew Petro was massively freaked, though.

Petro didn't say a word until he finished his tea. Every second of waiting for his reaction scared the kid more. The yelling was going to start any second. It had to. Once the glass was empty, Petro stood and faced Melvin. He put both hands on Melvin's shoulders and stared him down.

This was it. Melvin felt his eyes filling with tears. *Stupid tears.* He couldn't cry in front of Uncle Petro. Just as the levees were about to break, Petro pulled him into a hug. They both took a few deep breaths.

Petro talked first. "That was one of the bravest things I've ever seen."

Melvin was confused, and suddenly hopeful. Maybe he wouldn't get yelled or lectured at.

Petro continued. "Mostly, it was the single dumbest idea anyone in the history of the human race has ever lived through."

No such luck.

"If you ever pull anything half as stupid as what you pulled today, I will send you home and you will not be welcome back. Ever. Do you understand?"

Crap. He was back to being stupid and troublesome. "Yes, but …" Melvin wanted to explain about Choopy and the chickens, so it would make sense, resulting in less trouble.

Petro interrupted. "I don't want to hear any 'buts.' I don't care what happened. There is never a good reason for you to ride a twelve-foot alligator. I don't care if Choopy was being eaten, or even if I and every other person was about to be attacked. You should have stayed away and blown your whistle. You. Don't. Ride. A. Twelve. Foot. Alligator!" He said every word slowly and poked Melvin in the chest on every word.

The lecture was affective. "I'm sorry," Melvin said, and meant it.

"We have to tell your mom."

Steve didn't seem like much of a threat all of a sudden. "Why?"

"Well, for one thing, it's about to be all over Channel Five News. She and Briar deserve to know. I'm the idiot they put in charge of looking after you. They may decide they want you back, and for good reason. I'm not sure I'm ready for the responsibility of your safety. I couldn't live with myself if something happened."

Melvin wished he had just yelled or even slapped him around a bit, anything but dropping a guilt bomb.

"We might as well get it over with. See if you can get your parents on the computer. We can Skype them."

Steve's belly was a preferable place to be. "I'll try." He brought his laptop to the kitchen table. Somehow, both of his folks were at home at the same time, with the computer on. The one time he didn't want them to answer, they did.

After the usual few minutes of pleasantries, Petro ruined it by telling them what happened, from the beginning. He started with the Chinese alligators in the van on the way down and finished with the day's events. He told every story and adventure they had together, even the hog attack. Petro made it sound as if he lacked judgment and possibly shouldn't have taken on such a large responsibility.

Melvin didn't add anything, too afraid to open his mouth. The old guilt panther returned to chew his face off, starting with his new unicorn bruise.

After a few more minutes of torturous heart-string tearing, Shea asked Melvin to go to his room so they could talk to Petro alone.

Petro looked sad and defeated. His shoulders slumped and head bowed. The look he gave Melvin seemed apologetic as the boy walked to his room. His uncle was about to face the firing squad because of Melvin and he couldn't do anything about it. If he were cut by any more guilt, he would probably slip on his own guts as he walked away.

Choopy got up from the couch and limped after him. Good thing he didn't slip on Melvin's entrails and hurt another paw.

He closed the door and sulked on his bed. He couldn't watch the conversation like before, and was glad. The last time he spied, guilt beat him about the head and shoulders, too. The dog laid his too-toothy head on his lap. Melvin realized he would do the same thing if it happened all over again. *Stupid dog.*

Petro knocked. "Your turn to talk to the parental units." He didn't sound quite as sad as before. Maybe he was in shock. He probably hadn't gotten the full attack from Shea before. Melvin was used to it, but poor Petro couldn't have prepared himself.

Melvin sat in front of the death panel. *I hate that I have to meet my maker via computer,* he thought. It stinks to have one of my favorite, most trusted things be the deliverer of such wrath.

Then it occurred to him. He reached to the keyboard and hit the buttons ALT and P at the same time.

"Are you ready to face the consequences?" Shea asked, which translated to "Arrr ye ready to walk th' plank?"

Melvin had installed a program a few months ago that translated any spoken language into pirate speak. It typed the words on the bottom of the screen like closed captioning. He leaned over and muted the sound, so all he got was the pirate translation. If he had to get in trouble, maybe his computer could help ease the pain. It was only a one-way translation, so his parents didn't see the words on Melvin's screen.

"Be ye tryin' to gift us 'n ye uncle a heart attack? What were ye thinkin' when ye mounted on th' gator?"

Melvin put himself in a difficult position. He didn't want to hear what his mother said in her voice. He also couldn't laugh at the pirate translations. If he laughed, the jig was up and the conversation would only get worse. He had to keep a straight face to survive.

It was good Petro was in the other room. He wouldn't let him get away with it.

They lectured him for several more minutes on everything from safety to responsibility, or so he thought. There were lots of 'Shiver me timbers,' 'walk th' planks,' and countless 'arrrs' thrown in. They kept calling him 'Jim laddie', which was confusing.

Choopy walked up to Melvin, bandaged leg and all. He put his head in the boy's lap.

"Be t'is th' sea monster ye was nearly murderized over?"

"Yes, ma'am," he said. Now would be a good time to use all the ma'ams and sirs he could fit into the conversation. "This is Choopy. He saved me, then I saved him, or at least tried to."

Melvin knew not to say much. Short facts that put him in the best light were the only things to interject when he had to say something.

"I never thought I would be sayin' t'is to a sea monster, but many thanks to ye, Choopy," said Shea.

The dog looked at the screen, then licked Melvin's face from bottom to top. Melvin's hair stood up from dog spit.

Then odd things happened. Shea started crying and Briar started laughing. His mother slowly switched from crying to laughing. She did that a lot, sometimes in the reverse order, depending on what Melvin did in the first place. It was a sign that he might survive.

Briar talked while Shea pulled herself together. "Ye're stayin' thar 'til th' end o' th' season. We reckon Petro be doin' a fine ship, though he don' think so himself."

"Aye Aye, Captain," Melvin let slip.

"Shiver me timbers, Jim laddie! Do ye have us on scurvy pirate shout again? Arr! If'n so it's th' plank for ye'!"

CHAPTER THIRTY
Stupid TV

Melvin watched Petro work diligently over the next few days. His uncle did nothing but finalize the grant proposal to help the Red Hills salamanders. Petro never left his desk except to eat, sleep for a couple of hours, and stink up the bathroom.

The boy did the same, but on his video game. Melvin took frequent breaks to let Choopy out and change the dog's bandage. The wound looked a lot better and Melvin thought the pathetic pooch might have been milking him for attention. Choopy had become a full-fledged house dog. It didn't hurt that he rarely left Melvin's side.

The game was coming along better than Melvin expected. It was a simple Flash game with segments of video clips. The person playing had to watch the video at the beginning, then guide the character through each level. Until the task or level was completed, the player couldn't move on to play or watch the next clip.

Each part had a score, so points could be won according to how well the player succeeded. Points could be compared with other people's on a scoreboard, so players could play against each other.

For the first level, Melvin used the video clip of the orangutan spanking, kissing, and generally embarrassing Petro. If played right, Petro screamed, "Friend, not baby!" after each action. The louder he screamed, the more points were awarded. He worked hard on this level. He wanted people to keep playing. The video was funny enough to watch over and over, so it never got boring.

The player had to hit buttons on their phone to guide the orangutan into each movement at the right time. It was addictive to play. Other levels included Melvin throwing a towel into the Chinese alligator's mouth to save Joe the zookeeper, Petro catching the snake from the tree while Jimmy shot the boar, Melvin saving the Princess (Sasha) from snake poop (he hoped for another smooch for that one), Melvin putting salamanders down Cassidy and Petro's shirts while they made the kissy kissy, and finally Steve bowling through Mitch and Petro to run Melvin's face into the truck.

It would be good to have outside input. So, after a thorough testing, Melvin emailed the game link to his dad, Sasha, Cassidy, Chucky, Eric, and Twitch. They could download it onto their phones, assuming they didn't have an ancient model, like Petro. He would have emailed it to his mom but decided to let the sleeping worrier lie; besides, the only game she ever played on her phone was Solitaire.

Petro popped his head in Melvin's bedroom door. "My grant proposal is done! How about we go into town for dinner tonight to celebrate?"

"Good timing. I just finished working on my game," Melvin said.

They went to a place called Mama's that made the best nachos Melvin had ever encountered. Halfway through his second order, Chucky called. Melvin answered with a fart sound.

"Yo! Turn on the TV! You're about to be one of America's Most Wanted," Chucky shouted back.

"What?" Melvin was baffled.

"You're on Channel 5 News lookin' like a gangsta' riding a dang crocodile. Your uncle be lookin' like a straight thug, too. They sayin' you two some kind'a environmental terrorists. Dude, yo' moms is gonna flip!"

"When did you see that?" Melvin asked. He hadn't hung out with his best friend all summer and it took a second to translate Chucky-speak.

"It's on now, yo. I gots ta go. My dad saw it and doesn't want me talkin' with you no mo'. He says you're a bad influence. No worries, though. We still gonna kick it. Oh, and that game is off da hook!"

"Thanks. I'm going to try to find Channel 5," Melvin said. There were no less than eight flat screens in any restaurant in town. Melvin asked earlier if there was a city ordinance to have all the TVs. Petro told him it was so nobody would miss a second of the football games.

Chucky blurted, "One more thing, who's that fine honey in your game. You been holdin' out on me?"

"That's Sasha. She kissed me on the lips," Melvin said with a grin. He looked up to see Petro giving him the stink-eye. "I've got to go. Talk to you later."

"My boy's a player! Later, yo." Chucky hung up.

"We're on the news, and it's not pretty," Melvin said.

Petro got up and flipped the channel on one of the smaller screens. Mitch Mitchum popped up like a zit before prom. Apparently there was a lag between the news in New York and Alabama. So, the story was just starting.

"This is Mitch Mitchum, Channel 5 News, lead investigative reporter. I have a chilling story tonight, folks. As you will see in a few moments, I was attacked with such ferocity that I almost lost my life in the line of duty. Some might say I went too far to get to the truth. You be the judge."

The video showed Melvin riding Steve, who was charging one of the cameras. Then it broke for commercial.

Petro exhaled with a sound of exasperation. "What? This is such crap."

The few people in the restaurant turned to see what was annoying him. "Hey, that's those two over there," came a whisper. Then there were more comments. Everyone crowded around to watch.

Mitch continued. "I was doing a follow-up on a story I broke several weeks ago about two terrorists who viciously attacked people in our fine city with crocodiles. Well, I tracked down those hooligans. Mitch Mitchum always gets his story."

He paused to let his butt-chin glisten for the camera before he went on. "This is about the evil man, Petro Fitzpatrick, and his young, possibly brainwashed henchman, Melvin Fitzpatrick, an uncle-nephew team of terror. After a failed attempt to attack our city with reptiles, the two would-be assassins escaped to Alabama. I used my hawk-like reporting skills to follow them and caught this on tape."

The video showed Mitch interviewing Petro. The questions Mitch asked were ridiculous, such as, "Why were you attacking the fine people of New York?" Each question made Petro look as if he were plotting against the world.

It was a good thing Petro didn't answer many questions while the cameras were on. The few things he said were edited out of context. Mitchum villianized him. Then he showed a clip of Petro tackling Mitch. What he didn't show was Petro saved the reporter from being run over and possibly eaten by Steve.

Then he showed a clip of Melvin riding Steve right at them while blowing the whistle. Mitch suggested Melvin had trained Steve to attack with whistle commands. The reporter topped the story by making it look like he fought both Petro and Steve. The fight just happened to be off camera. Then a shot went to Steve trapped under the truck, and finally Petro saying, "Get away from my nephew and get out of my yard."

The story made them look like insane criminals, attacking random people with crocodiles to further Petro's radical views of environmentalism. It made no sense, but Melvin knew people believed what they saw on TV.

"This is such crap," Petro said. He was furious.

"Mister, I think you need to leave," said one of the customers. The small crowd that gathered around them had moved back several steps. They looked as if Melvin and Petro had stepped in a pile of yak poop and were going to run over any second to wipe it on their pants.

"The story was wrong. We never did that stuff," Petro said.

"Pictures don't lie," the man said. Three people stood up behind him to look intimidating. They seemed worried Petro would attack.

"Well, they did this time," Petro spat. "Come on, Melvin. We're leaving."

When they got home a police officer and wildlife control officer waited for them. The news really did travel fast.

"Petro Fitzpatrick? I need to see permits for the alligator in your yard. If you can't produce them, I will be forced to arrest you for harboring wildlife illegally. I will also need to confiscate the animal, pending trial. You may be charged with assault and battery, and endangering a minor." The officers sounded bored, but very serious.

They were ready to take Petro, Melvin, and even Steve into custody. Luckily, Petro kept spotless records on his animals and produced the state and federal permits to keep Steve. He was a licensed wildlife rehabilitator. Then they showed the officers the tape Melvin had recorded of what actually happened.

"Cool. I really didn't want to catch that gator," one said as they were leaving. "We've gotten at least twenty calls about you two being terrorists since you were on the news. The story stirred up the community like a nest of hornets. You need to fix it with the locals somehow."

"How?" Petro asked. He was clearly perplexed.

"Not my job, sir. Have a good day."

CHAPTER THIRTY ONE
Stupid Bur..eauc..rauc..Stupid Politics

Both Petro's and Melvin's phones rang constantly once Mitchum's ridiculous story broke. After taking calls from several reporters, random angry people, and even a creepy guy that wanted to "join the revolution," they decided to stop answering the phone unless it was a number they knew. There were almost as many calls from friends and family, giving support.

Sasha texted, saying he was cute on TV, which made Melvin almost forget the rest. Then he listened to a voice message from a stranger calling him all kinds of names, some of which might even make Eric blush. It scared him. He didn't understand how a person who didn't even know him could hate him, especially an adult. He saved all the messages. He wasn't sure, but thought he might need to let somebody hear them, somebody like the police or a squad of ninjas. Choopy stayed close, sensing his anxiety.

Petro didn't seem scared. He was, however, very, very angry. He talked to Briar on the phone for over an hour, which calmed him enough to stop muttering curses.

Melvin's dad was going to come down in a few days to visit, hopefully to help sort things out. The boy couldn't be happier, unless his mom came along, though he wouldn't admit it out loud. Apparently, a few reporters had stopped by their house in Brooklyn looking for interviews. The vultures were even bothering his mom, thanks to that idiot reporter. *Stupid Mitch Mitchum and his stupid butt-chin.*

The story had been so fantastical many other stations, both national and local (New York and Alabama), picked it up and were investigating for more gory details. Bloggers and newspapers (the old kind made of actual paper) were also snooping around.

Petro and Melvin were famous, but not in the cool rock-star, superhero way the boy had always daydreamed about. Melvin was the villain this time, and he couldn't even grow a huge mustache to twist while he laughed an evil laugh. So not fair!

That night Melvin had a nightmare about sitting in front of a judge in a courtroom. People threw rotten vegetables at him. He was convicted of being a communist environmental terrorist with an inability to grow facial hair.

His punishment was to be locked in a glass box in Times Square, naked, with only a toilet to sit on. His box replaced the Big Apple and slowly dropped as everyone in the world watched. He had to grow a tail while Mitch Mitchum and Ryan Seacrest gave live plop-by-plop commentary. This happened every hour, once for each time zone, every year for the rest of his life. He didn't know how he could possibly poop twenty-four times in a day; he just did. It was a long dream.

In the morning he went to Petro's lab to clean, and hopefully forget the awful nightmare. After an hour Petro was called to the administration building to meet with a provost, whatever that was. Melvin went with him. He was still scared to be left alone, especially without Choopy.

Melvin sat in the lobby of an old building that smelled like books. He watched Petro walk through a door and saw about ten people in suits sitting at a long table. They all frowned at his uncle as he entered.

Eric sat at one of the reception desks, clicking away at a keyboard. "Melvin, dude! That game you made is cooler than a poo-poo platter full of egg foo young! I played it until my phone died last night. Twitch laughed so hard she farted. The whole house smelled like chow mein. You should charge for downloads."

Melvin smiled for the first time since Sasha told him he was cute. Eric gave his game a huge compliment. He and Twitch were no mere newbs, either, which made it that much more credible. "Thanks! I worked hard on it. I'm not sure what to do with it. I haven't thought that far ahead. I was so concerned with building it that I didn't think about what I would do once it was done."

"There's a site you can upload it to. You'll need a PayPal account. You can charge anywhere from 99 cents on up every time somebody downloads it. It gets added to their phone bill, just like any other app. You would get to keep seventy-five percent of the money. The rest goes to the website. If it starts making money, they'll advertise it for free. Seriously, you will make major green once this game gets known," he said through a mouthful of meatball sub.

Eric was as big of a tech geek as Melvin, only more on the software and programming side. "Cool, I'll look into it. I don't have a PayPal account. I think my dad does, though. What are you doing here?"

"I'm working on the Auburn website. It's my part-time job. I've got a hard-line to the server from this computer, though, I could easily hack it from home. I'll forward you the link to the phone-app site. There are a few, but this one is best for not egg-rolling you over. What are you doing here?"

"Uncle Petro had a meeting in there." Melvin pointed to the big wooden doors his uncle walked through.

"Oh man, not good. We call that room the woodshed because people go there to be axed. Did Petro do something to get in trouble?"

"Did you not see us on the news? Mitch stupid-butt-chin-Mitchum made up a story about us. He made us look like terrorists or something."

Eric looked up from his sandwich and monitor. "Whoa, no, dude. That sounds like some deep triple-delight. Twitch would be devastated to lose her leader. I'll call a meeting of the minions to see what we can do."

"Aren't there just three of us?"

"Never underestimate the power of loyal minions, little dude. With our computer skills and Twitch's leadership, we can accomplish some serious Kung Pao with broccoli."

"Are you running out of Chinese food words?" Melvin asked.

"Yah, I'm going to maybe start bringing in some Korean or Indian. It's hard to express one's self with such a limited menu."

Melvin let Eric return to eating and working, though he noticed the guy's fingers never stopped typing even when he talked. *Impressive.*

Petro emerged from the door looking like the law of gravity had beaten him up and taken his lunch money. His shoulders slumped, his face frowned, he had sad eyes, and the rest of his body and demeanor drooped. He looked totally and utterly defeated.

"Come on, Melvin. Let's go home," he mumbled.

"What happened?" Melvin asked.

"I got suspended from my job. They wanted to fire me, but agreed to an investigation first. Most of them know me and believe I'm not what Mitch Mitchum portrayed. Some people think I'm too much of a liability and might cause the university's alumni to stop giving money. It's an election year and people will get away from anything that might associate negatively with their reputation. Stupid bureaucracy," he finished.

"What's a byorokrasey?"

"Politics. The worst part is they turned down my grant proposal. They didn't even read it. They saw my name on it and automatically denied it. Nobody wants to be seen giving funds to a suspected terrorist. The Red Hills salamanders are going to get turned into a passing lane and there's nothing I can do about it."

Melvin and his broken-hearted uncle went back to the house. On the way, the boy started to form a plan almost as big as Mitch's chin, but hopefully less like a butt.

CHAPTER THIRTY TWO
Stupid Lynch Mobs

A crowd had formed at the end of Petro's driveway. There were several news vans, a gaggle of angry people holding signs, and, thankfully, a couple of police officers attempting to tame the mob. The only things missing were torches and pitchforks. It was stupid Alabama. Maybe they were still trying to figure out how matches worked. Melvin hadn't seen so many people in one place since he left New York.

As they pulled up, the posse surged forward, pointing at Petro's truck. Some pushed microphones at the windows, snapping pictures and yelling questions. Others, the scarier ones without cameras and microphones, screamed and spat. Some of the signs said: COMMIES GO HOME, FITZPATRICK = TERRORIST, and MITCH SAFED MERICA FRUM THE DEBIL. There was a Photoshopped picture of Mitchum fighting an alligator. Melvin thought Petro might actually run that last guy over.

"Get in the back, Melvin. Those cops are fishing buddies of mine. They won't let anything happen; but just in case, I want you as far out of harm's way as possible."

The two officers tried to direct people out of the way so the truck could get by. The crowd was stirred up and didn't want to listen. Melvin squirted into the back as they began rocking the truck back and forth. He was scared someone was going to break a window and grab him, or worse. Petro honked his horn and put the truck into a lower gear. He meant to run these people over to protect his nephew. Things were out of control. That's when good old Jimmy Six-shooter stepped out of the crowd.

This time he wore more than just a man-kini. He had on a pearl-button shirt, blue jeans, his standard cowboy hat, boots, and was strapped with his trusty six-iron. He nodded to the policemen as he pinned a gold star to his chest that read 'Volunteer Deputy.'

The revolver pointed to the sky behind the crowd. A herd of people blocked the vehicle. Jimmy fixed that with a single shot, straight up.

The crowd immediately parted, and scattered, like roaches when the lights are turned on.

Jimmy waited until the horde turned to him. He holstered his gun and spat tobacco juice on the pavement. "The next one of you yellow-bellied, inbred, unschooled piles of vomit that takes a step toward these upstanding gentlemen is gonna be swallerin' hot lead." The man tipped his hat to Petro and Melvin.

"Jimmy's a volunteer fire-fighter, too. I guess now he's a volunteer sheriff's deputy," Petro explained.

The officers flanked the truck. One walked on either side in case someone wanted to test Jimmy's resolve. Nobody did. Petro drove slowly past the stunned masses and crunched down his road.

The policemen pulled their cruisers up to the driveway to stand guard.

Melvin exhaled in relief.

Petro held the steering wheel so tightly his fingers turned white. "Go straight in the house. Get Choopy and don't let him leave your side," he growled. Then he farted.

Melvin remembered he changed his uncle's ringtone again so it would rip one whenever a call came. It would have been funny with better timing.

Instead of laughing, Petro exhaled some frustration and answered after looking at the incoming number. "Hey, Cassidy," he said as he walked to the barn. He didn't growl at her.

Melvin hustled inside. Choopy greeted him with a face lick and an few inappropriate crotch sniff.

"Master, you have an incoming Skype," flashed across Igor's screen when Melvin logged onto his laptop. It was from his dad.

"Hey, Pops."

Both of his parents crowded in front of their home computer's webcam. They hadn't mastered Skyping, though Melvin had explained it at least a million freaking times.

His dad sat uncomfortably. The top half of his head was cut off from view. He was always nervous in front of a camera and seemed to think too much about what he was supposed to do with his hands. He kept moving them from his hips to crossing his arms to scratching his head. "Hi, Son."

Shea leaned in to the camera every time she wanted to say something and talked slowly and in a loud voice. "Hi, Baby! How are you doing? Are you getting enough to eat?" she said as though giving directions to a deaf person who didn't understand English.

All Melvin could see when she talked was her top lip and a close-up of the spinach stuck in her teeth. "I'm eating fine, Mom. You don't have to talk so loud or get so close."

"Oh, okay, honey." She leaned back, revealing his dad, who decided one hand under his chin with the other on his hip was the natural way to sit. It wasn't.

Melvin snorted and Briar self-consciously traded hand positions. "When are you coming down here?"

"Tomorrow or the next day," he said. "It depends on a few things with work. There's somebody here I want you to talk to. He says you'll recognize him." He swiveled the camera one way, then back the other.

The panorama stopped on a face Melvin recognized. It was one of Mitch Mitchum's cameramen, the one that winked at him as they drove off.

"Hi, Melvin. I'm Phil Bradshaw. You might recognize me from the other day. I was the cameraman for Channel 5. I'm sorry about what Mitch did to you and your uncle. He hired me a few weeks ago and I didn't really know what I was getting into."

Melvin was worried Mitchum had his parents at gunpoint. He was skeptical and showed it via the stink-eye, but listened to the man.

Bradshaw continued. "I've since quit working for Channel 5. Katie Abraham from Channel 3 hired me after I told her what actually happened the other day. She's working on an exposé to show the world how Mitchum reports. Sadly, Mitch owns the footage for the story he ran. So, we can't use it. I don't have an unedited copy of it even if I wanted to. Mitchum keeps it on his personal computer. We'd like to interview you and your uncle. If you give us an exclusive, we'll do what we can to set things right."

Melvin might have believed him, but still had adrenaline coursing through his body after an angry mob tried to lynch him. It would take more than a wink and a promise to gain his trust. *Who was this guy to be in his house with his parents asking for an interview?* Melvin wasn't exactly sure what chutzpah was, but knew this guy had it.

"Why should I believe you? How do I know you're not still working for the investigative butt-chin?" Melvin felt his anger and frustration building.

Bradshaw responded after chuckling at Melvin's comment. "I talked to your folks. We won't run any story until you and your family see it and approve it first. We will put it in writing. Listen, kid, I don't blame you for being suspicious. What Mitch did was unforgivable. Katie and Channel 3 seem to want to do the right thing. I know I do. So, talk it over with your parents."

Briar moved the camera back over so it was mostly pointing at the ceiling, but got the top of Shea's head.

She leaned in close. Melvin could see straight up her nose. "One of the Franks, the one from the second floor, was a lawyer before he retired. He'll write a contract to make Channel 3 do what they say," she said loud enough to be heard over a train whistle attached to a jet engine during a fire-drill.

Instead of moving the webcam back to the correct position, his dad moved in front of it, from the side. His mom shifted back. So the view Melvin had was of Shea's eye and part of her nose, and Briar's horizontal head. If awkwardness was water, his parents would flood the entire Eastern Seaboard.

CHAPTER THIRTY TWO

"Is Petro there?" Briar asked.

"Let me check." Melvin looked out the window to see his uncle pounding NO TRESPASSING signs into the ground with a Louisville Slugger. He seemed to be enjoying swinging the bat too much for Melvin to interrupt him. "He's busy at the moment."

"Ask him to call me when he gets a chance, please."

Melvin talked with his parents for a few more minutes. He ran some ideas past them about the plan he'd been forming. There was a lot to do in the next couple of days, and it started with a meeting of the minions.

CHAPTER THIRTY THREE
With Minions Like These ...

Since Melvin couldn't really go anywhere, he texted the minions and asked them to come over. While he waited, he turned on the local news. It was surreal to see people being interviewed in front of his uncle's house. Complete strangers were telling reporters how the Fitzpatricks were evil. They had never met and hopefully never would.

Behind one of the reporters, a Cadillac pulled up. Mrs. Weaver was so short that she had to climb down from her seat with a basket. She handed it to Jimmy and patted him on the back.

The reporter caught her, shoving the microphone in her face before she got back into the car. "Ma'am, how do you feel about living so close to terrorists?"

Mrs. Weaver's scowl could have scared away a stampede of bears with machine guns. "You should be ashamed of yourself! I've known Petro Fitzpatrick since he was smaller than a mouse fart. He's no terrorist. That boy's done nothing his whole life but try to help little animals. What's the thanks he gets? He gets idiots like you spreading lies for no reason."

Her voice grew and people in the crowd began watching her, realizing she didn't agree with them. They seemed confounded at the anger from the tiny woman, who had always put a smile on their faces in the past.

"I know a few of the people in this crowd. Well, guess what," Mrs. Weaver continued, shaking her knobby finger at them. "You're all off my Christmas list. No sweets for you this year or any other! For shame!" She got back in her car and drove past Jimmy and the deputies, who had their mouths full of buttery biscuits, to Petro's front door.

"Let her pass," Jimmy said, through a crumb-covered beard hole.

Several people in the crowd slumped their shoulders and frowned, realizing they had already had their last taste of Mrs. Weaver's baked treasures. The crowd didn't disperse, but seemed to lose some of its bloodthirsty excitement.

Petro opened the door, letting Mrs. Weaver in. He hugged her and gobbled one of her steaming muffins before she made it past the entry way.

"Henry said he'd be here as soon as he found his old scatter-gun," she said. She winked at Melvin and handed him a basket that smelled like cinnamon, butter, and heaven. "Don't worry. I hid that gun in the attic years ago. That blind fool doesn't even know we have an attic."

Melvin smiled through a mouthful of monkey bread. He didn't know food could taste so good.

Choopy's tail had been wagging since he heard her voice on the talking box. He was not a dumb dog-horse-thing.

"Don't worry, doggy. I brought something for you, too." She pulled a bone from a bag. Most of the meat had already fallen off, but there were still a few dangling bits.

Choopy's wagging tail left dents in the side of the couch and gave Petro a Charliehorse on his thigh as he trotted by with his prize.

"Melvin, go out to my car and get the box out of the back seat. It's a bit too heavy for my old bones, and be careful with it."

"Esshh am," he said through a mouthful. Roughly translated to "Yes, Ma'am" with a nod. Petro got his own basket of goodies, which was a good thing. Melvin wasn't going to share.

He ran to the car and brought back a cardboard box weighing about as much as his backpack full of books.

From it, Mrs. Weaver pulled the Booger jug Mr. Weaver had finished for Melvin. It had a blue-green glaze and looked beautifully horrendous. The facial features were highlighted by the troll-like color. He had no idea art could be ugly and cool at the same time.

Melvin was so excited, he blurted out, "Iss is ate!"

"Now, chew your food, boy. Nobody wants a sprayin'," she laughed.

He gulped the mouthful down, too excited to not talk. "This is great! I'm going to put it on top of the fridge. Thank you, and thank Mr. Weaver for me."

"Oh, I'll tell him you like it. I'm sorry about that dumb old reporter making up stories about you boys. We know he's fibbing. You just watch. He'll get what's what. Liars never last. I've got to get going. Keep your chins up."

"Anks," Petro squawked.

Melvin was happy to stuff his mouth full again, now that he only had to hug goodbye. Mrs. Weaver was probably used to people chewing in her ear.

Petro, Choopy, and Melvin sat in different corners of the same room. They ate their treats and glared at each other with looks that said, "Mine!"

Another couple of familiar faces appeared on the television. Twitch and Eric pulled up. They were swarmed with questions as they explained to Jimmy that they were friends and only coming to visit, not picket. There wasn't much explaining to do, since their bright orange t-shirts read PETRO'S QUEEN MINION and PETRO'S LESSER MINION, respectively.

Twitch stood with eyes the size of basketballs and a smile that could make a jack-o-lantern jealous. Eric towered over her, not seeming quite as excited. Then again, no one, not even a puppy with a sugar rush in a room full of tennis balls could get as excited as Twitch.

"So you two support the terrorists?" A reporter asked. The cameraman had to back up to get both Twitch and Eric in the shot. He was at least three feet taller than the red-headed spaz.

"Petro's not a terrorist! He's my boss. He's the best boss. He's our Supreme Leader, and I am his Queen Minion. He's so good, he doesn't even pay me! Wait, that didn't make sense. I like your tie. My grandfather had a tie exactly like it. He's dead. I hope that tie isn't the same one, because I don't like you. You're spreading lies about my best boss and you don't deserve my grandpa's tie. Good day." All the words shot out of her mouth fast enough to give a cheetah whiplash.

The reporter stood there, looking at his tie, as if it had just sneezed.

Eric leaned down to the microphone after Twitch was finished. "Yeah, if you think Petro and Little Dude are terrorists, you should just go eat a pork dumpling, with extra plum sauce. Peace!"

"So much for not looking crazy," Petro pouted. A few seconds later the dynamic duo knocked on the door.

The Fitzpatrick boys hid what was left of their home-made goodness from prying eyes and grabby fingers. Choopy stayed right where he was.

"I brought your uniform. You left it at the lab again," Twitch said, pushing the dirty orange, oversized T into Melvin's chest. "Oh, look! Da puppy gets to stay inside, now," she said, approaching Choopy.

"Grrr," Choopy said back.

"The dog's got a bone. Watch out. He'll snap you like a chopstick," Eric said, grabbing the back of her shirt before she became bone number two.

He pivoted behind her and released her shirt. She kept walking but towards Petro instead of Choopy. She raised her arms to hug her boss. "Our fearless leader isn't a terrorist! He's our ... He's our fearless leader."

Melvin couldn't let the chance get past. "Don't you mean Supreme Leader?"

Petro reintroduced her to his straight-arm, while ignoring his nephew's comment. "What have I told you about personal space?" he asked.

Her forehead thudded against his open palm.

"You like it," she pouted. "We're here to help, oh boss-like one. What can we do?"

"You've done plenty, thanks," Petro said.

"Dude, what the chow mein? We came all the way out here to help. If she doesn't get to help, it's going to be a long night for me. Let her help," Eric said.

"Okay, the chickens need cleaning," Petro said after a few seconds of thought.

"Yay! Chicken cleaning of justice!" Twitch said, and clapped her hands.

Eric smiled. "Cool. Let's get to it before we have to mow the lawn for justice."

"I'm going with them. I want feedback about my game," Melvin said.

"Take Choopy with you and don't go anywhere near the road."

Choopy looked up from his bone as if to say, I'm busy.

Melvin said, "Come on, Choopy."

The dog looked to his bone, then to Melvin. Finally, making up his mind, peed in a large circle on the floor in the corner of the living room. Then he placed his bone in the middle of it. Happy with the safety of his treat, he trotted after Melvin.

"You're cleaning that up! He's your bodyguard!" Petro yelled.

Melvin told the minions his plan. They each had input, but Twitch came up with the best idea. They had two days to complete the tasks. The Minion Mission, as it was to be known, had started.

CHAPTER THIRTY FOUR
Morse Code, Tractor Beams, and Sweet Justice

Melvin stayed locked in the house with Petro and Choopy for the next couple of days. He was glad his uncle lived far back from the road so he couldn't see the circus of reporters and protesting idiots who set up camp there. He worked diligently fixing bugs in the game and updating his old robot website, www.melvinsworld.com.

Eric had been in constant contact over the web. The lumbering minion proved to be amazing on the computer, teaching Melvin several new things. Eric sent links to sites he made for data and programs probably illegal in most states. The guy could find his way in and out of secured systems easier than walking through doors.

Melvin made a mental note to never make Eric angry. The guy had mad skills and with Twitch keeping him focused could be a serious threat to an enemy.

Petro moped around the house in a bathrobe and fuzzy bunny slippers. His beard grew in and he farted almost as much as he pouted. Being suspended from his job, turned down for the Red Hills salamander grant, and having everyone in the world but close friends and family believing he was a terrorist sent him into a stinky depression.

Choopy had been unbelievably gassy as well. Melvin was convinced his dog and uncle were communicating via Morse Code.

Each dash and dot consisted of butt-bursts that signaled duck and cover to Melvin's nose. He needed all this to be over, if only to end crop-dusting season in the house.

"What is that awful smell?" Briar asked as he walked in the front door with a package under his arm. He'd driven the old family wagon all the way from New York. He wasn't expected for a few more hours.

"Dad!" Melvin jumped from his chair, greeting his Pops with a hug.

"Good to see you, son. This must be the famous Choopy. Aaahhhhh!" Briar yelled as the horse-dog almost lifted him off the ground with a crotch sniff.

"Hey, brother," Petro said. It was the first time he'd smiled in days.

"You look like you've spent the last two weeks in a Sasquatch's butt. Clean yourself up. Katie Abraham will be here in a few minutes with her crew to interview both of you. Melvin, get some clean clothes on and paste down that cowlick. I'm going to open the doors and let a draft through. This place smells worse than Petro looks."

Melvin and Petro did as they were told. Good thing, too, because Cassidy pulled up with Sasha a few minutes later. It would have been plenty embarrassing for the girls to see them after marinating in farts for days.

"Remember when you dumped water on Shea and me on our first date? Paybacks are hell," Briar whispered to Petro as Cassidy walked up.

Petro looked as if he were on a flight to Mars and he just remembered he left the stove on and the bathwater running at home.

Briar and Melvin shared a grin.

"Hi, I'm Cassidy, and this is my friend Sasha," she said, reaching for Briar's hand.

"It's so nice to meet you. Gas Man and Koo Koo Butt have told me so much about you both," Briar said.

The girls giggled as the boys reddened. Melvin didn't know he was going under the bus with his uncle. *Not cool.*

Briar continued. "I'm Briar, Melvin's dad and Petro's brother. These two have not shut up about you ladies since I arrived. They've been clucking like hens. You would think they were sorority girls meeting to gossip in a bathroom during a homecoming dance. It's great Petro has finally met someone accepting of his little problem."

"And what problem would that be?" Cassidy asked.

Choopy sat behind the men, waiting to greet the new visitors. It was a small room, and he didn't have the space to get between. So he waited.

"Well, since my little brother was a kid, he's had a problem with flatulence whenever he was nervous. We hoped he would grow out of it, but it only got worse. So whenever he talks to a girl he likes, especially the first few times, he just about rips the seat from his pants. That's how he got the name Gas Man."

Petro stood with his mouth open looking like a dead fish trying to figure out calculus.

Choopy had perfect timing, letting go a three-second squeaker right behind Petro.

"See, there he goes now," Briar said, smiling.

Petro finally found a few words. "That was Choopy, not me!"

"Take some responsibility for yourself, Man. He always tried to blame it on the dog when we were kids, too," Briar finished.

Sasha cackled, "Gas Man and Koo Koo Butt!"

Cassidy had a single tear rolling down her cheek as she burst with laughter along with the girl.

Melvin thought she cried from laughter, but it could have been brought on by Choopy's particularly sour announcement.

"If you get any redder I'm going to have to take you to the burn unit. Your brother is hysterical," Cassidy said, leaning up to kiss Petro's smoldering face.

Briar smiled, seemingly pleased with himself. "I'm good-looking, too."

Petro tried to defend himself. "He's paying me back for dumping a bucket of water on him and Shea on their first date."

Cassidy laughed. "Your son did a pretty good job of getting us on one of our first dates. He put salamanders down our shirts."

Briar high-fived Melvin. "Wow, you still want to hang out with this guy after that and the gas? You two must be in loooove."

Petro and Cassidy both blushed, looking at the floor, the ceiling, and anywhere but at each other.

Sasha and Melvin followed their cues. "Ooooh, in loooove!"

The two broke into fits of giggles.

Then Petro really did fart, or at least his phone did. He had asked Melvin to change his ringtone back, but he conveniently never got around to it.

"Hello," Petro said in a huff. "Thanks, Jimmy. Let Ms. Abraham and her crew through. We're expecting them."

A couple minutes later, Katie Abraham was in Petro's front yard with Phil Bradshaw, Mitch Mitchum's former cameraman.

They all went outside to meet her. It was hot and muggy, but not any more unbearable than hell on a Tuesday.

Katie got out of her car as if in slow motion. On TV she was pretty. In real life, she was a supermodel wrapped in bacon, dipped in caramel, and sprinkled with chocolate chips. She had long, curled blond hair, eyes bigger than basketballs, and other equally impressive parts.

Katie walked up to Petro, holding out her hand. "Hi, I'm Katie."

"Ahhhh," Petro said.

"Ohhhh," Briar said.

"Huhhh," Melvin said.

Cassidy elbowed Petro in the ribs. "Sorry, I think they're a little star-struck."

Petro looked at Cassidy and shook the cobwebs and legs from his mind. He held out his hand. "Nice to meet you, Ms. Abraham. I'm Petro Fitzpatrick." He introduced her to the rest of the gang without any extra awkwardness.

Katie said, "Thanks for allowing me to interview you and your nephew. I know you're nervous about reporters after what Mitchum put you through. I don't blame you. I promise to let you see the story and give you the ultimate yea or nay as to whether it gets aired."

Briar already had papers for her to look over and sign, just in case. To the Fitzpatricks, trust and reporters went together like llama turds and cottage cheese.

Phil Bradshaw walked by with several bags of equipment and a tripod. "That's the kid who told Mitchum to wipe his butt-chin," he said with a laugh.

Katie smiled and leaned down to Melvin. "I'd like to interview you first, if you don't mind. We can set up right over there. Your dad and uncle will be here with you if you're scared."

Melvin tried with all his might to stare only at her face. He had no idea what she just said. "Uh, okay." She had two tractor beams locked onto his eyes. He was fighting a losing battle when she finally straightened up.

"You're catching flies, boy," Briar said. He turned Melvin to a couple of rocking chairs Petro brought from the porch. Melvin sat in one and Katie the other.

The rest of the group stood off-camera as Phil finished setting up to shoot. Melvin focused and cleared his head. This was his big chance to complete the mission and clear their names.

Katie began the interview. "So, Melvin, are you a terrorist like Mitch Mitchum would have the world believe?"

"No, not at all," Melvin said.

"What were you and your uncle doing with those crocodiles in New York?"

Melvin went into great detail explaining what they were doing and why. Katie's questions weren't leading or sneaky like Mitch's. They were to the point, allowing Melvin to tell his version of the story. He added he had his own video of the altercation between Mitchum, Steve, and Petro.

"Thank you for that, Melvin. Is there anything else you want to add?"

"Yes, actually," Melvin said, looking to his uncle.

Petro looked surprised but didn't interrupt.

"My uncle has been trying to save a salamander that only lives here in Alabama. He couldn't get a grant to fund his research, so I decided to try to earn money for him. I made a video game you can download onto your phone. It's only a dollar to download. A couple of friends helped. The website is www.melvinsworld.com. You can find it there, along with some other interesting links. My friends tell me the game is pretty cool. It's the first one I've made."

"That sounds very sweet of you, Melvin." Katie smiled.

"One more thing," Melvin said, leaning over and grabbing the microphone.

"Uh, sure," Katie said.

"All the money will go to the Scotty Zimmerman Memorial Fund set up to help my uncle save the Red Hills salamander."

Briar awkwardly walked into view as if he were a robot needing an oil change. "Here you are, son of mine," He said, handing Melvin the package he brought with him. He turned to the camera said, "Hi, Shea!" and waved with both hands. Then he shuffled away.

Melvin pulled a frame from the bag his dad handed him. It was a picture of Petro and Scotty as kids, with fantastic mullets. Scotty held a Red Hills salamander and both boys were smiling. They must have been about Melvin's age when the picture was taken. A plaque at the bottom read IN MEMORY OF SCOTTY ZIMMERMAN.

Phil got a great close-up shot of the plaque, then panned over to Petro, who wasn't expecting any of Melvin's plan. He had tears in his eyes, then he farted. He forgot to turn his ringer off. The tension was broken and everyone laughed as Petro handed out hugs.

The camera turned back to Melvin and Katie. "Well, you don't sound like a terrorist to me," Katie said.

"Thanks, I guess," Melvin said.

Petro walked over and picked up Melvin. He hugged him so tightly that his back popped. "Thanks, Kid."

Katie continued the interview with Petro. As she did, Melvin ran inside to email the info on his website, the game, and the footage of what really happened to Katie's personal email address she gave him earlier.

The plan was coming together.

CHAPTER THIRTY FIVE
Stupid Kid and his Stupid Game

Briar turned into the gopher for all of Melvin and Petro's needs outside the house. His face hadn't been plastered to every television in the country with the word TERRORIST stamped across his forehead. So he could run into town with relative ease and little harassment. He had some difficulty getting in and out of the driveway through the idiot horde, but had no major confrontations. That's what he told Melvin, anyhow.

Apparently, the reporters were gone, and only the whackos remained. The police took shifts, not allowing the psychos to get within fifty feet of the property line. It was a good thing Petro was well liked by most of the local officers.

Briar had been in a particularly upbeat mood during his visit. Most of the hours Melvin's dad spent in the house was playing on his phone and giggling to himself. When he wasn't doing that or running errands, Briar made a game of taunting the protestors. He waited until the middle of the afternoon to bring the cops big glasses of sweet tea, ice cream cones, and fresh-cut watermelon.

The afternoon sun in early August was tough to take, especially if one was holding misspelled signs on a seldom-traveled country road. The painful realization to the protesters that they were only picketing to pine trees and armadillos might have been another reason they began disappearing. On the last day only five or six smelly jerks were out there. They had lost their voices from yelling about the end of days being brought on by environmental terrorists. Briar's pampering of the lawmen, and taunting of the straggler protesters is probably what sent them on their way, finally.

The media frenzy slowly sputtered to a halt. Mitch Mitchum switched to another story about a woman in California selling dog meat from her so-called shelter. Melvin guessed what actually happened was a hot dog stand opened on the street near her building. He had lost faith in what he saw on television, especially from reporters like Mr. Butt-Chin.

"Good news," Petro said. "The university called. I'm off suspension. There were enough people on my side to slide the vote my way."

"That's great," Melvin said. "Why the change? Sweet, sweet Katie Abraham's story hasn't even aired yet."

The three Fitzpatrick males sat for a moment in distracted silence, daydreaming about the reporter.

Briar finally snapped out of it. "Any word on your grant?"

"Still no money. I doubt they're even going to consider it again. The university coming around is one thing. It's full of actual smart people. The grant was through the state government. They tend to be more political. There are a few good people, but apathy is rampant."

"Stupid Alabama," Melvin said. "Maybe we'll make some money off the game. If Katie," pause, sigh, "puts it in her report, maybe people all over will want to play it."

"I really appreciate what you did, Melvin," Petro said. "I know you worked hard on your game all summer. I'm sure it'll make a few hundred dollars, but I doubt it will go any further,"

Melvin's excitement dwindled. He felt like someone peed on his birthday cake. All the planning and organizing after the game was finished was almost as much work as building the game itself. Every second he worked on website coding, account building, and all the tedious tax-exempt status crap he had to do to set up a charity was for nothing. His uncle had dismissed it with a few words. Melvin remembered he was just a kid. A stupid kid.

"Wait a second, bro," Briar said. "Have you played the game? I've been playing it since Melvin sent it to me. I can't stop. It's too much fun."

"No, I haven't seen it. My phone isn't new enough to download stuff."

Melvin felt a little better, but decided his dad was simply giving both of them a pep talk.

Briar shook his head. "I've played the whole thing through a few dozen times. The Friend not Baby level is unbelievable. I've never laughed so hard in my life. The Salamanders down the Shirts part is genius. Once word gets out, I think this game will really take off."

"The what levels?" Petro asked.

Melvin forgot to mention to his uncle about the premise of the game. It was all video clips from his adventures in stupid Alabama.

Briar handed his phone to Petro. "Here, play."

Petro's brow furrowed. He looked suspicious of the gadget, as if it was going to bite him or teach him French. He pushed start.

Melvin heard the sound from the game and his uncle yelling "Friend, not baby" from the speaker.

It must have been odd for Petro to see himself on the screen. For the first couple of minutes, he didn't look happy. Eventually, a louder scream came from the phone. The corners of Petro's mouth lifted in a small smile, then he snotted uncontrollably from an unexpected laugh. Slime shot from his nose and landed on Briar's sleeve, who had been watching closely.

"Gross!" Briar protested.

Petro rubbed his nose on his own shirt sleeve, while continuing to play with both hands. "This is the funniest thing I've ever seen, you little punk," he said, presumably to Melvin, since his eyes never left the screen. "How did you do this? I was expecting Pac Man, or at best Space Invaders, not me getting spanked by an orangutan."

Petro completed the level and handed the phone back to Briar. He was clearly in a better mood. "I'm sick of sitting in the house. Let's get out and celebrate."

Melvin was glad his uncle didn't want to kill him from using such embarrassing footage in the game. "Yeah, let's go to Mama's and get some nachos!"

"Nachos it is," said Briar.

Pulling out of the driveway and not seeing anyone protesting was a relief to Melvin. He wasn't scared with both his dad and uncle, even if the policemen weren't standing guard anymore. He felt normal as they walked into the place where the original story broke a week prior.

The three Fitzpatricks walked to the cashier. "Three orders of nachos and three Cokes, please," Petro said.

In the late afternoon a large group of boisterous college students occupied the corner tables. Over pitchers of beer they yelled excitedly to each other while they watched one of the big screens. Melvin thought they must be watching a game, though he couldn't see the television from his angle.

"What flavor of Cokes, dudes?" the kid behind the counter asked.

"Coke coke, please," Petro said.

Melvin couldn't figure out why all the soda pops in the state were referred to as Coke. The South confused him more all the time.

The guy handed out the drinks, pausing when he looked closer at Petro. "Dude, don't I know you?"

"I don't think so," Petro said.

"I recognize you from somewhere. Do you teach Lit 101?"

"No, I work for Auburn, though. Maybe you've just seen me around campus," Petro said as they turned around to walk to a table.

"Dude! I know who you are!" the guy said as if he'd found a twenty-dollar bill.

Melvin got nervous, thinking about how people might react if they believed what Mitchum had reported. They were in public and the rowdy group in the corner might cause some serious problems. Petro and Briar stiffened as well. Each stepped in front of Melvin, for his protection, Melvin thought. It could get dangerous, very quickly.

The kid making nachos said, "I'd recognize your butt anywhere!"

CHAPTER THIRTY FIVE

"Excuse me?" Petro said.

"Hey, everybody! Do you know who this is?" the guy yelled to the group in the back.

The gaggle of students quieted, turned, and studied Petro. Trouble had arrived and had been drinking beer. There were way too many people to fight off if it came down to it. Two and a half Fitzpatricks to fifteen drunken frat boys were not good odds. There were no police for protection. It was just the three of them against a crowd with intoxicated judgment.

Petro pulled a chair out, maybe to use as a weapon. Briar did the same, both facing the crowd.

"I know that guy," one of the more muscled frat boys said, standing up.

It was a showdown like in old western movies, but this time the posse of bad guys had the white-hats cornered.

"You're the guy from TV," someone said from the back of the crowd. "Will you sign my shirt?"

Melvin was utterly confused. Petro and Briar were ready for a fight, and the biggest guy kept walking closer.

"You're the 'Friend, not Baby' guy from the game!" he said.

Petro and Briar exhaled. Melvin smiled. They had not expected to be recognized from the video game.

A smaller guy walked over, pointing at his own chest. It had a picture of Petro's head and the caption said MY MONKEY SPANKS ME. "You're from Melvin's World. I can't get enough of it. I hope you don't mind we made some shirts. Would you mind signing mine?"

"Uh, sure. I guess," Petro said. He still seemed confused. "How did you know about the game?"

"It's on the university website's front page. We've been having competitions for the past couple of days between the Delta Chis and the Beta Theta Pis. Look." He pointed to the big screen in the back. Someone had connected their phones to a laptop and uploaded the images onto the TV.

"Cool! Don't know how, but Eric got it on the website," Melvin said, as he stepped in front of his uncle, all fear replaced with pride.

Stupid Alabama by Michael P. Wines

"This is my nephew, Melvin. He made that game," Petro said.

The guy at the laptop said, "The kid's got skills! Great job! I figured it was some corporation with a team of writers. Where did you come up with the ideas?"

"I just took the video, cut it up, and added Flash and sound," Melvin said, cowed by the attention.

"You mean this video is real? Props, dudes!"

Briar stepped in. "So, how many people have downloaded the game?"

The laptop guy shrugged. "I don't know, at least four fraternities and whoever they told. It's all over MyFace."

"Check your Paypal account. See how much money you've made," Briar said to Melvin.

He was already on it. He typed the password into the tiny screen on his phone. "2,427 dollars in two days!"

CHAPTER THIRTY SIX
Stupid Kindness

Melvin was given the honor of playing against the winner of the night's competition. He plugged his phone into the laptop as the room went silent.

Melvin cracked his neck and popped his fingers before turning to his opponent. "Good score, for a newb." He savored the word, combining it with a sly smile and sideways glance.

"Burn! You're getting trash talked by a eleven year-old!" one of the guys blurted.

"We'll see if this kid's legit," the evening's high scorer said, with a slight quiver in his voice.

Melvin ripped through the game. Every detail and all the timing poured from his fingers like arrows from Robin Hood's bow. He had created it. It was his baby. No one could beat him, no matter how much they practiced. Once he got rolling, he typed in a secret password between levels. It replaced Petro's regular head with an oversized mulleted version he had scanned from long-lost pictures. The high score was smashed like a power line in a Godzilla movie.

The frat boys bought Melvin several rounds of nachos once they realized he was too young for beer. Several indistinguishable but sweet sorority girls took pictures of themselves with the boy and his uncle. They made weird duck faces and peace signs as the cameras flashed. Melvin thought it was some sort of tic they had or a bet they lost. *Why else would they make such unattractive facial gestures?*

As the festivities wound down, Melvin's phone chirped. It was a text from Chucky.

"Yo, Playa'! You 'bout to be on the news again! When did you talk to Katie Abraham? That honey is hotta than a laser shot into a volcano on the sun! What she smell like? Did you smell her? Tell me! Did you give her my number? Give her my number, and smell her, and tell me 'bout it."

"Uncle Petro!" Melvin said. "Katie Abraham's story is about to come on. I thought we were going to be able to see it before she aired it." The four-hundred pounds of nachos and Coke-flavored Coke began bubbling in his stomach.

"What? I haven't seen it or heard about it. I'll call her and find out what's going on," Petro mumbled.

A few seconds later Melvin's uncle dialed the number from her business card. "Hello, Ms. Abraham? Yes, this is Petro Fitzpatrick, from Alabama. Your story is about to air and we didn't get see it first. I thought," he paused. "Yes. Oh, she did. I wasn't aware of that. Thank you. Goodbye."

Melvin and Briar waited for the verdict as Petro stowed his phone.

"She said she cleared it with Shea after she stopped by to interview her," Petro said.

"Oh, that's great," Briar said, fully trusting his wife's judgment, or at least seeming to.

"Oh, no!" Melvin said, thinking about all the horrible things his mother could tell a reporter. "That's it. I'm dead. She probably pulled out baby pictures."

"Not to worry, son. I'm sure your mother wouldn't let anything bad be said about you," Briar said, pulling out his phone. He called the number marked SHMOOPY on his contacts list.

"Hey, honey. So the story is about to be played on the news. Did you get to see it before the reporter gave it the go-ahead?" Briar asked Shmoopy.

Yick, Melvin thought.

"Oh, so you told her to go with it because she was such a nice lady. I see. Well, we hope you're right. Love you. We'll be home soon, if we don't have to go into hiding." Briar winked at Melvin.

Melvin gulped, sacrificing a swallow to the gods of the angry nacho geyser threatening to erupt. There were so many things that could go wrong with the story. Katie Abraham could be just as mean or crazy as Mitch Mitchum. That was the worst-case scenario. They might have been tricked by her pretty face, and other parts.

Their backup plan of the signed waiver was void, since the reporter got permission from Shea. His mother was the sweetest person, and always believed the best about people whether she knew them or not. She was generous and trusting, with a deep-down kindness that biased all her decisions. Basically, she was a wacko, Melvin thought, and may have unknowingly ruined his life. *Stupid kindness.*

"No worries, kid. Your mom's always right about these things," his dad said, patting him on the slumped shoulder.

Petro turned one of the fleet of TVs to Channel 3 News.

A graphic came up. HOME-GROWN ALABAMA TERRORISTS rolled across the screen. *Crap.*

"This is Katie Abraham with a story about a story. I'm reporting to you on a pair of terrorists from our Bible Belt. A tale was told about the Fitzpatricks, a fiction too unbelievable to be reality. The truth, it seems, is even more fantastic than Mitch Mitchum, the perpetrator of the original story, could invent in his wildest dreams. You see, he didn't tell you the whole story about our home-grown environmental terrorists. I'm about to."

The show went to commercial. Melvin and Petro sat in stunned silence. Briar stood behind them, smiling. He seemed to have no worries.

After three political ads, two personal injury lawyer slots, an infomercial on armpit hair removal, gross, three truck commercials, thirty seconds about the miracles of Gas-X, funny, and several days of beers playing football, the story returned.

An image of Melvin riding Steve straight at the screen popped up. "Mitch Mitchum broke a story several days ago about this terrorist, Melvin Fitzpatrick. He said the boy and his uncle were building an army of communist crocodiles to overthrow the government. He even had videotape of the evil Fitzpatricks attacking him. I did my own investigating. Many of the people from the community, the family, and friends of this evil little boy testified. I am proud to say, I got an exclusive interview with the pint-sized terrorist you won't see on any other channel. Stay tuned."

Hours of commercials were followed by days of ads. Mama's had become quiet. There was definitely something happening, but not a sound was perceived. Petro looked as uncomfortable as Melvin. Briar, however, seemed to have no worries.

Katie Abraham's beautiful, possibly traitorous face finally returned. Again, she showed Melvin, looking crazy atop Steve. "Is this little boy a terrorist? Channel 5 would have you believe it. I have the entire footage Mitchum based his story on, from a source so secretive they wouldn't reveal themselves to me. After the interviews, some more digging, and watching the entire footage, I present to you the real Melvin Fitzpatrick."

She cut to tape. It was the video from Melvin's phone of the fight between Petro and Mitchum, with Melvin riding Steve. It was another angle of the same story, the way Mr. Butt-chin had told it. Then they showed the whole version and Katie described what was actually happening. It showed Melvin distracting Steve with the chickens, and Choopy protecting him. Finally, in slow motion, Melvin jumped on the massive gator to save his dog and warn the bickering men about the approaching beast.

It proved both Petro and Melvin saved Mitch from Steve instead of running and letting him get eaten. The gods of Mount Nacho had been mollified for the moment and the threat of chunky, cheesy eruption quelled.

"I had the chance to interview Petro Fitzpatrick, the uncle. Channel 5 would have you believe he's a terrorist. Here's what he said out the situation and his nephew."

The tape switched to Petro's front yard and the rocking chairs. "Mr. Fitzpatrick, are you or have you ever been a terrorist?"

"No."

"What about your nephew, Melvin? Is he a terrorist?" she asked.

"That boy? He's as bad as his mother, but he's no terrorist." Petro seemed to be distracted by the buttons on Katie's shirt. A loud throat-clearing came from off camera, possibly from Cassidy. Petro snapped out of the blank stare at the reporter's blouse.

"Will you explain what you mean by that? Why is he as bad as his mother?"

"He's selfless and kind. The kid only came down from New York to stay with me for the summer because his parents couldn't afford to send him to computer camp. He's smart, too. He's been designing a video game. I've never seen anyone so focused. I can't believe what he's going to do with it. All the work he's put into that game, and he just wants to give it away to help save a salamander nobody cares about. When I was a kid, all I did was play in creeks and ride my bike. Melvin is different, just like his mom."

A frog crawled into Melvin's throat. He did his best to ignore it. His new rep didn't need any tarnish.

Katie Abraham continued, sitting on Melvin's couch at his house in Brooklyn instead of the rocking chairs in Alabama. "This is Shea Fitzpatrick, Melvin's mom. Tell me what you think about your son and the controversy surrounding him."

Shea grabbed the microphone, almost putting it in her mouth to talk. "There is no controversy, not to me, and not to people who know him. He's such a good boy. It seems like only yesterday I was cleaning poop from his cute little fanny. Now, he's inventing computer games and noticing girls. Pretty soon, he won't even want to wear super-friends underwear or play with his little dolls. He's growing so fast, and I think his body is doing things it's not used to. You know, pretty soon he's going to hit puberty. But he'll always be my little boy, my little Koo-koo Butt."

"Oh my god, Mom! Staahhhp!" Melvin yelled at the screen. Shea had reached reputation-destroyer-level-one-thousand. He was sure at any second there would be secret video of him pooping.

Giggles and snickers came from the watching group of sorority clones. Melvin was pretty sure he heard the words *Koo-koo Butt* and *fanny*.

Finally, Katie switched to the interview with Melvin. He looked very small on the big rocking chair and noticed the cowlick stood up the same way his father's and uncle's did. Whenever he was asked a question, he gushed about his game, and his uncle and about the charity he helped set up.

The story went on to give details about the game, where to download it, what the money was going to, and a snippet about Scotty Zimmerman.

Channel 3 News switched back to the studio for Katie to finish the story. "Things aren't always what they appear. This little Alabama terrorist turned out to be an adorable hero. Mitch Mitchum, if you're watching, Melvin has something he'd like to say to you. I'll leave you with his words, unedited."

Melvin remembered the interview. He hadn't said much about Mitchum, if anything, and wasn't sure where she was going with this.

A picture of the boy formed on the screen. His head was bleeding and he was dazed from bashing into the truck on the back of Steve. He was looking at an angry, disheveled Mitch Mitchum. "You need to wipe the butt on your face. It's kind of gross."

The gathered crowd in Mama's cheered. Petro and Briar lifted Melvin onto their shoulders. The frat boys clapped and sorority clones pursed their lips in duck faces as they photographed each other.

Melvin wondered how Katie got the footage Mitch had on his computer. His phone chirped again. It was from Eric.

"You're welcome, eggroll."

CHAPTER THIRTY SEVEN
Mitchum Got the Last Word and It Was Loud

The fallout from sweet, sweet Katie Abraham's news story was bigger than Mitchum's original fabricated fiasco. For one thing, Mr. Butt-chin was fired from News Channel 5. According to News Channel 3, several groups were filing lawsuits against Mitch for libel and slander, which are fancy words for he's full of butt-nuggets and likes to spread them around.

The angry mobs of reporters and crazies Mitch once used as attack dogs had turned and were biting at his own heels. Apparently, there were so many people following the once mighty reporter, he went into hiding.

Melvin giggled every time he saw Mitch's frustrated, angry face on the television. He didn't get much time to laugh at his arch-enemy, however. Most of the following days were spent watching the Scotty Zimmerman Memorial fund grow. In three days since the story aired, profits jumped from $2,427 to over $600,000 and climbing.

Briar had a wonderful time turning away reporters who had previously been on the Butt-chin bandwagon. They all wanted to interview the shiny new non-terrorist Melvin Fitzpatrick, game designer for the salamanders. Melvin's dad remembered every reporter's face who had previously called his family terrorists, and denied them access with a smile.

Stupid Alabama by Michael P. Wines

Melvin and Eric had to build new servers for Melvin's World. So many people visited the site to download the game or donate to the charity that it crashed and had to be fixed. There were even a few generous people who didn't want to play the game. They simply wanted to help. A whole new way to give money had to be added.

Petro's original grant proposal was only for $100,000. He said he was going to spend the following semester deciding what to do with the cash. The extra money was going to help other species in need, like the Eastern Indigo snake and Alabama Red-Bellied turtle, but there were tons of details still to be worked out. Melvin's uncle seemed overwhelmed by the sudden prospect of being a conservation biologist with extra money. There was never any such thing before.

Once the servers were built and the website ran smoothly, Briar told Melvin it was time they headed home. There were only a couple weeks before school started and his dad had missed a week of work already.

Petro had been at the lab most of the night and all morning, working with a group of excited biologists. Suddenly, he was popular around campus. He returned with lunch from Mama's. As Petro handed out sandwiches and nachos, he slipped Melvin an extra bag with a wink. It contained a huge serving of hot, steaming onion rings.

"Eat these in your room. Think of it as a little surprise for your dad on the way home," Petro said.

Melvin gobbled the fart fuel like a shark at an underwater bacon buffet. He savored the nachos. After the technical details had been worked out, he packed his things and stuffed them in the car.

Cassidy, Sasha, Twitch, and Eric came to see them off and stood in the yard awkwardly awaiting his departure. Sasha snuck in a quick smooch for making her the princess in the game.

"I knew it would work," Melvin said after the kiss, and right before she smacked him.

He felt a familiar bubbling in his bowels, so he hurriedly said his goodbyes. Petro hugged him, but not too tightly. Choopy licked him and, for once, didn't pee on his leg.

As they were about to drive off, Melvin remembered the booger jug on the fridge and ran back in to get it. He stepped in the front door and turned to the kitchen, where he was grabbed by a strong set of hands.

Mitch Mitchum picked Melvin up by the arms and lifted him to eye level. "You ruined me, you little brat! Now I'm going to ruin you."

His eyes were crazy and he smelled like he'd been wearing the same cheap suit for days. There was a twitch in his butt-chin. The former reporter didn't seem to be all there in the head, like he had a nick in his record or a scratch in his CD.

Melvin freaked. It wasn't the kind of fear Rusty Castleman had given him, or even Steve the alligator. This was a new horror. The man was there to hurt him, possibly kill him.

Mitchum slapped a piece of duct tape over Melvin's mouth before he could scream. His dad, uncle, friends, and even Choopy were all outside. There was no help for him. He strained to get away from the psycho, but Mitch was too strong.

Melvin's panicked mind went to self-defense. All he could think of was the snake biting his uncle at the demonstration several weeks prior. He couldn't bite, like he did against Rusty. His mouth was taped shut.

Mitchum threw Melvin over his shoulder like a sack of corn. Then Melvin remembered the snake's other defense mechanism. He couldn't spray musk all over the predator, but he had a loaded onion ring bomb ready to detonate.

As the crazed man carried Melvin toward the back door, probably where he snuck in, Melvin defended himself. He didn't just let the gas bomb go. He didn't pull the pin and step away. He launched the raucous fart like a sniper with a bazooka at point blank range.

Mitchum's head was two inches from Melvin's single-shot butt-barrel when he turned into the devil's accordion. The sound could have been mistaken for a stadium full of elephants with megaphones. The smell was a perfect blend of stagnant sewage, orangutan armpit, hippopotamus bile, and yak vomit, formed into a wet spike of methane powerful enough to blow out the sun.

Melvin wasn't sure if the fart blew him off Mitchum or blew Mitchum out from under him. Either way, he was free, back on his feet, and out of the grasp of the diabolical Butt-chin. He ripped the tape from his mouth and screamed like a nine-year-old girl with her hair on fire.

Mitchum stood up, dazed and confused. His perfectly formed hair had been blown to the side as if a tornado had licked its thumb and smeared it that way. The crazy idiot still somehow managed to lunge at Melvin, grabbing his shirt.

Melvin kicked and flailed with all his might. Luckily, his size seven and a half tennis shoe landed squarely on Mitch's smaller-sized grapes. Melvin thought, hoped even, one of them might have popped. Regardless, Mitchum was down and out.

Choopy was barking outside. Briar bolted in the front door, grabbed Melvin and pulled him away. Petro wasn't far behind and finished subduing the broken man.

"Are you okay? Are you hurt?" Briar asked.

"I'm fine. Mitchum grabbed me, so I had to defend myself," Melvin was still scared out of his mind. His blood was at least seventy-five percent adrenaline, but he felt good.

"What did you do to him, and what is that smell?" Briar asked.

The answer was the same for both questions. "Onion rings," Melvin said, as he cracked his knuckles dramatically. "I farted in his face, then kicked him in the junk."

"Go outside and call the police," Briar said, not smiling.

Melvin did.

Choopy tackled the boy as he stepped out the front door. Melvin told the rest of the gang what happened after he made the 911 call.

Briar and Petro stayed inside with Mitchum. It was probably for the man's safety. Later Melvin was told Choopy had tried to claw through the door as soon as he went inside. The dog probably would have killed the reporter.

The police came and dragged Mitchum to a patrol car in cuffs. The man had several more scrapes and bruises than Melvin remembered delivering. His left eye was swollen, his nose trickled blood, and his lip was bloody and puffy. He also walked with a limp. Maybe Melvin kicked him harder than he thought.

Petro and Briar followed the police out of the house with their hands in their pockets, seemingly calm and content. Petro hugged his nephew much harder than before, the fear of blow-back gone. "So, I'll see you next summer," Petro said.

Melvin wasn't sure if it was a question or a statement of fact. "Stupid Alabama," Melvin said, with a smile. After answering the officer's questions for over an hour, retrieving the booger jug, and saying another round of goodbyes, Melvin started the long trip back to Brooklyn.

A couple days later, Mitch Mitchum's disheveled mug shot was all over the Internet. According to Channel 3 News, the man was in the psychiatric ward of the Lee County, Alabama, jail mumbling the words *Stupid onion rings* over and over. The attempted kidnapping victim, a eleven-year-old computer whiz named Melvin Fitzpatrick, had beaten the sanity out of him.

Luckily, most of the reporters swarmed Alabama instead of Brooklyn to get the scoop.

CHAPTER THIRTY EIGHT
Stupid Kitten Whiskers

"Yo! You gonna get tons o' honeys now, bein' famous and all! How about tossin' a few my way?" Chucky said as they walked down Bedford Avenue in Brooklyn.

"Yeah," Melvin said as they turned the corner. "I'm sure designing a video game to help salamanders is something girls look for in a guy. Come on, let's cut across on Lincoln to the park. I've been cooped up in the apartment for three days with my mom and her hugs. Ehhg."

"Check it! I tol' you, dog! You're famous!" Chucky said, pointing at a magazine rack.

Droid Gamer's Weekly had a picture of Melvin on the cover holding a cell phone in one hand and a salamander in the other. It wasn't a Red Hills salamander, but nobody knew the difference or cared. The title read: *Melvin Fitzpatrick: The Environmental Anti-Newb.*

"Cool! They just took that picture yesterday. I've gotten more swag since I got home than I knew existed. Everybody wants me to rate their games or wear their shirts," Melvin bragged. He was wearing a throwback T with an ancient image of PacMan. It was cool to be old-school.

A familiar voice emerged from behind the distracted boys. "You don't impress me, Fartspatrick! I've got a score to settle with you."

Melvin and Chucky turned to find Rusty Castleman leering over them. His half-grown mustache hadn't filled in any, but the bully had grown at least eight feet over the summer. His posse of thugs had grown as well. Chucky stepped back.

"Scoot back, jerk. Have you showered once over the summer?" Melvin said as he pushed some room between himself and Rusty.

Those familiar, vacant, dirt-brown eyes flared, along with his pubescent-haired nostrils. "I'm going to beat you so ..." Rusty started as he poked Melvin's bony chest. The bully's fist was as big as the head it would surely connect in a few seconds.

Melvin interrupted and slapped his hand away. "I said back up. How about you go away and let me finish doin' what I was doin'? Got it, Crusty?" He tried to add a little of Chucky's street-speak for intimidation factor, but doubted anyone noticed.

"What?" Rusty asked, confused that Melvin didn't cower under his usual tactics.

"Did I stutter? Now, back up, you wannabe hairy-lipped, yellow-toothed, can't-pass-the-eighth-grade-twice, girly-fainting pansy! I'm busy!"

Rusty seemed confused by Melvin's aggression. "What are you doing that's so important?" he asked. He might have been deciding in which spot to hit Melvin first, and his question was to stall while he decided. Either way, it didn't matter.

Melvin grinned and whistled. "Walking my dog."

Choopy bounded around the corner with a dead rat the size of a raccoon. No! It actually was a raccoon! The horse-dog was adjusting nicely to city life. He stopped a few feet in front of Rusty, growling. Instead of dropping the dead varmint to show his teeth, he bit down. The carcass was cleaved in half with a sickening crunch. Each side fell away, trailing viscous guts from the dog's bloody jaws and splattering on the sidewalk.

Rusty looked down to see the tail twitch on the back half of the raccoon. Then Choopy bared his teeth.

The bully didn't run or say a single word. His eyes widened as a circle of pee soaked through his pants.

The stunned silence was broken by Chucky laughing uncontrollably. "Oh, girl, you need a diaper!"

"Sit. Stay," Melvin said.

Choopy obeyed, licking his chops and maintaining eye contact with Rusty, who was slowly snapping from his wet, catatonic state.

"Listen, Rusty," Melvin said. "I know I won't always have my dog with me, but I will have the video of you wetting yourself like a little-miss-oopsie-pants doll. If you so much as fart and it wafts towards me, I'll put it up on my website for the world to see." Melvin pointed to Chucky, who held up his phone to show the incident had been recorded. "Now, go home, take a shower, and shave those four stupid kitten whiskers off your lip."

"Yo, good plan, Homes!" Chucky said, pushing a button on his phone. "That goes for me, too. You can't play a playa! You dig? Now, run on to yo' mama, like the man said."

Rusty turned and walked away with a few pants adjustments and some under-his-breath mumblings. His posse of thugs had dispersed when Choopy showed up.

"Yo, why you keep that beast off a leash?" Chucky asked, as he walked a wide circle around Choopy and his oozing pile of raccoon parts.

"I tried to put a leash on him, but he just bites it off. I even used chain and he gnawed through it after a couple of minutes. He likes to be on his own, anyhow. Uncle Petro and Dad decided after the Butt-chin attacked me I might need some protection for a while. So, we brought him home." Melvin patted his dog.

"Sounds like my boy's set to be king of the seventh grade," Chucky said, popping his collar.

"Yeah, right. But, it would be nice to sleep one night all the way through. I'm not used to these car horns, stereos, trains, and people yelling at all hours. Is it too much to ask for some peace and quiet? A cricket chirping or a frog croaking would be a lot better."

Melvin smiled and thought, *Stupid Alabama.*

MICHAEL P. WINES was born in the great wide North. He moved from Flint, Michigan, at age eight to a tiny town in middle Tennessee. The first thing he remembers about the South was seeing a blue-tailed skink scurry up a grapevine, which he had never encountered up North. He decided he had moved to the jungle and has spent most of his life since exploring it. After more than two decades of living all over the Volunteer State, he found himself in Auburn, Alabama, still fascinated and freaked out by the Southern culture and ecology. Though he claims to be a Yankee at heart, he is often found covered in red dirt at a rockabilly show, folk-art festival, eating BBQ (only Memphis style, obviously), or chasing some slimy, scaly Southern creature through a sandy pine forest.

Mike is working his way through a master's degree at Auburn University. He studies rare and endangered reptiles and amphibians. He's helped catch crocodiles in Costa Rica, pythons in Florida, alligators in Georgia, and cottonmouths in Alabama. He focuses on the Red Hills salamander (the Alabama state amphibian) and the Eastern Indigo snake. His lab mates call him The Hatchmaster for his freakish ability to incubate reptile eggs, while Mike more often refers to himself as the mascot of the herpetology lab.

Before graduate school, he spent several years as a keeper at the Memphis Zoo, where he took care of the Komodo Dragons, venomous reptiles, spiders, giant tortoises, crocodilians, and a few fish and fuzzy critters. He developed a weekly stage show titled: "Living with Venomous Reptiles." Finding the best way to educate people on wildlife was to entertain them with it, his first snake-poop joke was born.

Mike's only true talent is the ability to not mind looking like an idiot while trying something new. This natural ability has led to many hobbies, several of which seem to be going pretty well, others not so much. One is writing, and may one day be his career. He's had several magazine articles published. In 2011 one of his short stories was published in a book called *Summer Gothic - A Collection of Southern Hauntings*. Besides the writing, Mike likes to make cigar-box guitars. He can't play a lick (his neighbors and dog, Gretta, will testify wholeheartedly), but that hasn't stopped him from trying. He's not a bad woodworker as can be seen at his website: www.wineswoodworks. com. Mike might be the worst gardener of all time. If he ever had a green thumb, it must have rotted and fallen off years ago. He also plays a mean game of dodge ball.

Made in the USA
Charleston, SC
14 July 2013